## In the boreal forests, untouched since time began . . .

Maggie joined her husband Rob on a research mission into the wilderness of north-
ern Maine. Instead of finding a land of beauty
and peace, they found themselves caught in
a nightmare—one that Maggie knew would
never end.

# PROPHECY

# PROPHECY

David Seltzer

BALLANTINE BOOKS • NEW YORK

Library of Congress Catalog Card Number: 78-74246

ISBN 0-345-28034-2

Manufactured in the United States of America

First Edition: February 1979

To
Hector M'ral

# Prologue

SNOW FELL UPON the Manatee Forest, ushering in the awesome silence of winter. It fell for five days and nights, burying the trees that provided work for the lumberjacks, icing the river that provided food for the Indians. The men of the forest retreated, huddling for warmth within the confines of small shelters, subsisting on meager supplies, until the coming of spring.

The other creatures of the forest were better prepared. Through millions of years of evolution they had adjusted, with body structure and bio-rhythm, to the famine and cold that lay ahead. The insects ensured the safety of future progeny by depositing their eggs beneath the water and below the frostline, where they would be impervious to the elements above. The birds would migrate to warmer climes; the cold-blooded reptiles and amphibians would assume the same body temperature as the environment, freezing solid, then thawing to life with the coming of spring. The few warm-blooded creatures who could survive on the meager vegetation buried beneath the snow would remain awake through the winter, their bodies and numbers thinning as they foraged the bleak terrain. Those that demanded a greater supply of food would hibernate, falling into a deathlike coma with heartbeats and respiration that could barely be perceived.

Hidden beneath the white blanket that blurred the border between Canada and Maine, tens of thousands of animals lay slumbering in the darkened silence of their dens. Some would emerge with new off-spring that had been born while they slept; others would not emerge at all, expiring quietly from old age or starvation, permanently sealed in their earthen tombs. Concealed from the eyes of man, these secret pockets that held life in suspended animation were used over and over through the years, some of them dating back centuries in time. They ranged in size from the teacup-shaped nest of the chipmunk to the ten-foot-wide cavern of the bear.

But this year there was a new hibernation den. And it had a size and configuration unlike any ever built before. Nestled within craggy cliffs at the edge of a frozen lake, it loomed almost thirty feet high and twenty feet wide, and the air within it was thick with the strench of rotting carcasses. The tenant's sleep had been restless. It was eager for the coming of spring.

As the sun moved closer to the earth, the snow that covered the Manatee Forest began to thaw, stimulating the forest's creatures into wakefulness. From its subterranean sanctum dug in the mountains above the tree line, a seven-hundred-pound black bear awakened early and stalked in search of prey. The ground was still covered with a thin white crust, creating a trail of paw prints behind him as he descended to the lake, broke the ice with his massive paw, and drank his fill of water. Satiated, he surveyed the environment, detecting the sound of bark being torn from the base of a tree. Following the sound, he spotted a massive buck feeding in the distance, its stately antlers turning as it sensed that danger was near.

The bear moved slowly, knowing that the deer could not escape him; the deer seemed to know it, too, its posture sagging with resignation as it watched the lumbering specter of death approach. At the last moment the deer spun and the bear charged; the pursuit was silent, save for the muffled impact of paws and hooves upon the snow and the grunt of exerted breath as the bear quickly overtook its prey. With a single swipe the bear's claws ripped into a rear leg and the deer went down, blood seeping into the snow as it struggled, then stopped, watching the bear move in for the kill.

It would not be a swift death. The bear did not have to hurry. There was nothing in this forest that could steal its meal away.

But as it ambled forward, it heard a sound from directly behind. It was an abrupt squeal, a voice unlike any the bear had ever heard. A shadow suddenly loomed overhead, and the bear spun, squalling like a frightened fieldmouse. It tried to run but was jerked upward with such force that its body ripped from its hide, the skinless torso taking flight and slamming hard onto the ground. The legs continued to pump, running in place, even after the head had been neatly sliced from the shoulders.

The wounded deer staggered to its feet, dragging limp hindquarters, finding safety in a thick stand of trees. There it turned and watched with dispassionate eyes the sight of its predator being turned into prey.

The head of the bear was devoured on the spot, the body carried back to the den among the cliffs. There it would be eaten at leisure, its bones thrown onto the pile of carcasses that would grow higher throughout the spring, creating a macabre scaffolding that would reach to the top of the thirty-foot walls. The architect of this cavern had no taste for hooves and claws; they had been severed and left rotting on the earthen floor.

Before long, hands and feet would lie rotting there, too . . .

# 1

To Robert Vern, the coming of spring in Washington, D.C., meant more than cherry blossoms and the start of punting season on the Potomac. His own experiential calendar marked the change of season with a shift in the nature of human misery. Winter was the time of gas leaks, child battering, pneumonia, and asphyxiation; spring was the brief overture to the rat bites and sewage problems of summer.

In his four years of working for the Department of Public Health, he had seen the tenements go from bad to worse. And he was swept with a sense of personal failure. He was a doctor. His patient was the entire ghetto. And its heartbeat was failing, despite his efforts.

In the complicated tangle of cause and effects, a change in national mores was having a dramatic effect on urban development. The young middle-class working corps, who had once paired up, gotten married, and lived in suburbs where they could send their children to "good" schools, were staying single now, invading the heart of the city and creating a land boom on which every owner of real estate was prospering. Areas once designated for public housing were being rezoned, and the ghettos were getting squeezed. In a single one-block tenement area where two thousand blacks once lived, there were now six thousand. Families of eight were inhabiting single rooms, spilling out onto the fire escapes, and sidewalks, so desperate for housing that they were at the complete mercy of the slumlords. If they complained that there was no water, they would be thrown out into the streets.

If there was one single group of people whom Robert Vern felt vengeance toward, it was slumlords. On his never-ending rounds of the tenements he saw the mark of their greed everywhere. He filed lawsuits against them and faced them down in court; ultimately, even if they were penalized, they always won. They owned the real estate and it was in short supply. The tenants knew better than to appear in court and be identified.

Then there were the politicians. The endless stream of sunlamp-tanned bureaucrats who showed up to have their pictures taken at the openings of housing projects, then became unavailable to assist when the projects lost their funding and turned into crime-ridden ghettos. There seemed to be no solution for it, and no end. No one, except Robert Vern, seemed to care.

To the community of people among whom he worked, Vern was an irritant, an idealist who refused to grow up. He even *looked* younger than his years; his six-foot frame and boyishly handsome face would have been more credible carrying a football on a college campus than a doctor's bag in Washington. The age of youthful enthusiasm was gone from the capital, dead with Kennedy and the Peace Corps; but Robert Vern was still imprisoned within that time capsule, fired with the belief that the sheer energy of one man who knew right from wrong might ultimately prevail. His social conversation was diatribe, his zeal frightening. Few dared to befriend him for fear of getting caught up in his combat with the world.

And yet, in his dealings with the impoverished and disinherited, he was a man of consummate gentleness. He literally ached for them, sometimes even felt guilty for having been born with all the possibilities in life that they would never have.

He had spoken to a psychiatrist once, at a fund-

raiser for community mental health services, and after
a lengthy conversation the psychiatrist had suggested
that Rob go into therapy. He observed that Rob suffered from what he called a "Savior Syndrome," a
neurosis that makes one behave in a God-like manner to compensate for some kind of guilt or for the
lack of a simple feeling of human self-worth. Such
people, the psychiatrist went on to explain, can feel
worthwhile only when they associate with the weak
and helpless. Those who need them.

The superficial analysis had irritated Rob, but he
knew that it touched upon a basic truth. There was
plainly a disparity between what he was *trying* to accomplish, and what he *could* accomplish. It made him
fear that he was acting more out of his own needs
than those of others. At the age of thirty-nine he was
at a crossroads, his mind given to analyzing not only
where he was going, but where he had been.

He remembered that even as a young boy he had had
a desire to heal. When he bought tropical fish for his
aquarium he always passed over the healthy ones,
choosing instead those that were covered with white
spots or limped through the water with battered fins.
He toiled over them day and night, curing icthiomy-
atosis and dropsy with the same kind of dedication he
had witnessed in his own father, a country doctor,
who had died when Rob was twelve.

He had gone to college on scholarship, then on to
medical school. After graduating with honors, he
spurned the rewards of private practice to minister
to the needs of those who could afford no medical
treatment at all. He went to Brazil with the Peace
Corps, where he became expert in the diseases borne
of environmental squalor; then, two years later, to
New York, where that field of expertise became his
specialty. He worked at Bellevue Hospital, an institution that is to the medical profession what the Ford
Motor Company is to automobile production. An as-
sembly line, through which patients move so fast and
continuously that they all begin to look alike and the

doctors themselves lose their sense of identity. Rob worked a twenty-hour day, and it was there, on a night when he was feeling lost and alone, that he met a young woman named Maggie.

Maggie Duffy, now Maggie Vern, Rob's wife of seven years, was at that time a student at the Juilliard School of Music. She had brought her cello and two friends with violins into the Children's Ward, to serenade on Christmas Eve.

After all these years, it was still Rob's fondest memory of her. She was playing Brahms, her cheeks wet with tears from the sight of the children; she used a Kleenex, which she kept tucked under the cello strings at the very top of the instrument near the tuning knobs, to dry her tears between selections. When she played, it was as though she were completely at peace; a single entity expressing a single feeling. That feeling was compassion.

They spent that night together, walking the cold, deserted streets of Times Square, feeling, in the uncommon emptiness of Christmas Eve, as though they were the earth's only two survivors. With a sense of urgency, as though they might never cross each other's paths again, each told the other the entire story of their lives. And by dawn of Christmas morning, over coffee and cherry pie at the Automat, each secretly knew that they had found their life's partner.

It was Maggie's optimism that Rob most admired; her naïveté, her openness, her vulnerability. In many ways she was like an innocent child; easily hurt, quickly consoled, exuberant one moment, pensive the next—responding immediately and instinctively to everything around her. Whereas Rob dwelt in the province of the mind, she followed the dictates of her feelings. Together they were a perfect combination.

Their first apartment in New York was just off Columbus Circle: Rob used to watch Maggie through the kitchen window, dragging her cello behind her as she walked to her morning class at Juilliard. She often took a glass of water with her to nourish a small plant that had somehow managed, against all odds, to crack through the asphalt directly in the middle of the street and survive the traffic. She would pause there and give it an encouraging word or two, leading passers-by to believe she was daffy. She was not daffy. She was Maggie. And Rob loved her now, as then, more than anyone he had ever known.

But the intimacy they experienced during their years in New York was gone. The move to Washington had been like stepping out of a field of flowers into a raging river that swept them apart. Maggie had become first cellist with the Washington Symphony, occupied with rehearsals by day and performances by night; Rob was swallowed up in the never-ending battle that he now seemed to be losing. In recent months, he was often asleep when Maggie came home from her concerts, and gone before she awakened. No longer did they spend time drinking wine and talking about their feelings; no longer were there the long nights and late mornings when they dismissed the problems of the world and made love. Their contact was fragmented and shallow, their conversation had become practical, their lovemaking perfunctory and infrequent. It was disturbing to both, but neither spoke of it. It was a cycle they couldn't seem to break.

Maggie was putting in extra hours now, rehearsing for the opening of subscription season; Rob was beleaguered by a heavier-than-usual flood of emergency calls. For the last three days they had communicated mostly by telephone, and through notes left on bed and refrigerator. The message was simple, somehow sad. The note always said, "I love you."

As Rob sat now in the passenger seat of a speeding ambulance, responding to an emergency call from the tenements, he forced his thoughts away from Maggie. The distressing distance between them was something he felt helpless to control. He turned his mind back to the problems of urban decay, and came up with a thesis that somehow consoled him. Even though the tenements were being squeezed by the influx of nonmarried working people, perhaps the collapse of the institution of marriage would have one positive effect. With fewer marriages there would be fewer children. Fewer innocent victims caught in the un-stoppable whirlpool.

But the thought of children brought him back to Maggie. It was the most difficult subject between them; the mere mention of it made them see each other as adversaries. Maggie was thirty years old and becoming anxious. Rob had seen enough starving infants to realize that overpopulation was the earth's most urgent problem; he believed it was unfair to bring a child into such a difficult world.

He closed his eyes now, trying to find some peace. The ambulance slowed; the driver beside him sighed with frustration.

"I should've taken A Street."

Rob followed the driver's gaze up Pennsylvania Avenue, where a demonstration in front of the White House was blocking traffic.

"Back up."

But it was too late. They were hemmed in.

"Turn on the siren," Rob ordered. "Push right through."

As they inched forward, Rob gazed at the demon-strators. They were American Indians, a hundred or so of them, their faces made up with garish war paint, some carrying bows and arrows, their voices raised in shrill, murderous cries. Seeking any target as an outlet for their anger, a group of them charged the ambulance, banging on its hood. One young mil-itant danced around it with a spear in his hand.

"Jesus Christ," muttered the ambulance driver.

Rob kept his eyes forward. He knew the syndrome. The rage born of helplessness. He'd seen it in the tenements, too. Any white man, no matter what his motives, represented the Establishment. It was always those who came to help who bore the full brunt of anger. Firemen were shot at by snipers, social workers were threatened with their lives. The good guys had the same skin color as the bad guys, and the bad guys were beyond reach.

"What the hell are they trying to prove?" asked the driver.

Rob didn't answer. He suddenly remembered he'd promised Victor Shusette that he would attend the hearing on Indian Affairs. He checked his watch. It was too late. He wouldn't make it back in time. An emergency call from the tenements usually meant that a life was hanging in the balance. Now, with the traffic jam, he didn't know if he'd make it there in time either.

"I showed it to the man, he say it was chicken pox!"

The black woman who shouted at Rob was enraged, and rightly so. Her six-month-old infant, whom Rob was examining in its crib, was covered with festering rat bites. Crowded around them in the one-room tenement dwelling were the woman's five other children, no more than a year apart in age, and a mob of people from the street, drawn by the sound of the ambulance. The room was filled to capacity; the heat was unbearable.

"I say to him, there's *rats* in here!" the woman cried out, with tears in her eyes. "He say to me, this is chicken pox. I say to him, there ain't no chickens in here, there's *rats* in here! And them rats bit my *baby!*"

Rob eased the stethoscope from his ears and felt the infant's pulse.

"You know what he say to me?" the black woman shouted. "He say the rats got to have room to live, too!" She burst into sobs, her children clinging to her. "That's what that bastard landlord said to me! The rats got to have room to live, too!"

Rob looked for the two ambulance attendants, their white faces barely visible at the back of the crowded room. He gestured to them and they began pushing through.

"What you gonna *do?*" the woman demanded.

"I'm going to put your baby in a hospital."

"Then what?"

"He'll get well."

"And then he'll come back here and get bitten *up* again!"

"Not if I can help it."

"You can't help shit!" the woman sneered.

Rob stood firm and took it. She pushed her face close to his.

"You been here before," she snarled. "You said that before."

"No," Rob answered, "I've never been here before."

"Last winter. Upstairs. That lady who died of pneumonia when they turned the heat off. You took a dead body outa here and said we'd have the heat turned back on."

Rob remembered. "The heat *was* turned on," he said quietly.

"For one week! Then it was turned off!"

Her angry eyes locked into his, and Rob's guts tightened.

"You gonna take my baby away and fatten him up so we can serve him to the rats again?"

"Where do I find your landlord?"

"That's one goddamn good question!"

"Do you know where he lives?"

"Sure. He lives in *Virginia*. He lives with you *rich* rats up there!"

"I'm trying to help you—"

"Bullshit! Bullshit! You makin' a livin' here, is all! You don't care what happens here!"

The room went silent and she buried her face in her hands. Rob touched her shoulder and she angrily pulled away. "Go on, *take* him!" she cried. "Get him adopted or somethin'! I don't want him to have to come back here!"

"Will you come with me to court?" Rob asked.

"No!"

"I can prosecute your landlord if you'll come and complain."

"He'll throw us all out!"

The woman was right. She knew from the experiences of others that the visibility of any individual here was dangerous. That was why, when their frustration reached a breaking point, it was expressed by mobs.

"Get outa here!" she screamed at Rob. "And take my poor, sick baby *with* you!"

Rob nodded in defeat and signaled the ambulance attendants to head for the door. He followed them but paused, gazing back at the weeping woman surrounded by her children.

"She don't mean what she says," a man said from the crowd. "It ain't your fault that you can't help us."

Rob felt a sudden swelling in his throat. He turned and left the room.

Outside the tenement, the streets were filled with bodies stripped to the waist in the unseasonably warm weather. As Rob pushed through them toward the ambulance, he knew that if it got too warm too fast, it would be chaos here by summer. The shower of bricks and bottles that rained down on government vehicles came in direct proportion to the duration of summer heat. By all indications, it would be a deluge by July.

Taking his seat in the back of the ambulance, he paused to wipe his forehead, then turned his attention to the baby. Its eyes were riveted upward; it had suddenly ceased to move. The ambulance siren began to wail and Rob lunged for his bag, pulling out a syringe with trembling hands. Then he stopped, his face white with fear, and lowered his ear to the infant's unmoving chest. He listened for a moment; then, suddenly, unexpectedly, Rob began to cry. The baby began to cry, too. It was alive. And Robert Vern realized how close he was to cracking.

# 2

"THE SITUATION IN our forest, Mr. Senator, can be likened in the following way . . ."

In the Senate Subcommittee Hearing room, five Senators sat behind a long table, illuminated in an island of light, listening to the words of a young American Indian who testified with eloquence and passion. He was there to protest the theft of his tribal land, a three-hundred-square-mile wilderness area that was about to be leveled by the lumber industry.

"If I came to your home, you would likely welcome me. If I needed food and shelter from you, it would likely be given. Indeed, if I demanded my own room within your house, and if you had such a room, you might be kind enough to give it to me."

The Indian paused, his voice becoming tense.

"But if I claimed that your house and everything in it belonged to me, and I ordered you out, you would no doubt become angry! And that is exactly what is happening to the original people of this land!"

A smattering of applause rose from isolated spots in the darkened viewers section, quieted by the sound of a gavel. Victor Shusette strained to see his watch. It was plain that Robert Vern was not going to be here. Shusette would have rather not been here either. At the age of fifty-six he felt too old and tired to face the pressure of the position that his Agency was being placed in. The Environmental Protection Agency was supposed to be nonpolitical. But it was being forced into a hotbed of politics.

"I can appreciate your feelings, Mr. Hawks—" a Senator said.

"Can you appreciate the *facts,* Mr. Senator?"

"That's what I want to deal in. I want to deal in the facts . . ."

"Then let us deal in *these* facts. The purchase of all Indian land in the Northeast Territories was accomplished under the provisions of Treaty Nine . . ."

The Senator raised his voice. "Will you let me finish, please—?"

"And Treaty Nine was never ratified by Congress!"

"Mr. Hawks—"

"There has never been another treaty in the history of this country that has been implemented without the full approval of Congress. This is *your* constitution I'm talking about! These are *your* laws I'm talking about! This is *your* so-called justice I'm talking about. And I'm asking you a question!"

The Senator had begun to bang his gavel.

"I'm asking you a question! Would this have been done to people whose skin is white?"

Another burst of applause came from the darkened auditorium. The gavel continued banging until there was silence.

"Are you finished, Mr. Hawks?"

"I'm finished with this speech, if that's what you mean."

Laughter rang out; the Indian was smiling. He knew just how to leaven the proceedings when it was needed, knew just when to make his attacks and when to retreat. A few of the Senators were smiling, too. They knew they were being manipulated by a master in the craft of verbal combat.

John Hawks was not an easy man to reckon with. He was articulate and poised, and he had righteousness of his side. No one knew exactly where he had come from; his rise in the ranks of militant spokesmen had been meteoric. Three weeks ago no one had heard of him. Today he was the chosen representative of the group calling themselves O.P. It stood for

Original People. A hastily formed amalgam of Masaquoddy, Ashinabeg, Yurok, Wampanoag, and Cree, tiny tribes along the Maine-Canadian border who were trying to protect their land from a company called the Pitney Paper Mill.

"What I was about to say, Mr. Hawks," the Senator continued, "is that although I can appreciate your feelings, the blockade you've constructed in your forest is against the law."

"The law will not bring justice," Hawks declared.

"The blockade will lead to confrontation."

"Abstinence from confrontation will not bring justice."

"You're aware that the Supreme Court has issued a restraining order against this blockade?"

"Which Supreme Court is that, Mr. Senator?"

The Senator looked at him warily. "The Supreme Court of the United States."

John Hawks sat back and smiled. "That's not a very high supreme court, Mr. Senator. My supreme court is much higher."

Whistles and cheers resounded in the darkness; Victor Shusette had heard enough.

Leaving the Senate chambers, he walked out onto the front steps of the old Senate Building and squinted into the sun. The branches of the cherry trees were turning white and their fragrance wafted through the air, but it did not bring him the pleasure that it had in the past. This spring he was facing a problem. After a lifetime of building the Environmental Protection Agency into a respected force, he was now watching it being suddenly placed in jeopardy. In the land dispute between the lumber company and the Indians, the Agency was being used as a pawn. The Pitney Lumber Company was planning to exercise its right to harvest the timber in the Manatee Forest; the Indians were standing in their way. The lumber company had the money with which to win the legal war, but the Indians had gained national sympathy. The result was that the Supreme Court was unwilling to make a decision. They had turned to Shusette to provide them with an Environmental Protection report as a means of breaking the deadlock.

It was not as simple as it sounded. The lumber companies employed over half the working people of Maine. The working people of Maine supported their Senators. Their Senators had control of the purse strings that kept the Environmental Protection Agency alive. One Senator in particular, the Republican from Maine, had already started working the territory. Shusette had received an invitation to go fishing at his private cabin on the Kennebec River on the opening day of salmon season. It was easy to resist this kind of obvious bid, but there were others that were not so easily ignored.

In Washington one hand, it was said, washed the other. Fittingly, Shusette had noticed, politicians were a breed of one-handed men. They seemed to rely on their right hand. For handshaking, gesturing, and pointing fingers in people's faces. The left hand was usually kept in a pocket or in a tight fist, no doubt concealing what the handshaking, gesturing, and finger-pointing was all about.

In the case of the Republican Senator from Maine, the left hand concealed a grab bag of threats and promises. The promise that if Shusette's Agency wrote a positive, or sufficiently ambiguous, report, he'd honor their sacrifice of the first round by giving up the next. If, for instance, they reported that wide-scale timber cutting in the Manatee Forest would *not* be detrimental to the environment, the Senator would support a suggestion that the cutting be "limited" rather than total. If, on the other hand, the Environmental Protection report came in totally negative, the Senator could wage war on the Agency with the full financial resources of the timber lobby behind him. He could campaign to discredit their report; he might even introduce legislation that would curtail their future involvement in the controversy over cutting trees.

The showdown between the Pitney Paper Mill and

a handful of Indians calling themselves the Original People was not just a minor skirmish. The results of this isolated land dispute had precedent-setting ramifications, and the Environmental Protection report would provide a powerful weapon for one side or the other to use. Shusette wondered how many of his field workers had already been contacted by the timber lobby, received invitations to parties, or been given hints of political jobs. They were a dedicated group and, as far as Shusette knew, incorruptible. But the pressure on whoever took this job would be enormous.

It was for all these reasons that Victor Shusette had thought of Robert Vern. He was from outside the Agency; his integrity was unquestionable, his dedication to the cause of human justice was beyond compare. He had no political ambitions and could face down any politician. And he had the healer's gift of dealing with the kind of emotional turmoil that existed in the Manatee Forest. Moreover, he had reached the end of the line in Public Health. Shusette knew that Robert Vern was psychologically ready for a change.

"Rob?"

Victor Shusette moved tentatively down the darkened hospital corridor toward the lone figure leaning against the wall. It was past midnight, and he had looked everywhere for Rob, had even called his wife just an hour ago, awakening her to find that he still hadn't returned home. On an off chance he drove to the hospital and found that Rob had been there since two in the afternoon, trying to save the life of the tenement infant.

The silhouetted figure before him *looked* like Rob, but Shusette couldn't be sure. He had never seen Rob standing still before. Since they'd first met in the Central Commissary a year ago, their conversations had always been conducted in transit; Shusette hurrying to keep Rob's pace as he ran from one point to the other. The man standing before him now was plainly exhausted, drained of every bit of life and energy.

"Victor," Rob said. "What brings you here?"

"Mohammed comes to the mountain." He paused to assess his friend. "You all right?"

Rob nodded. "Have a cigarette?"

"You smoke?"

"Not since I was twenty-two."

"Taking it up?"

"I might."

Shusette produced a cigarette and Rob lit up, taking a puff without inhaling, not liking the taste.

"I'll take it."

Rob gave it to Shusette, then moved to a bench, where he sat with exhaustion.

"How's the baby?" Victor asked.

"Weak. How'd you know about the baby?"

"I keep a close eye on you."

Rob was beyond banter. He lay down on the bench, one arm crossed over his eyes, as though settling in for the night.

"Not going home?" Victor asked.

"Waiting for an EKG."

"Too tired to talk?"

"No."

"I'll let you alone if you're too tired."

"I can listen."

Shusette paused, glancing down the hall in search of a chair. There was none. He slid down to the floor, sitting against the wall. From a distance they would have looked like a couple of derelicts.

"I wanted to tell you about that hearing this morning."

"I'm sorry I missed it."

"I am, too. It was really something. The Indians are going on the warpath."

"A few of them attacked my ambulance."

"They've got good reason. To be angry, I mean."

"Don't we all."

"This paper mill . . . the Pitney Mill . . . bought timber rights to a hundred thousand acres of forest, under the provisions of Treaty Nine. The Indians claim that Treaty Nine was never ratified by Congress."

"I read about it."

"The Indians have blockaded access to the forest, keeping the lumber company out . . . the Supreme Court's filed a restraining order against the blockade . . . everybody's ready to kill each other, and the whole thing is holding for an Environmental Protection Report."

Shusette paused, letting Rob absorb it. He didn't want to go too fast.

"That's a land dispute," Rob mumbled. "What does the Environmental Protection Agency have to do with a land dispute?"

"It's a judicial cop-out. No one wants to make a decision."

"Political football," Rob mumbled.

"The Superbowl," Shusette added. "Whoever writes this one up is going to make or break the lumber industry. I'd say it could make or break the earth's entire environment. The land environment, anyway."

"Then all you have left is the ocean and the sky."

"Wouldn't mind winning one out of three."

Rob sat up, rubbing his eyes. "I sometimes envy you, Victor."

"Why is that?"

"Earth, water, and sky. Seems very simple to me."

Shusette was amused. "Does it?"

"The issues are right out there. You go into battle, and you win or lose."

"Usually lose."

"But the losses are decisive. And so are the victories."

"That's true."

Rob rubbed his face, issuing a long sigh. "Me . . . I just do 'housework.' I'm like a maid in a house full of destructive kids. I clean up one room, and by the time I move to the next, the first one is messed up again." Rob's face was somber, his voice soft and without expression. "I stand in the middle of this mess, and I shout, 'This has got to stop.' And no one listens." His eyes roamed to Shusette, who was visible only as a cigarette puffing in the near darkness. "What does it take to get someone to listen?"

Shusette shook his head.

"My wife once told me," Rob continued, "she met an artist. A painter. And he told her that a great work of art is never finished. It's just abandoned." He smiled sadly to himself. "I wonder if the same is true of great intentions."

"Sounds like you're about to give up."

"Do I?"

"Are you?"

"Maybe."

Shusette struggled to get up from the floor, his bones aching as he hobbled to the bench and sat down next to Rob. "Want to know something?" he asked.

"Sure."

"If I could have planned your side of this conversation, I couldn't have done it better."

Rob glanced at him, not understanding.

"I've been waiting for you to get fed up with what you're doing."

"Why?"

"I'd like you to come over to the EPA."

Rob shook his head.

"It's bigger, Rob. The stakes are higher. You're spending the night here trying to save one sick baby when you could be holding the lifeline of the entire species in your hands. You go to court to clean up one room in a tenement when you could be using that same energy to clean up the entire planet that tenement stands on."

Rob was silent.

"You want potency?" Shusette continued. "I'm prepared to put a job in your hands that could affect the entire land mass of this country." Shusette locked into Rob's eyes. "I'm talking about putting you in a pivotal place in time, and events, where you can have an effect on your entire world."

Rob remained silent. Shusette knew he had a hook in him.

"I'm talking about this land dispute."

"It's not my field, Vic."

"I trust you."

"Trust me about tenements. Not about trees."

"I can teach you what you need to know. There's nothing mysterious about it, it's all written down in books."

Rob studied Shusette's face in the darkness. "Why me?"

"Because you have intelligence and you have tact. And you have integrity."

"That's very flattering, but it doesn't answer the question."

Shusette rose and stood before him. "I'll tell you the truth. I'm walking through a mine field on this one, and if I don't step carefully, the whole Agency can get blown up. The timber lobby is breathing down my neck. The politics are hot and heavy. That forest is turning into a war zone."

Rob was skeptical. "It can't be that bad . . ."

"Not for *you*, no. You're accustomed to war zones. I've got all the tree experts I need. I need someone who can deal with people. That's what you're expert at. If you'll let me bone you up for a few days, there'll be nobody better equipped to do this than you."

Rob pondered it in silence, then rose. He paced the corridor, his footsteps echoing in the stillness. He was tempted by Shusette's offer and it made him feel disloyal. As though, by entertaining the thought of change, he was somehow cheating on the people who counted on him. He thought about the black woman and her baby. And his promise to help them.

"What are you thinking?" asked Shusette.

"I feel like a married man dreaming about a mistress," Rob replied.

"Maybe that's a good way to think about it. Just a mistress. Just something to try."

Shusette could see that Rob was wavering. "Just give me two weeks of your life," he said. "I need you on this one."

# 3

---

THE STREET DEMONSTRATION conducted by the American Indians in front of the White House had reached a fever pitch by the following day. Maggie Vern watched it from a taxi as she headed back to the doctor's office she had visited two days prior. Rob had not returned home at all last night, remaining at the hospital to monitor the life-and-death struggle of the tenement infant. He had called to tell her that he would likely be returning there again tonight after putting in a full day at his office. It was just as well. She was in no condition to face him.

At the doctor's office she waited in the company of women in varying stages of pregnancy, keeping her eyes riveted on the page of a magazine. Her palms were moist and her toes hurt from being curled in her shoes, which was a habit of hers when she was nervous. Sometimes she wouldn't even realize she'd had a tense day until her toes started aching at night. For the past two nights, while she waited for the test results, her toes had been throbbing.

She knew that if the test was positive, she would have to deal with something she didn't have the strength for. Her husband was a powerful man, articulate and passionate, always able to convince her that his way was right. As far as having children was concerned, she had heard him recite the litany many times. There were ten million unwanted children in the world. Population control was the responsibility of everyone, regardless of their economic means. The society was failing. The environment was failing. It was irresponsible to bring another child into the world.

In the early years she had agreed with him. His beliefs were her beliefs. She found excitement in sharing his sense of purpose. She was raised in the sheltered environment of upstate New York, exposed to only the homogenized people and products of an upper-middle-class world, and to her Robert Vern had been a magnetic and dashing figure. A man of the world, alive with passion, filled with the belief that he could shape the future in the palm of his hand. It made her own life seem trivial, her horizons limited, her intellect insubstantial. Her feeling in those early years was gratitude; it was miraculous to her that this giant of a man could have loved her.

The gratitude had now eroded into a smoldering resentment, but the feelings of inferiority still persisted. Maggie felt a sense of shame that she could not rise above her own needs. She felt selfish for wanting to be happy.

Ironically, the life they led in Washington was one that anyone looking on from the outside would envy. They were each accomplished in their fields, recognized for their work, and they occasionally rubbed shoulders with people who made history. Maggie had played her cello at the White House; Rob had sat on a dais with Andrew Young at a seminar on World Hunger. To all who knew them, they appeared as independent, strong, and fulfilled people. The very essence of what modern marriage was supposed to be.

What Maggie knew was that it was no longer a marriage at all. It was a bed-and-board arrangement between two people who lived separate lives, and whose values were growing more divergent with each passing day. When they found themselves together, they talked of daily events, masking their crying need for intimacy. They never talked about their feelings any more, their secret hopes and dreams. It was as though that were a forgotten language; a language of their childhood that didn't apply to their roles in the adult world.

Maggie had thought for a while that time itself would bring them closer together. But it was not happening, and she felt she could wait no longer. In recent weeks she had been waging a battle with depression. Not the kind of feeling she once referred to as the blues. This was different; a desire, when she awakened each morning, to close her eyes again and find oblivion in the deathlike darkness. She had even thought, at odd times of the day, for no apparent reason, of suicide. Of being found dead in some bizarre way. Once when she saw a blood-donor truck, on that day of the year when everyone is suppose to give blood and get a boutonniere in return, she wondered whether if she went from hospital to hospital giving blood, she might simply expire. A noble death. One that Rob might approve of. Giving her all to those who needed it.

The depression lifted, however, when she realized she was no longer menstruating and might be pregnant. For the first time in months she felt the loneliness leave her. She felt somehow warm and loved. Loved by Rob, even though he knew nothing about it.

She had not intended to become pregnant. She had merely relaxed her precautions. She and Rob were so rarely together, in the same bed at the same time, with enough energy to make love, that the exercise of inserting a diaphragm became in itself a rejecting experience. When it had to be removed, unused, in the morning, it accentuated her feeling of being un-wanted.

Maggie knew that if she were pregnant, it would provoke a crisis beyond any she had ever faced. It would cause anguish and recrimination, and would possibly confront her with the kind of decision that she did not even dare to think of. Rob would refuse to have a child. And the need within her was over-whelming.

"Maggie?"

The doctor who summoned her was someone she had known since they first moved to Washington. Peter Hamlisch had been Rob and Maggie's next-door neighbor in their first apartment in Georgetown. When Maggie had come in earlier that week she was turned over to a laboratory technician. This was the first time in three years that she had seen Peter.

"My God," he said. "Look at you."

"That bad?" Maggie smiled.

"That good. Come on in."

She followed him down a corridor and into his office, where he closed the door, gesturing toward a chair. Maggie remained standing.

"I can't believe it," he said. "Has it been two years?"

"Going on three."

"How's Robert?"

"Fine. Working hard."

"Still keeping the same hours?"

"Oh, yes."

"And how 'bout you?"

"Busy."

"We keep meaning to get to the symphony . . ."

"That's okay."

"I saw your picture at the White House . . ."

"Bad picture."

He smiled, delighted to be with her. "You look glorious. But then again, pregnant women always do."

It took a moment to sink in. Then it hit like a body blow.

"Sit down." Hamlisch laughed. "I didn't know you'd be so surprised. Women are usually very certain about these things."

"Are you sure?" Maggie asked in a shaky voice.

"Yes," Hamlisch answered, somewhat puzzled by her tone.

Maggie slowly sat in a chair, feeling so many con-

flicting emotions that they all blurred into numbness.
"You all right?"

She nodded, trying to force a smile, but was unable
to sustain it.

Hamlisch's intercom buzzed, and he hit one of the
buttons. "Hold the calls," he said. Then he turned his
eyes to Maggie.

"I take it this isn't good news."

Maggie shook her head, not knowing how to respond.

"I assumed it was a planned pregnancy," Hamlisch
said. "I wouldn't have been so casual about it."

Maggie's fingers touched her parched lips. She
didn't trust her voice.

"It's not the end of the world, you know," Hamlisch
said. "You're very early in your pregnancy. Women
deal with this every day of the week."

She shook her head quickly, pressing her hand to
her eyes in an attempt to halt the tears that she feared
would slip past them.

Hamlisch put his hand on hers, and the moment of
touch released her emotions. She wept quietly, the
sounds soft, childlike.

"I want you to sit in this office for the next fifteen
minutes," Hamlisch said. "I have one patient to see.
Then I want to take you to lunch."

They didn't go to lunch; Maggie had no appetite.
Instead, they walked the hot streets of Washington,
Maggie wiping her eyes as she talked, until she was
finally talked out. She described, in every way she
could think of, how and why her marriage was wrong;
how and why she so desperately needed Rob and
didn't know how to reach him. She felt disloyal to be
divulging her unhappiness, but somehow relieved to
hear herself expressing it.

Hamlisch had listened, mostly in silence, occasionally asking a question, encouraging her to continue until he was sure she had said everything there
was to say. He was compassionate and understanding.
And he cared for both of them.

They stood now by the long reflecting pool in front of the Washington Monument, a place Maggie had once journeyed to by bus to join twenty thousand black people in their demand for freedom. The grass had grown back now where it had once been trampled down; a group of small children floated toy boats in the water as Maggie and Hamlisch looked on.

"You know," Hamlisch said with a sigh, "I once heard a description of Albert Einstein. Someone said he was a 'visionary' not so much because of what he saw, but because of what he *refused* to see."

"That wasn't Einstein, it was B. F. Skinner," Maggie replied softly.

"Was it?"

*"Scientific Monthly.* Rob gets it."

Hamlisch sat down at the edge of the reflecting pool. Maggie sat beside him, using a wadded-up handkerchief to wipe her eyes.

"I was thinking of Rob when I said that," Hamlisch added.

"I know."

"He has blind spots, but men who accomplish things always do."

"So you think I'm selfish?" She did not ask it defensively; more as confirmation of what she herself believed.

"I think you're in a bind."

She dipped her handkerchief into the water and wrung it out, pressing it to her forehead and eyes. "God, I've cried so much lately, I think I'm going to get dehydrated."

"Do you love him, Maggie?"

"Yes." Her answer was without emotion or hesitation. It was a simple fact of life.

"What if you have to make a choice?"

"I'm unable to make that choice."

"Is it possible that if you waited . . . ? To have a child, I mean? Maybe in a few years he'd feel mellower about it."

"I couldn't do that."

Her eyes went blank. "I'm unable to kill anything. I couldn't do it." She turned to Hamlisch, trying to make him understand. "I already love it. And I feel like it loves me." She shook her head, feeling foolish. "Is that just nonsense?"

"No."

"No matter what happens, I'll never . . ." Her voice broke off and her posture stiffened. "No matter what happens, it's going to be born."

Hamlisch watched her closely. "Then I guess you've made a decision."

She didn't respond.

"When are you going to tell Rob?"

Maggie rose and moved slowly away from him. "How long before it shows?" she asked.

"Two months. Maybe three. Women who want to conceal it can sometimes go to four."

He read her thoughts.

"It's not a good idea, Maggie. I've seen women do that. Unmarried women, usually, who try to ignore it until it's too late for an abortion. They weaken themselves emotionally. The one time in your life you have to be adult is when you're pregnant."

"When *is* it too late for an abortion?"

"Don't do that, Maggie."

She knew he was right.

"No matter how he feels about it," Hamlisch said, "it's his life, too. He has a right to make his decisions, just as you have a right to make yours."

"Just a thought," Maggie whispered.

"Go to his office right now," Hamlisch advised. "Get it out in the open."

"I'm frightened, Peter," she whispered.

"He'll say no, and you'll get angry. I think anger is more appropriate than fear right now."

He took her hand and they walked to the street; Peter spotted a passing taxi and hailed it down. She directed the driver to take her to the Public Health Building.

But Rob was not in his office when Maggie arrived.

She waited a full two hours and in that time the anxiety built up within her to a point where she knew she couldn't face it. At the last moment she fled. The confrontation would have to wait. She would carefully choose her time.

It was 2:00 A.M. when Rob returned home. The tenement infant had died. The infection caused by the rat bites had been complicated by anemia. The heart had given way to a conspiracy of assaults. Rob had seen infant deaths before. This one had hit him particularly hard, accentuating his sense of futility.

He moved quietly into the bedroom, not wanting to awaken Maggie. The moon's soft light spilled through the window, illuminating her face as she lay in slumber. He sat on the bed beside her and brushed a wisp of hair from her eyes, noticing a faint mark running from the corner of her eye across the bridge of her nose. It was a path traced by tears. She had been crying.

He studied her for a long time, swept with sadness that he did not know the reason for the tears. He thought to awaken her, but decided against it. Tomorrow was Thursday. She had an early rehearsal. He leaned down and kissed her, hoping it would somehow reassure her that she was safe. Then he slipped off his clothes and lay quietly beside her.

Sleep was difficult, for his mind was in turmoil. He thought of the offer that Victor Shusette had made to him. Perhaps a new job was what he needed. The only other alternative to the work he did now was private practice. It was somehow inevitable, but to Rob it seemed like retirement. He was still young enough to accomplish something on a global scale, and there would be other benefits in working for the EPA. No more emergency calls or all-night sessions at the hospital, no more early-morning appearances in court. It would mean he'd have more time to spend with Maggie. Perhaps that in itself was worth it.

As he drifted into slumber, he was thinking about trees. Soon, he was dreaming.

He saw himself walking through the tenements. The tall, lopsided buildings with their zigzag fire escapes were nestled in the midst of towering trees. The fire escapes were filled with bodies. Black bodies. Hundreds of them. And they all held spears. Maggie was beside him and she was frightened. The black bodies began streaming downward, their faces covered with war paint, their voices rising in a shrill cry. Rob grabbed Maggie in his arms and ran into the forest, but became lost in the trees. She screamed and clung to him, begging him to save her, but suddenly they reached a drop-off and could run no farther. Rob paused and looked up into the sun. And, directly from the center of it, a spear came searing down at him.

Rob awoke panting. His body was bathed in sweat. He rose on trembling legs and pulled the curtains. to shut out the moonlight. But the moon was so bright he could still see it's shape through the curtains. Returning to bed, he managed to close his eyes again, and this time fall into dreamless, exhausted slumber.

# 4

---

THE SAME MOON that lighted Robert Vern's bedroom shone down on the Manatee Forest, gently illuminating the tops of the endless expanse of trees. The wind was warm, rustling the surfaces of the lakes, creating tapestries of glittering sequins from the reflection of the moon.

From the time of the planet's creation until now, this three-hundred-square-mile plot of earth had been allowed to remain as God meant it to be. The morning sun still filtered through the trees, given definition as clear as laser beams by the fog; the towering black spruce and red balsam still spiked a mountainous skyline. Dawn still came with the discordant orchestration of loons, dusk with the faintly drumrolling wingbeats of the ruffled grouse. And darkness was still punctuated with the sudden and unexpected cry.

It was the place where the Manatee River flowed into the Espee, creating a watershed known to the Masaquoddy, Ashinabeg, and Wampanoag Indians by sixty different names. All of them describing the bountiful life that existed within.

But in recent years, the Indian names had given way to others. The largest body of water, the lake with a small island in its center, once known as Lake Wabagoon was now called Mary's Lake, named for the wife of Morris Pitney, an industrialist from Georgia who'd come in 1930 and founded the Pitney Paper Mill on the shores of the swift-running Espee River. The pond

once called Talak'tah was now listed on Forest Service
relief maps as Flat-Iron Pond because it reminded
Mary Pitney of the steam iron she pressed her husband's pants with.

The Pitneys were dead now, but their imprint on
the landscape was permanent. The Pitney Paper Mill,
now passed into other hands, had grown on the charts
of stockbrokers and Wall Street economists into a
corporate conglomerate, one of five absentee landlords who owned over half the land in Maine and
looked upon its forests as a cash crop waiting to be
harvested. The towering pines that were once called by
the names of Indian ancestors, each one considered an
individual personage, had now been counted and mea-
sured, classified by size and weight, and labeled with
price tags.

The major products of the Pitney Paper Mill were
wrapping paper, disposable grocery bags, and toilet
tissue. For the latter product, and the noxious fumes
that hovered along a three-mile section of the Espee
River, the Indians referred to the paper mill as *D'hanat
Y'oah 'tha*. The Farting Giant.

Unlike the Indians of the American Western Plains,
the American Forest Indians had been a passive
people, conditioned perhaps by the gentleness of their
environment to accept changes within their lives and
to accommodate trespassers who came to live within
their borders. Thus the small tribes of Masaquoddy,
Ashinabeg, Yurok, and Wampanoag were content to
give the paper mill its small share of the massive
forest. As long as they gave wide berth to the lumberjacks with their trucks and chain saws, the two civiliza-
tions lived separate lives, occasionally crossing each
other's paths, gazing at one another with nothing more
than curiosity. The lumberjacks felled trees and processed them into pulp; the Indians netted salmon and
dried them in the sun. It seemed there was little connection between the two.

When the once benign temperament of these Indians
began undergoing an insidious psychological change,

they still failed to make the connection. The Indians were confused by it and feared that if it became known that violence was beginning to sweep through their ranks, they would be accused of drunkenness: the historical verdict of the white world, used to avoid any responsibility for Indian outrage.

It was true that the growing aberration in behavior, which they called *katahnas* (seizures), resembled the effects of intoxication. Dizziness, hallucination, loss of coordination and, often, unexplainable outbursts of rage. One man turned on his own wife and children, another ran into Mary's Lake and drowned. At first the incidents were isolated and infrequent, vaguely explicable in terms of the movement of the stars and the personalities of the men whom these *katahnas* struck. But now it was becoming more generalized—and more frightening because it was harder to recognize. The once dramatic symptoms were becoming muted, the entire community falling under a kind of lethargy and haze that would lift for periods of time and then descend again like a cloud of smoldering gloom.

There was another secret kept by the Masaquoddy, too; unspoken because it brought shame to those who had suffered it. A growing rate of stillbirths and deformed children. By tradition the Indian women bore their children in the forest alone, and thus for a long time maintained the awful secret even from each other. The evidence of their changing chemistry was buried in shallow graves throughout the Manatee Forest.

The first member of the tribe to gather enough evidence to become alarmed was Romona Peters, a full-blooded Masaquoddy woman, twenty-eight years of age, who bore the Indian name Oliana. It meant Spring Fawn. With her light skin and doelike eyes, she was given this name by her grandfather, Hector M'rai, the former chief and now oldest living member of the tribe. But Romona's fawnlike appearance was misleading. She had the courage of a vixen. At the age of twelve she was raped by a lumberjack in the forest and, by herself, went into the town of Manatee to report him to the sheriff. It was her first lesson that the word "justice" had little application to the American Indian.

From then on, she strove to accumulate enough knowledge to become a force of change. But the goal remained elusive. Having to leave school at the age of thirteen, which was customary for Indian women whose labor was needed in the village, she used the Androscoggin Public Library as her school, spending every available moment there, poring over books that she rarely understood, attempting to grasp as much of the vocabulary and ways of the white world as possible. As she passed through her teens, the library was the focal point of her life, her heaven and her hell. She was often taunted by her white contemporaries there, snickered at as she trod a continual path from the reading room to the big dictionary on the pedestal, trying to understand what she was reading. The carpet was worn thin there and she was blamed for it, finally forbidden by the librarian to use the dictionary more than once a night. This random quirk of cruelty, more than any other factor, curtailed her one opportunity for progress. Eventually she gave up. The frustration and humiliation were just too painful.

But now, as a result of recent events, she had gone back to the library. Having seen a woman return from childbearing in the forest in a state of near shock, with her arms empty and her stomach flat, Romona questioned her until the woman brought her to the grotesque remains. It was a stillborn fetus, almost full term. But it looked more like the product of a whelping than a human birth. The head was outsized, the eyes large and flat, without lids. The fingers were long and tapered, resembling claws; the legs were like hindquarters, rounded and much shorter than the arms.

The woman begged Romona not to reveal her secret, and Romona agreed. But she persuaded the next woman who was about to go into labor to let her serve as a midwife to the birth. It happened again.

A different variation this time, not so severe. But once again, the stillborn fetus had animalistic qualities. At the same time there were successful births; natural, normal children. But like a discordant tune played softly beneath an orchestration, the stillbirths and deformed fetuses continued to appear; occasionally some were born alive, their first outcries quickly muted by frightened mothers in the forest.

It was Romona's instinct to seek help, but her experience with the official white world was sufficiently frightening to make her hesitate. She did not want to go there until she was fully armed with as much knowledge as possible. It was for that reason that she returned to the library, certain that the answer to the changes in he physiology of her people could be found somewhere in that vast storehouse of information.

It was difficult now, even more so than when she was a child, for Romona to steal time for her forays to the library. She had the full care and charge of her aging grandfather, Hector M'rai, who was also suffering from the crippling effects of the *katahnas*. In the last six months his mind had gone dim and his hands had begun to tremble. It was not merely the product of his age. From spending a lifetime at his knee and under his tutelage, Romona Peters knew that her grandfather was not a man destined for senility.

Among the Masaquoddy people, Hector M'rai was a legend. He had lived through six incarnations, still spoke the ancient language, and was a storehouse of Indian lore.

He lived apart from the rest, in a compound he'd built with his own hands, following construction designs that he alone remembered. He called his campside *M'ay-an-dan'ta*. The Garden of Eden. It consisted of three tepee-like shelters, built of rough-hewn logs and animal skins; they were as different from the falling-down corrugated-board shanties that his people lived in as night is from day. In the midst of this changing forest the camp was an oasis where time stood still. A kind of museum. A shrine to a life that no longer existed.

It was difficult for Romona to tear herself away from M'rai, for she feared each time she left that it might be the last time she would see him alive. But each night before sundown, she journeyed into town to pore through the encyclopedias and medical pamphlets at the public libary. She knew that the *katahnas* and the stillbirths were somehow linked together, and she sought always to find that link.

It was in the preface to a book on nutrition that she caught her first clue. It said that food intake was the single most causative factor in both human health and *behavior*. Beyond that, it said that the actual *cultural characteristics* of an entire community of people could be influenced by what, as a group, they ingested. It described a tribe in Africa, called the El Molo, who had, in recent years, become aggressive and given to epileptic seizures when frightened, due to protein starvation in a land that had been poached of wild game. *Protein*, it said, bridged the synaptic gap in the command-chain of neuromuscular response.

She copied down every word she didn't understand. On a single page there were sixty-seven of them. Some of them, like "synaptic gap," weren't even in the dictionary .

The book also had a section on prenatal care. Once again there was a mention of protein, this time as a prime factor in the development of a healthy human fetus. Romona went to the card catalog that she had used as a child and found that there was an entire book on the subject of protein. At the back of the book there was a table of protein-enriched foods. Suddenly she was confused—highest on the list of protein-enriched foods was fish. There could not be a lack of protein in the Indians' diet, for they were fishermen. Eighty percent of what they ate was fish. She struggled, with every bit of logic she could summon, to make sense of it. Diet was the key. But what, in their diet, was causing the biological havoc?

She knew that the diet of the Masaquoddy people had remained for centuries virtually unchanged, with the exception of canned goods, which were new to this generation. The canned goods were all bought from the same store, the only one in Manatee that catered to Indians. Was it possible that the Masaquoddy were being poisoned? No. The cans were sealed.

She never knew how close she had come to making the connection when her quest for knowledge was suddenly cut short. Overnight a sudden storm of violence had erupted between the Indians and the townspeople; it became dangerous for Romona Peters to venture into town.

A group of lumberjacks had happened upon an Indian in the forest whose behavior was stuporous and disoriented. He was somehow lost in the midst of everything familiar to him, literally turning in circles, bumping into trees. They had laughed at him and taunted him, provoking a rage. He attacked them and they beat him within an inch of his life. The beating led to a reprisal. Ten days later, the body of a lumberjack was found, in similar condition, beaten by a group of Indians. The word spread quickly: the Indians were drunk and spoiling for a fight. The lumberjacks were only too happy to give it to them. In retaliation, they raided a small Indian fishing village. Shortly after that, two lumberjacks failed to return from a night crew. They had vanished in the forest. And it was said that the Indians had killed them.

After thousands of years of living in peace with their environment, the Indians now lived in a state of fear; afraid to go to their nets in the morning, dousing their fires at night, listening to the wail of two bloodhounds that searched the Manatee Forest for some sign of the missing lumberjacks.

As Romona Peters sat in the darkened silence of her grandfather's encampment, she listened to the cacophonous duet of the bloodhounds and watched the three searchlights of the rescuers who followed them. They looked like tiny fireflies on the distant mountain, dancing and darting through the trees. Every night for a week she and her grandfather had followed the progress of the rescue team. They knew tonight that something was different. There was an urgency in the sound and movement that had not been there before.

From the Indian village two miles away, the entire population of the Masaquoddy people also watched, sensing, as Romona and M'rai did, the sudden build-up of tempo. In fact, the movements of the rescuers were being monitored by thousands of pairs of eyes. The animals of the night, predator and prey, huddled in silence, tensing with the increasing crescendo.

The rescuers themselves felt it, too. After a week of listless wandering, the dogs had suddenly been seized with the kind of hysteria that meant their goal was near. A scent had wafted by them at sundown and they had taken off like cannon-shot, their voices shrieking with eagerness, their massive bodies straining against the harnesses that linked each to a human rescuer, tied to it at the end of a forty-foot leash.

When excited by scent, the bloodhounds were hard to control; their two-hundred-pound bodies functioned as mindless extensions of the nose. The eyes ceased to function, the mind ceased to work; the animals were enslaved, seeking union with the source of the scent like drug addicts following the lure of opiate. In their frenzy, darkness had no meaning, nor did obstacles. Were they not literally tied to human masters, they would have smacked blindly into barriers or sailed off cliffs.

As the dogs' voices now rose with heightening urgency, the men behind them lurched and staggered, branches lashing at their faces as they were dragged across the perilous terrain. They were on unfamiliar territory here, high in the mountains and moving dangerously fast; but they were unwilling to slow the

dogs for fear of their losing the scent. Behind the
two leashmen, each tied to a dog, ran a third man,
struggling beneath the weight of a two-way radio
strapped to his back.

"Slow them down!" he gasped.

"They're hot!" one of the leashmen shouted back.
"It's got to be close!"

The dogs came to an incline and their movement
slowed. But when they reached the crest and started
down, gravity abetted their eagerness, pulling them
with the speed of roller coasters. The men were now
running full-tilt, swept with a momentum they were
helpless to stop. And then they saw it. An angular
path of white water roaring through the forest and
coming to an abrupt end in the darkness just ahead.

"Water. It's a waterfall!"

"It's a drop-off!"

"*Stop* them!"

The leashmen heaved backwards, digging their heels
into earth. But the dogs refused to be stopped, pulling
even harder against the resistance, coming closer with
each moment to the gaping chasm that loomed in the
moonlight ahead.

"JESUS . . . !"

"I can't . . . !"

"*Help* me!"

One of the men grabbed a tree trunk and managed
to hold firm, snapping his bloodhound backwards,
jolting it into a daze. But the other leashman stumbled
and fell, clinging to the leash as he was dragged
forward, helpless to do anything but cry out as his
dog hurtled toward the ledge.

In a sudden, breathless moment, the radioman took
flight, leaping directly atop the dragged man. At the
same moment, the bloodhound sailed off the edge of
the cliff.

His flight lasted but an instant before it was halted.
On top of the cliff, the human anchor had held.

Just five feet from the cliff's edge, the radioman

clung tightly to the man beneath him. The dog swung silently in midair.

"Help us!" the radioman shouted. They were slipping, inch by inch, toward the ledge, the leash vibrating as the dog beneath them struggled in fear. The second leashman fumbled with his belt, quickly unhitching it and tying it to a tree. His dog was lying on the ground, dazed from the jolt, its eyes staring upward at the moon.

*"Help* us, goddammit!"

The second leashman ran from the trees, falling across his companions and grabbing the taut leash, heaving back on it with all his weight. Clinging desperately to one another, they inched back like a six-legged crab, until they had put ten feet between themselves and the cliff, and stabilized themselves behind the stump of tree. The man who had been dragged was cut and bruised; the other two clung tightly to him, for the two-hundred-pound dog was still suspended from the end of the leash that was connected to his belt.

They gazed at each other with frightened eyes, numbed by the near fatality.

"You all right?"

"I couldn't get the release . . ."

"I've never seen them do that. . . ."

"Whatever they're after is down in that gully."

"If it's down there, it's a dead man."

"They don't bay like that for a dead man."

"Let's get the dog up."

With shaking arms, they grabbed the taut leash, snaking their hands through it to get a firm grip.

"Heave!"

They pulled in unison, gaining three feet of slack. Then they grabbed hold again.

*"Heave!"*

They pulled again. But this time, to no avail. It was as though the dog's weight had suddenly increased beyond their strength. Digging their heels into the dirt, they continued to pull, their teeth gritted with exertion, their eyes meeting in confusion. It was becoming a struggle, a test of strength, as though something were pulling from the other end.

"Oh, God . . ." one of them moaned as they were abruptly dragged forward.

"Hold me!" cried the leashman who was tied to it. "Help me!"

One of them thrust an arm into the dragged man's belt, locking himself into the combat. The other man let go, but the dragged man grabbed onto him, clinging to him like a drowning man going under.

"No . . . !" one of them sobbed as they were dragged unstoppably forward. And with a sudden jerk their bodies left the ground, catapulting into the air, their screams echoing as they cartwheeled downward into the chasm.

Only one of them lived long enough after hitting the ground to see what it was that had pulled them. It stood over him, emitting a quiet squeal, and raised an arm that revealed a skinfold beneath it, with veins traced like tree branches, back lit by the moon. It was all the man saw before his head was severed from his body, the chemical reaction called memory quickly dissipating as the head smashed against a tree.

# 5

As JOHN HAWKS sat in grim silence, gazing out the window of the train that took him from Washington, D.C., to Maine, he saw dawn breaking over the stately pinnacle of Mount Katahdin. It was a sight he had not seen for seven years.

That last visit to the place of his birth, when he was twenty-one, had been a profound disappointment. He had been seeking ancestral ties, re-immersion into a culture he had forsaken. But he found that the Masaquoddy people had fallen into cultural limbo. The village he remembered from childhood as beautiful and magical had become a garbage dump; a collection of huts made from cast-off materials, the ground littered with unusable machinery and the skeletons of defunct automobiles.

Proximity to the white man's world had taken its toll. The incipient feeling of inferiority had created an appetite for mimicry. Washing machines were purchased even though the village had no electrical power source, transistor radios abounded even though nothing but static could be picked up because of the barriers of mountains. Automobiles were bought and junked there because no gasoline could be afforded. White Woolworth brassiers could be seen intruding between the earth colors of the women's animal-hide jackets and their rich brown skin.

And yet, in spite of all this material weakness, the Masaquoddy still had their pride. Pride enough to

44

avoid contact with the whites. Pride enough to resent
John Hawks for having been a part of the white world.

It was likely that there was white blood in John
Hawks. It was his blessing and his curse. It had
entered too far back in his lineage for him to trace,
but it was discernible on his face. His features were
fine, his skin was light. He had once taken secret delight in the knowledge that he could pass for white.
But now he hated that knowledge, for it had filled his
life with confusion.

It was because of his looks that he had been selected
by Mary Pitney when he was twelve to be taken from
the Masaquoddy village and educated at a boarding
school in Portland. As owners of the lumber company
on the shores of the Espee River, the Pitneys considered themselves philanthropic people. They were
in their seventies then, and wanted to make sure, before it was too late, that they earned their passports
to Heaven. There were two other Indian children
selected. One was from the Yurok tribe, one from the
Ashinabeg; Hawks was the third. The Yurok killed
himself when he was a teenager. The Ashinabeg died
in Vietnam.

Hawks was the only one who survived the ordeal;
he survived it by deception: losing his tribal accent,
dressing as the white children dressed, and learning
that it was better to be white than red. For many
years he made a conscious effort to forget where he
was born; he even invented a history of descendance
from a wealthy Bostonian family, who, he said, were
all deceased. The Pitneys had died by the time he was
sixteen, leaving him an educational fund administered
by a bank in Portland; he himself was an orphan.
There was no one, except his inner self, to remind
him of the truth.

But the lifetime of deception took its toll. Passing
for white in a country heavily populated with Indians,
he was often privileged to conversations normally re-
served for whites only. The jokes were torturous, and
he forced himself to laugh at them.

After boarding school, he won a scholarship to the University of Maine in Orono. It was there that the truth came out and humiliated him. He had become enamored of a girl who was wealthy, well-bred, born and raised in Boston. Having heard his story about coming from a wealthy Bostonian family, she took it upon herself to research the facts. Hawks left college immediately after, with the sound of laughter ringing in his ears.

Angered and ashamed, Hawks went back to his village, but found that they would not accept him, either. He dressed in buckskins, and tried to reinterest them in living the way that Indians once lived, but they considered him a joke. Like a bird telling a wolf how a wolf should be. There was only one person who extended kindness to him. Her name was Romona Peters. She and her grandfather, among all the people in the village, were the only ones who tried to maintain a hold on Indian life.

To Romona, John Hawks represented everything that she herself was unable to be. He had education and a knowledge of the world outside of the forest. She, in turn, had a purity that he envied. She was Indian through and through, and had no desire to copy the ways of the white world.

The attraction between them was instant and, even though it was forbidden by Indian law, they became lovers. But the very differences that brought them together drove them apart. It was in 1971, and the Pitney Paper Mill was sending out the first signal that it would one day make a claim to the entirety of the Indian land. Workmen were tearing down the old, outdated pulping mill and building a gigantic factory on the shores of the Espee River. John Hawks alone knew that it meant trouble. From his exposure to newspapers and television, he was familiar with the land-grab that was going on in the Pacific Northwest, and saw that the new factory, when completed, would be capable of gobbling up the entire forest. He attempted to rally the Masaquoddy people behind him, but they resisted. Even Romona was against him. She was a pacifist, and claimed that confrontation would lead to their downfall. Beyond that, she felt that confrontation was premature. She believed it was Hawks's anger at the Pitneys for disrupting his life, rather than the reality of a new factory, that was provoking his rage.

There were bitter words between them, and John Hawks left Manatee Forest, he thought forever.

He went to where the action was, observing other tribes who were battling industry for their land. As he witnessed successive battles and defeats, he learned that there was only one tactic that halted the momentum of land-grab. That tactic was violence. Not that there was victory in violence. There would never be victory, no matter what. But there was satisfaction in violence. As much as Hawks liked to trade verbiage with the industrialists and politicians and beat them at their own game, he knew that ultimately they considered him harmless. Like a dog that had been taught to walk on its hind legs, but would ultimately have to return to all four. It was only when the dog showed his teeth that he was respected.

Having followed the trail of destruction from forest to forest and tribe to tribe, Hawks had wound up in Washington, where demonstrators were finally massing, to join a chorus of protest against the theft of Indian land. To his surprise he found representatives there from his own part of the world eager to have someone unite them and act as their spokesman. It was the opportunity Hawks was waiting for. He had predicted what had come to pass; they looked to him now to save them.

It was not only that he was given the power to represent his people. He was, at last, given validity as an Indian. In spite of some throwback genes and a vocabulary that sounded like the white man's dictionary, he could now declare to the world that, in his heart, soul, and spirit, he was at one with his people.

His three meetings with the House Subcommittee on Indian Affairs were token gestures, both on his part and on theirs. The war of words was heavily loaded on the side of government. "Justice" had as much meaning as "tennis court." A concept valid to only those who could afford it. It was plain that the industrial complex felt it could mow down the forest like grass beneath a lawnmower, with little or no resistance from the people who rightfully owned it. They were about to find out differently. For John Hawks was prepared to fight.

As the small train wound around the base of Mount Katahdin, Hawks thought about Romona. He wondered if she was still there, if she would welcome him. He had thought of Romona often over the years; for periods of time he'd thought of her constantly. He knew that if, as a child, he had not been taken from his village, he and Romona would have grown up together and been married. He would have been a fisherman, she the mother of several children. He cursed the Pitneys for the confusion they had caused him; he was glad for the opportunity to fight back.

He remembered a conversation he'd had with Romona's grandfather seven years ago, when the old man gave him a stern warning about the forces of anger. "It is not the purpose of one family to vanquish another," M'rai had said. "For one family to point the finger at another and say 'This is the villain' is as destructive as having that finger pointed at you yourself." Hawks had replied that if a man refused to fight for what was his, he *deserved* to have it taken away from him.

"If it is truly yours," the old man replied, "you do not have to fight for it."

"No one's going to help us, old man," Hawks remembered saying.

"The forest will help us," M'rai had replied. "Katahdin will help us."

Hawks had been amazed at the old man's childishness. But that was his beauty, too; his belief in the ancient legends.

Katahdin was perhaps the first legend that any Masaquoddy child ever learned: the mythical beast whose physical makeup was a mixture of every creature that God ever created. It was said that in times of need, Katahdin would awaken from his slumber to defend whichever of God's creatures needed protecting.

Hawks closed his eyes and envisioned the old man standing in a desecrated wasteland where the trees once stood. He wondered if, finally, the old man would lose his childlike belief in Katahdin.

"It's a 'boreal forest,' Maggie. You know what that means?"

Robert Vern stood in the bedroom of their small Georgetown apartment, packing a suitcase as he spoke, his voice raised over the sound of an orchestra coming from the living room. There, Maggie sat in a stiff-backed chair, playing a cello solo to an accompaniment that blared from the speakers of her portable tape recorder. It was Schumann's Cello Concerto, a difficult selection that was to open the subscription season of the Washington Symphony. It was because she had been chosen to play the solo that she was unable to accompany Rob to Maine.

"Maggie? You hearing me?"

Rob waited for a response, but none came. His voice had been loud enough. She just wasn't answering.

Her dark and silent mood had begun a week ago, and Rob was deeply troubled by it. It had apparently started the night he noticed her tears.

He had remained at home the following morning to speak to her about it, but she was uncommunicative, passing it off as nothing more than a bad dream. But he knew it was something more. On successive nights he had noticed a bottle of Valium on her bed table;

she had never before used drugs to go to sleep. Twice
he pressed her on the subject; both times she avoided
it. It was as though she had become afraid of him.
Sometimes when she watched him, there was accusation in her eyes.

He was frightened now of pressing too hard, for
when he searched his mind for a possible answer, his
stomach tightened with fear. With all the time they
spent apart, it was possible that Maggie had become
attracted to another man. It was something he couldn't
deal with. In the seven years of their marriage, he had
remained faithful; he was deeply committed to her and
could not bear to think that she was not the same.
If, in fact, she had a lover, Rob knew it was his own
fault. He had taken her for granted, just assumed she
would always be there.

The thought of it caused him so much anguish that
he pushed it from his mind, forcing his attention back
to the job at hand. Picking up a stack of thick books,
he placed it next to his medical kit. The titles of the
books were *Soil Erosion, Hydroculture, Industrial
Hazards;* just a few of the dozens he'd been poring
over since he'd accepted Victor's offer to go with the
EPA. He was uneasy about the decision. It somehow
didn't seem right. He felt he was in over his head, in
a field that didn't really suit him. Nevertheless, he'd
given his work, and was committed to no more than
the two weeks ahead of him.

For the past six days, he'd immersed himself in
research, getting special dispensation to stay in the
Washington Library after closing hours, and had spent
a weekend with a veteran field worker in the forests
of New Jersey. He had learned how to collect soil
samples and analyze them for water absorption and
mineral content; he could identify over forty members
of the Pinaceae genre of trees. He could even determine
the age, health, and amount of waterfall over a ten-
year period by examining the under bark of a tree.

Now, a few hours before his departure to Maine,
he felt he was close to being ready. The books would

provide the rest. He'd start studying them on the plane.

Closing his suitcase, he sat for a moment on the bed, listening to Maggie play. He often envied her her occupation because it brought her peace instead of frustration. When she played the cello, she was able to express feeling simply, directly, and with immense clarity. She was a gifted musician.

Rob rose from the bed and walked to the open door, gazing in at her. She was facing him, and caught his eye.

"It's beautiful," he said.

She responded with a nod and continued playing.

"Brahms?" he asked.

"Schumann."

"Lot of cello."

"He loved the cello," she answered as she continued to play. "He said it was the one instrument that can be embraced like a lover."

"It's kind of quiet over dinner, though," he said.

"Tell me about it."

He saw it in her eyes again. The accusation that he had failed her. He moved inward, sitting on the arm of her chair.

"You know . . . if this job is something I like . . . you'll have me around the house again."

"Will I?"

"Um-hm. Trees don't get sick in the middle of the night, I'm told."

"Bet they do. They just can't tell anybody."

Rob was seated just behind her. He was taken with the tilt of her neck and the fragrance of her hair. Tentatively he leaned down and kissed her shoulder.

She stopped playing but didn't turn; the music on the tape recorder continued as she gazed forward.

"What is a boreal forest?" she asked.

Rob was stopped for a moment, then remembered he had called out the question from the bedroom. "You heard me."

"Uh-hm."

"Why didn't you answer?"

"Can't shout when you're playing 'Schumann.' "

"A boreal forest . . . is something that hasn't been touched since the beginning of time."

She lowered her head, not answering.

"That make you sad?" he asked.

"I guess."

"Why?"

"Because I can relate to it."

He touched her and she turned to him.

"What is it, Maggie?" Rob whispered.

Her eyes misted, and she turned away.

"Just blurt it out."

"I can't do that," she whispered.

"Why not?"

"Because it's not that simple. It's . . . complicated. It's not just something I can say."

She searched his eyes, trying to make him understand. "I need hours. I need days. I need to *be* with you. Feel close to you. I need the kind of time we don't seem to have."

He drew her gently to him, her head pressing against his chest.

"Remember how we used to sit and talk?" she asked sadly. "Just . . . endlessly? Just say whatever popped into our minds? My God, we used to sit up all night drinking wine . . . and when morning came we'd pull down the shades . . . and before we knew it, it was night again."

He nodded.

"Why don't we do that any more?" she asked plaintively.

"We're two busy people, Maggie."

"One of us is lonely."

Rob slowly shook his head. It was an expression of helplessness.

"I don't know what to do, Maggie . . ."

"I know how you feel about your work, and I admire that . . ."

"It's more than my work . . ."

"Exactly. It's as though you had a mistress. At least if it were a mistress, I could compete."

"I don't have a mistress," Rob said softly.

"Of course you don't, but . . ."

"Do *you?*"

The words had come out before he could stop them.

"Do I what?"

"Have a lover?"

She was taken aback. "Of course not."

He studied her expression carefully. "You sure?"

"Well, if I'm *not* sure, he couldn't be much of a lover, could he?"

"I'm serious."

She couldn't help laughing, but she stopped when she saw how pained he was.

"I've only loved one man in my life," she said quietly. "Isn't that a silly thing at the age of thirty? If I admitted that to any one of the girls in the orchestra, they'd laugh me off the stage. Do you know, there's a girl there who—" She stopped herself, suddenly bursting into laughter.

Her abrupt shift of mood was so inappropriate that Rob was disoriented by it. But he couldn't help laughing with her.

"There's a girl there who . . . what?" he asked.

"For starters, she plays the clarinet. If you get the symbolism."

"Yes."

"Well, she doesn't like pills or diaphragms. The pills make her sick and the diaphragms aren't a hundred percent effective. I mean, people *do* get pregnant even when they use diaphragms."

"Not usually."

"But it does happen, am I right?"

"In theory."

Rob maintained a smile, but there was something wrong with the conversation. Maggie was babbling.

"Well, anyway, she thinks you can get pregnant with a diaphragm, and so she buys these . . . you know . . . what do you call them? For a man? Condoms?"

"Um-hm."

"She goes to the university dispensary and gets them by the dozens. I saw them. She keeps them in her purse. They come all connected together in plastic, like machine-gun bullets or something, in a long chain, and she orders a hundred of them at once, and she just opens her beach bag and they feed them in over the counter."

She stopped and suddenly laughed again, slapping her hand to her mouth. "Can you *imagine?*"

"Nope."

"You know how many men she's slept with? Between five hundred and a thousand. That's what she told me. Can you imagine? That she's not sure about a mere *five hundred?*"

It was so bizarre that Rob began to laugh again.

"Who is she?"

"I'm not going to tell."

Their laughter faded and they sat gazing at each other, the classical music still playing softly in the background. Their eyes held, the mood softening to the moment when one of them had to speak. But neither wanted to.

"Do you know what just happened, Rob?" Maggie whispered.

"What?"

"You and I laughed with each other. How long has it been since we did that?"

Rob nodded in saddened agreement. "Long time."

"That's what I *need,* Rob. To feel easy with you. And free. And relaxed. If I could just have some time for that, then I could say everything that's on my mind."

"What *is* on your mind, Maggie?"

She stiffened, feeling her toes curling in her shoes. "You're leaving in three hours. I need more than that."

"Come with me."

"I can't."

"We'd have two weeks, Maggie. No telephones. No emergencies. They're putting me in a log cabin. On an island. In the middle of a lake. Nothing around but trees and water."

"How can I do that?"

"How can you not?"

Maggie knew she was trying to avoid the inevitable. She was subconsciously doing what Dr. Hamlisch had warned her not to—trying to avoid the subject of her pregnancy until it was too late. If she went with Rob, it would have to be revealed. And she would have to face the conversation that she most feared. But perhaps, in that setting, it could be handled. If it could be handled anywhere, that would be the place.

"How cold does it get?" she asked.

"You didn't answer my question."

"Yes, I did. I want to know what to pack."

# 6

---

THE MORNING SUN was muted by a cloud bank that
hung low over Manatee Forest. The humidity was
rising and there were distant rumbles of thunder
across the mountainous horizon. The voices of two
loons on Mary's Lake resounded within the cloud-
lidded enclosure as animals of all sizes and shapes
trundled out from the tree line to go through their
early-morning rituals of washing, drinking, and feeding at the lake.

Up in the mountains, at the foot of a cliff, a
family of raccoons tasted human flesh, snarling and
fighting over the bits and pieces of decaying meat
strewn across the ground. The body of a man suspended above them, his neck tangled in a leash,
created no fear in them. The uniquely human smell
had departed within hours, leaving just the stench of
a rotting carcass, tantalizingly out of reach of the
ravenous raccoons.

On the plateau above them, a chewed leash tied
to a tree was all that was left of the one bloodhound
that had survived the massacre. He had gnawed
through the thick tether and followed his nose back
to the nearest point of civilization. There, at a forestry
station, a ranger had summoned the sheriff, whose
men repeatedly attempted to entice the dog into leading them back into the forest. But the animal refused.
He would not even turn his head in the direction
from which he had come. Two days had passed with

no sign from the rescue team. In another few days it would become evident that they were never going to return.

The sheriff of Manatee County was making every effort to keep the new disappearances quiet, but there were certain people who were privileged to the information. One was Bethel Isely, the managing director of the Pitney Paper Mill.

Isely was forty-four years of age, born and raised in Atlanta, Georgia, schooled in public relations, hired just six months ago to bring his wife and three children from Atlanta and work for the Pitney Paper Mill. Though he knew little about lumbering, he was an expert in the art of swaying public opinion. Under his auspices there had been two barbecues for the townspeople, and a large grant of money dispensed to the three local churches. The few dissenting voices initially heard in regard to the paper mill's planned expansion had been smothered beneath a cascade of literature on the positive effects of culling and harvesting trees.

Isely took his job seriously, and believed what he had to believe. There were good arguments to be made both for and against timber cutting, and he could righteously argue the side that provided him with his livelihood. The fact that his livelihood had never been better added to his conviction. The Pitneys had given him a house, two cars, and a salary of seventy thousand dollars a year.

He knew, however, that it would all be in jeopardy if the man who was arriving today from the Environmental Protection Agency filed a negative report. Taking every precaution, he had put in extra hours, researching every aspect of timber cutting that he could think of. He even researched the man himself, discovering that Robert Vern was an M.D. and had a wife named Maggie who played the cello. Leaving no stone unturned, he even learned a thing or two about cellos and symphonies. He hoped that Vern was bringing his wife, for then Isely could more easily convince him to turn the visit into something of a vacation.

Isely was well prepared, ready to answer any question, willing to make himself available to Vern full time. The Pitney Paper Mill was a model of efficiency and high standards. He could truly be proud of what he had to show.

As he dressed to go to the airport, he glanced out the window to check the sky. By the look of it, the spring rains were about to begin.


Not far away, John Hawks was making plans, too. But not for the arrival of Robert Vern. He did not know that the man from the Environmental Protection Agency was arriving today; even if he had, it would not have altered his course of action. The barricade was going back up. From this day on, no vehicle from the lumber company was going to be allowed to use the main road into the forest. Hawks knew they could ferry their men in by boat along the Espee River, or fly them by float plane into Mary's Lake. But it would cost them time and money, and substantially cut into their efficiency rate. The road blockade would squeeze them into taking the Indians seriously.

Hawks had been in the forest for only twenty-four hours, having gone directly to the village and summoned an army of ten able-bodied men. It was different now than it had been seven years ago. The Masaquoddy had finally gotten angry enough to fight. They were being victimized from all sides; accused of being murderers when they were not, of being drunks when they were not.

Hawks had had little time to digest the myriad problems that besieged the villagers, but had listened with concern as they told him of the *katahnas,* the seizures that struck without warning, confusing the minds and bodies of their people. They showed him a man who was in the throes of it. He was racked with fever and raging with hallucinations.

At this particular moment, the *katahnas* were not widespread. Fearing contact with the lumberjacks or townspeople, the Indians had stopped going to their fishing nets, and were living within the confines of their village, subsisting on whatever small game they could catch and their surplus of canned goods. As mysteriously as they had come, the *katahnas* had suddenly tapered off. Only one man in the past three weeks had been affected.

Hawks did not know what to make of the strange affliction and, because it was in a period of recession, failed to understand its alarming proportions. He would investigate it another time. On this day his priority was the blockade.

With his army of stalwarts, he now moved through the forest toward the main road. The men ranged in age from sixteen to thirty; none of them in their lives had ever stood up to a white man before. Hawks had cautioned them to leave all weapons behind. They would defend the forest with their lives, but they would not be accused of threatening life. The only semblance of a weapon among them was a long-handled ax, brought for the purpose of making shelter in the event of rain.

As they moved silently through the forest, they passed close to the encampment of the old man, M'rai. Hawks could see the crossed poles of his tepees protruding through the tops of the trees. When he first arrived at the village, Hawks had inquired about the old man, and was told that M'rai, too, was suffering frequently from the *katahnas*. They said his mind had grown dim and he often hallucinated, wandering alone through the forest at night, and spinning tales of the beast Katahdin, who, he claimed, came to drink at the shores of his secret lagoon.

The so-called secret lagoon was a sacred place to the Masaquoddy; by tradition, the private sanctuary of the oldest man in the tribe. It was said that everything grew large there, larger than life. But Hawks remembered sneaking in as a child and being pro-

foundly disappointed to find that it was just another
pond in the forest.

The myth of the secret lagoon had once reached
the ears of some flower children from New York, and
they had gone there planting marijuana seeds in the
hope that they would grow to gargantuan size. They
were chased off by the Indians; the sheriff's deputies
had plowed up the ground with picks and shovels to
make sure the seeds didn't blossom. Hawks wondered
if a few of the seeds might have survived. If the old
man was chewing cannabis while he meditated at the
pond, that could well explain his visions of Katahdin.

As they now came closer to the old man's encampment, Hawks paused and gazed in through the trees.
It was just as he had left it: in the midst of this
troubled forest, an oasis of peace and beauty. Three
huge, conical tents made from animal hides stood in
a circle, a large fire pit, rimmed with stones, in the
center. A line strung between two poles held drying
animal skins and strips of jerky; an elegant, handmade
archer's bow leaned against a tree. It was a bow that
Hawks himself had used when, as a child, he was
tutored in archery by M'rai.

The smell of animal fat hung in the air; another re-
minder of Hawk's youth. As he stood there, he felt
transported in time.

"Noa'hgna'aught N'hak'tah," one of the men behind
him said. He was warning Hawks that no one was
allowed in the old man's encampment without invitation. The language of Hawks's childhood was still
familiar to him; he had some command of it and
could make himself understood.

"D'hana'ht Yo'ahtha," Hawks replied as he pointed
in the direction of the road. The men moved off,
leaving him alone. Since he had arrived back in the
forest, Hawks had refrained from asking anyone about
Romona. He could not pass by without knowing if she
was there.

Stepping forward into the compound, Hawks called
her name.

*"A'hanspanitah Oliana . . . ?"*

After a moment, one of the tent flaps pulled back, and she appeared. She was more beautiful now than he remembered her. Her dark hair had the sheen of a forest animal's; it draped gently against her shoulders with the contour of a graceful waterfall. Her body was lean and agile and stood straight as only an Indian woman's could. But her eyes were vulnerable and filled with hurt.

She stood in silence, overwhelmed to see him. "Thank God," she whispered.

"I'm back to stay."

"I'll fight with you now, John," she whispered. "I'll fight beside you. We're dying in here."

"Come with me now."

"Where?"

"The first battle is today."

Without hesitation she followed, watching Hawks move in front of her through the forest as though he belonged there. He was all Indian now; she could see it in the way his feet touched the forest floor. There was much she wanted to tell him. About the stillbirths and the sickness. But he was filled with single-minded purpose now. She would wait until he was ready.

As the small twin-engined Cessna dipped beneath the cloud cover, Rob and Maggie looked out its small window, catching their first glimpse of the forest below. Maggie's cello was propped upright in an empty seat behind her, Rob's doctor's kit beside it. The symbols of the two personalities that had kept them apart for so long were riding separately behind them.

Hours earlier, in a hurried call to the symphony conductor, Maggie had promised to continue practicing the Schumann on her two-week vacation if they would substitute for her until she returned. The conductor complained, but Maggie was firm; the assertiveness of the moment had acted on her like a shot of vitamins. She felt confident and proud of herself for taking a step toward solving her dilemma.

For his part Rob, too, was grateful that she had come. In the limbo of sky-transit they were more at ease with each other than they had been in months. They had held hands all the way, recounting fond and funny memories, both reveling in their closeness. They were swept with a feeling of well-being, a sense that everything between them was going to be all right.

"Isn't it beautiful . . ." Maggie whispered as she gazed down at the lakes and trees below.

Rob nodded, awed by it. "I forgot the world could look like this."

"Maybe that's our trouble, huh? Can't see the forest for the trees?"

He smiled appreciatively.

"Really," she mused, "I think we get so caught up in *details* that we forget what life is all about."

"What *is* life all about?" he asked. He was half joking, but sincerely wanted to hear her answer.

"Us. What's inside of us. If that's empty, then there's nothing."

"You feel empty inside?"

She kept a straight face. "No."

"Me, neither. Not right now, anyway."

They glanced at each other, and he kissed her cheek.

"Can this be true?" she asked. "Have I done something right lately?"

He laughed and cradled her head against his shoulder, his eyes drifting to the window.

"You know," he mused, "yesterday I walked the streets of a city where six thousand people live in a single block, stacked up on top of each other and side by side, asking only for enough space to lie down at night and stand up in the morning."

Maggie glanced up at him. His eyes were on the forest.

"Today I'm flying over three hundred square miles of wilderness that a handful of people are claiming is all their own." He shook his head, unable to fathom it. "Children die of malnutrition while farmers pour surplus supplies of milk down the drain . . ."

"Why do they do that?"

"To drive the prices up."

"How awful."

"That's what it's all about. Profit. The tenements . . . the trees . . . starvation . . ."

His voice trailed off, his eyes etched with despair.

"Can I tell you something?" Maggie asked softly.

"Mmmm."

"It's wonderful that you worry about those things. It's something I don't seem capable of doing." She paused, wanting to make her thoughts clear. "But the part that worries me is that you sound as if you feel personally responsible."

"I guess I do."

"There's only so much you can do, Rob. The world is too big."

He nodded and glanced at her with appreciation.

"Ever read *Small Is Beautiful?*" she asked.

"What's that?"

"It's like it sounds. It's a book."

He looked at the unopened book in his lap. "Bet it can't compare to *Hydroponics and Industrial Hazards,*" he joked. "Now, *that's* an exciting book."

"Don't tell me the ending," she quipped.

He smiled sadly to himself and shook his head. "I fear what the ending is. I really do."

The plane swooped low and the Androscoggin airport came into view. It was no more than a dollop of cement surrounded by wilderness; on the gravel road leading to it, Rob saw two yellow cars kicking up a cloud of dust as they headed fast toward the landing strip.

Within minutes the plane was on the ground, Rob and Maggie stepping out into the bracing wind. It was like a tonic to them; they pointed their noses directly into it, closing their eyes as it washed over them.

"Smell it!" Maggie groaned in ecstasy.

"Pine."

"Mmmmmm. I'd like to bottle it and take it home."

"There's plenty out there. Look at those mountains."

Near them on the runway, a man and woman were tying down their private plane while their two children, a boy and girl of about ten and twelve, squealed with delight as they picked through their belongings. The boy caught Rob's eye and called over to him:

"You going camping?"

"Well, sort of," Rob answered. "We're going to be in a cabin."

"We're going to be outside! On a mountain right beside a waterfall! It's gonna take three days just to walk there!"

"Sounds hard," Maggie responded.

"That's the fun!" the boy exuberantly shouted back. Beside him, his sister was shielding her eyes as she gazed into the sky.

"What the heck is *that?*" she exclaimed.

Rob and Maggie looked skyward, amazed at what they saw. Dangling on the end of a rope suspended from the bottom of an approaching helicopter was a huge dog. A bloodhound, its four legs pumping air as though it were swimming instead of flying, its tail rotating as if, by instinct, trying to function as a propeller.

"It's a dog!" laughed the boy. "A flying dog!"

Maggie laughed, too, and turned to Rob. "What do you suppose they're doing?"

"Damnedest thing I ever saw," Rob mumbled.

He looked around the airstrip to see that others were as amazed as he, everyone squinting upward into the brightly overcast sky.

Then Rob spotted the two yellow cars he'd seen from the air. They bore the emblem of the Pitney Paper Mill and swerved directly onto the landing strip beside them.

"Mr. Vern?"

The man who spoke from the driver's window of the first car was round-faced and rosy-cheeked, prematurely bald, with a bright, engaging smile. He stepped out, revealing he was soft around the middle, and walked with a duck-footed gait, his hand extended as he approached them.

"Bethel Isely," he said. "Pitney Paper Mill. Have a nice flight?"

Rob knew that he was to be met at the airport, but didn't know it would be by representatives of the paper company.

"Uh . . . yes . . ." Rob mumbled as the man pumped his hand, "This is my wife, Maggie Vern . . ."

"Mrs. Vern . . ."

"Hello."

"Mighty glad you came along, Mrs. Vern. Be a shame to miss out on a treat like this."

He spotted the uneasy look in Rob's eye. "Hope you don't mind my coming. Some of the locals don't know exactly how to get where you're going, and I thought you might need some help."

Rob was slow to respond. "To tell you the truth, I don't know if I feel right about being met by the paper company . . ."

"Fine, fine. I'll call you a cab. They don't usually go into the forest, though."

"Well, how does one get in there?"

"Private car. That's the ticket. We'll rent you a car. I thought I'd save you that trouble by bringing an extra one for you, but that's fine. I want you to do what you want to do."

"That's very nice of you," Maggie said.

"I didn't want you to have any trouble," Isely responded. "I even packed in some supplies so you'd have everything you needed for a few days. My wife insisted on sending some home-cooked food, and I said, 'No, no, these people are going to think we're putting pressure on them.' "

"I'm really sorry to seem ungrateful," Rob said.

"I understand completely," Isely responded. "That a Rogeri?" he asked, pointing to Maggie's cello.

"Montagna," she replied with surprise. "You know cellos?"

"I know wood. That's got a balsam back, a spruce belly, and a maple bridge. Three different types of trees in there."

"Very impressive," Maggie replied.

"You know," Isely continued, "there wouldn't be near as much music in the world if people didn't harvest trees."

Rob had to laugh. "I'm glad you're not putting any pressure on," he said.

"Am I comin' on too strong?" Isely replied with a smile.

"It's all right," Rob said. He liked the man in spite of his pushiness.

"Well, I'll be right up front," Isely said. "Your trip here is real important to me. I wanted to come here so you wouldn't think I was your enemy. Us lumber people are human, too. We don't want to do anything wrong, any more than you want us to."

"I appreciate your saying that."

"You want to rent a car, it's fine with me, but I'd prefer to take you. Just let me have your ear while we drive to the lake, then I'll let you alone."

Rob caught Maggie's expression. She clearly didn't want the man to feel slighted.

"Okay," Rob said.

"Fair enough," declared Isely. Then he turned toward his cars. "Kelso? Take these people's bags. Johnny, you handle that cello and be mighty careful with it. It's worth a heap of money."

Five men climbed out of the second car and began grabbing luggage. They wore plaid shirts that showed long undershirts protruding from the sleeves; their boots were caked with mud. They were obviously lumberjacks.

"Mrs. Vern? You want to sit in front?" Isely asked.

"Could I ask you a question?" Maggie responded.

"Anything at all."

She squinted toward the sky, her eyes following the bloodhound, which was now hovering almost directly over them, being lowered slowly toward the ground.

"What's that dog doing up in the air?"

"Those choppers can't take a sudden weight shift. They carry the dog underneath so they'll know he's staying in one place."

"Where are they bringing him from?" Maggie asked.

"The mountains."

"Do they usually fly them out?"

"Well, he was in pretty deep."

Both Rob and Maggie sensed that Isely was avoiding something.

"Somebody's pet?" Maggie asked.

"Well . . . not exactly."

Rob caught Isely's eye. "What's the mystery?"

"Oh, no mystery, really. That bloodhound, he was a part of our Search and Rescue Team. I *figure* that's the dog. I don't think there's any other bloodhounds in these parts."

"Someone was lost?" Maggie asked.

Isely nodded. "People from our company, as a matter of fact. Couple of lumberjacks. Went out on a night crew and never came back."

"Did they find them?"

Isely's face sobered, his eyes following the bloodhound's descent. "No, sir."

"What do you suppose happened to them?"

"Oh, I don't know—got lost, I guess," Isely said, dismissing it. "We ready to go here?"

They followed him to the car, Maggie's eyes still fixed on the bloodhound, who was pawing the air as his feet neared the ground.

"So they're just giving up? The rescue team's coming back?"

Isely paused, wondering whether or not to tell them. "There is no rescue team any more."

Rob and Maggie exchanged a glance of confusion.

"I don't understand," Rob said.

"Three men and two dogs went in there. Only one dog came out. He showed up at a ranger's station; no sign of the people who brought him in there."

"What happened to them?"

Isely shook his head. "Guess they got lost, too."

"A rescue team?" Maggie asked. "Is that possible?"

Isely had gotten himself into it now, and there was no getting out. He gestured Rob and Maggie to the side. "We're being honest with each other here, so I'll tell you the truth. This particular forest isn't too safe right now. That's why I thought I'd better take you in."

"Why is that?" Rob asked.

"The Indians are angry in there. They're trying to keep the lumber company out any way they can."

Rob and Maggie listened intently, uneasy with what they were hearing.

"There's no need for you people to worry. They wouldn't mess with people from the government. This is sort of a family matter that's going on here."

"You're saying the Indians did something to those people?" Rob asked.

"That's awful hard to prove. There's no evidence. Things with the Indians are real sensitive right now."

"Have you questioned them?"

"The sheriff has."

"And what do they say?"

"They say they don't know anything about it. They say those people were taken by Katahdin."

"What's Katahdin?" Rob asked.

Isely shook his head with grim amusement. "One of their legends. They call it Katahdin."

"Like a 'Big Foot,' you mean?" Maggie asked.

"Yeah, except this one's a little uglier. The size of a dragon, the eyes of a cat, they've got everything thrown in except the kitchen sink. Speakin' of the kitchen sink, my wife baked you a pie. I got it in the car."

He walked around to the driver's door and got in

the car. Rob and Maggie exchanged a long look before
they did the same.

"The idea of Katahdin," Isely continued as he
closed his door, "is to frighten the lumberjacks out.
They're almost as superstitious as the Opies."

"Opies?" Rob asked.

"O.P.'s. Original People. That's what they call
themselves. The Ashinabegs, Masaquoddy, Wampanoag, Yurok—they've all joined together now and
call themselves the Opies."

He put his keys in the ignition and started the
motor.

"But what about those people?" Maggie asked with
concern. "The ones who disappeared?"

"I can only tell you, if it had been up to me, I
wouldn't have sent a search party in. I'd have sent a
posse."

"So you're convinced the Indians did it."

Isely looked across Maggie, into Rob's eyes.

"They stagger around drunk half the time in there,
Mr. Vern. It's a damn sad thing, but it's true. My
men have seen them bumping into trees in that forest.
We heard that one Indian man ran right into the lake
and drowned. Another man showed up at the hospital
with knife wounds all up and down him, from being
attacked by his own brother."

Rob and Maggie sat in silence.

"I'm afraid the only explanation is booze."

"Where do they get the booze?" Rob asked.

"We don't know. Since the craziness started, nobody in town is allowed to sell it to them."

Maggie turned to Isely with apprehensive eyes.

"So what you're saying is . . . that those people
disappeared because the Indians *did* something to
them."

"A rescue party doesn't get lost, Mrs. Vern. Neither
do my lumberjacks."

He shifted gears; the two cars moved slowly out
of the airport.

The drive from the airport took them through the town of Manatee; its one business street looked as if it were created for a postcard. There were three churches, two stores, a post office, a library, a jail; all were lined up side by side. But there was also a quality of loneliness. Few people were on the streets; the branches of the trees were still bare, the wind vocalizing as it swept through them.

Four miles beyond the town, they turned onto a dirt road, the car behind them following close, engulfed in their dust as they rumbled into the wilderness. Isely explained that the road they were traveling on disappeared every winter and had to be cut fresh with bulldozers each spring. It was an imperfect job; Isely held tight to the steering wheel, which lurched in response to boulders deeply imbedded in the narrow corridor that stretched through the endless expanse of trees.

The talk had turned to the subject of lumbering. Rob was impressed by Isely's knowledge; there wasn't much he didn't know, including the EPA standards and regulations concerning pulping procedures.

"Now, this stuff about the paper companies ruining the forest is pure myth," Isely said as they penetrated deeper into the forest. "We've been operating a small-scale pulp operation upriver on the Espee here for twenty years now. We plant seeds every time we harvest, and that land is more stable today than it was when God himself made it."

Rob took this with a grain of salt. He knew from his own research that it took a hundred years to regrow a black spruce just to the thickness of a man's leg. Isely glanced over at him and read his skepticism.

"To give him his due," Isely added, "God didn't have modern science to help him. He didn't have hydroponics, silvaculture techniques, and chemical analysis procedures to determine soil erosion."

"Oh, I think he did pretty well under the circumstances," Rob said.

"What with his limited education," Maggie added.

Isely laughed. It was his special talent to join the laughter when he himself was the joke.

"Where you people from? Born in Washington?"

"New York," Rob answered. "How 'bout yourself?"

"Right here."

"You have a Southern accent."

"Damn! I thought I'd lost it. I was just testin' to see if you could tell."

Rob chuckled. There was something endearing about the man.

"I'm from Atlanta. Lived there all my life. That's how I tied into this job. I started doing public relations for the Pitney company there."

"Why Atlanta?" Rob asked.

"That's where the head offices are."

"The Pitney Paper Mill is based in Georgia?"

"Oh, yeah. All the lumber companies are from out of state. But we own over half the land in Maine, so to us it's just like home. It's our own back yard and, believe me, we're going to tend it."

To Rob, this particular piece of information was chilling. The forests of Maine were owned by absentee landlords. It was the same situation that existed in the tenements. The lumber companies, with the protection of distance, could be as ruthless as the slumlords. They didn't have to look at, or live with, the misery that their actions might cause.

The car suddenly slowed; Isely breathed a sigh that sounded like fatigue. Ahead of them on the road, a ragtag group of Indians had materialized from the surrounding foliage, clearly intending to block the car. They were dressed much like the lumberjacks, in plaid shirts, boots, and blue jeans; they stood tall and firm, shoulder to shoulder. They were plainly ready to do battle.

"What's happening?" Rob asked as Isley stopped the car.

"Somethng against the *law* is what's happening."

"Who are they?" Maggie asked.

"The O.P.'s I was telling you about."

"What do they want?"

"We'll find out."

One among them stepped forward. He was tall and fine-featured; his clothing was fresher than the rest. His buckskin jacket had fringes on the shoulders; his belt buckle was shiny and new. Rob's powers of deduction told him that the man was new to this forest. He approached their car, sauntering with the kind of take-your-time authority an arresting officer on the Washington Causeway would. He paused at Isley's window, putting his hand on the sill. Rob noticed that his fingernails were clean. He wondered if he was an Indian at all.

"Mr. Hawks?" Isely asked.

"That's right," Hawks replied.

"Heard you were headin' our way . . . nice to see you."

The man leaned down, studying each of their faces. "Who are you?" he asked Isely.

"My name is Bethel Isely."

"So you're Isely," Hawks said. It was plain he didn't like the name.

"This is Mr. Vern and his wife," Isely explained. "They're from the Environmental Protection Agency. I'd appreciate being let through."

Hawks's eyes fastened onto Rob. The power within them was frightening. Maggie averted her gaze, looking out through the windshield. She saw that one of the Indians was a woman. The two had found each other's eyes. Romona glared at her intently.

"I was told you were coming here to work *independently*," Hawks said to Rob. "That's what the Senators said."

"I am working independently," Rob replied. He was surprised at the sound of his own voice. It seemed weak and uncertain compared with the Indian's.

"Why are you in this car?" Hawks challenged.

Rob gritted his teeth. He had known it would be a mistake.

"He's in this car because I persuaded him, Mr. Hawks," Isely replied. "I met him at the airport and I brought him here because I was afraid that something like this might happen."

"You made a bad choice," Hawks said. "No car from the lumber company gets through."

Isely responded with a snort of amazement. He looked at Rob, then back to Hawks.

"This is against the law, Mr. Hawks," he warned.

"How do you select which laws can be broken?"

"I'm not going to sit here and argue with you. The Supreme Court issued a restraining order against this blockade."

"The Supreme Court never ratified Treaty Nine. This land is ours. We have a right to stand here."

The Indian woman was approaching now. She came and stood directly beside Hawks, as if to support him in case he might be weakening.

"Hello, Romona," Isely said coldly.

"Mr. Isely," she replied in kind.

"You a part of this, too, Romona?"

Her mouth tightened. "By birth, Mr. Isely."

"You're gonna get yourself in a heap of trouble," Isley said.

"That's a fact, Mr. Isely," she replied.

Her eyes met Maggie's again. Maggie was withered by her glance.

Isely emitted a long sigh, turning his eyes forward.

"Can we walk in?" Rob asked Isely.

"Ten miles?"

"Isn't there some other road?"

"I'm afraid there isn't."

"Let's back up," Rob said.

But Isely ignored him, turning to Hawks.

"John, I want to tell you something," he said.

"Mr. Hawks," Hawks corrected.

"Mr. Hawks . . . You've got one minute to tell your friends to get out of the way."

"I'll do it right now, Mr. Isely." Turning to his men, he gave them a signal to move aside. They did, revealing a heavy metal chain, strung, and padlocked, between two trees at either side of the narrow forest road.

Isely flushed, his entire body bristling. "I guess it won't do any good for me to tell you to unlock that chain, will it?"

"Try it," Hawks said.

"Will you please unlock that chain?"

"No."

Isely quickly stepped out of the car. "Kelso?" he called to the car behind him. "Cut down those two trees, please."

Inside the car Rob and Maggie exchanged a frightened glance. Behind them, the sound of a motor suddenly broke the silence. One of the lumberjacks, the biggest among them, got out of the car with a portable chain saw already buzzing in his hand.

Suddenly there was movement everywhere. The Indians backed away, the lumberjacks stepped forward, Hawks raced to the chain, where he picked up a long-handled ax, holding it up as a warning.

"Now, John—" Isely began, but he was interrupted by Hawks.

"I'm Mr. Hawks!" Hawks shouted over the din of the buzz saw.

"Mr. Hawks, this is downright silly!"

"You're not going through!"

Hawks's eyes were wild, and there was fear in them now. Rob scrambled out of the car, grabbing Isely by the arm.

"I said I don't want to go through there."

"I *do*."

"I don't see the point."

"The point is not to be intimidated."

"Look . . ."

"If we turn away, we'll have one hell of a mess on our hands. They'll go back and tell their people they won, and next time there'll be three times as many standing here. This is going to get snubbed out right now."

"If anyone is hurt here . . ."

"No one's going to get hurt here—they're bluffing." He turned to his men. "Kelso! Take 'em down!"

The lumberjack with the buzz saw moved forward. Rob could see from the expression on his face that he was eager to do battle. He was bigger than Hawks and outweighed him, and he was out for blood. He was literally smiling, his tobacco-stained teeth showing in a menacing grin as a small, eager sound, like a child's giggle, climbed upward from his gut.

Romona stood beside Hawks, her fists clenched at her sides, her jaw rigid, as though braced for a blow. Hawks reached out and gently pushed her aside, standing his ground as the lumberjack bore slowly down on him.

"Rob!" Maggie cried from the car.

"Don't let this happen, Isely!" Rob shouted.

"Will you move aside, Hawks?" Isely called out.

Hawks raised the ax, holding it angularly across his chest. "You'll cut my head off before you cut these trees!"

"Have it your own way!" Isely replied. "Kelso. Hit that tree!"

"Wait a minute!" Rob cried. But his voice was drowned out by the sound of the buzz saw hitting bark.

What happened next was a blur. As the chain saw hit bark, Hawks knocked it upward with the handle of his ax; for a moment the two men stood as gladiators. Then their weapons collided. Sparks flew as metal hit metal.

"Stop!" Maggie screamed.

But it was too late. The men were locked in combat, circling, feinting with their weapons, the onlookers running forward, all crying out at once.

"John, don't!" Romona cried.

"Stop him, Isely!" Rob pleaded.

"Kelso!"

The air was alive with clanging metal, the onlookers

fading back in horror and disbelief. The buzz saw
lunged and the ax swung in a wide arc, both men
spinning and dodging, widening their arena of combat.
The lumberjack was on the offensive; Hawks used his
weapon defensively, deflecting and lurching as the
chain saw sliced past his head.

With a resounding blow, the buzz saw collided hard
with the ax head; Hawks was knocked off balance,
stumbling backward, hitting the ground. The lumberjack leaped toward him, but Hawks's foot caught him
firmly in the chest, thrusting him backward into the
air. Hawks sprang to his feet and streaked after him,
shrieking in a bloodcurdling war cry as he spun the
ax overhead. The lumberjack fell back against the
hood of a car and Hawks flew at him, pinning him
with the ax handle pressed hard against his neck.
The lumberjack was helpless now, his eyes bulging
as Hawks pressed harder.

"That's it!" Isely warned. "Let him up!"

"Drop the saw!" Hawks shouted.

"Drop it, Kelso!" Isely commanded.

But the lumberjack would not. Baring his teeth, he
snarled like an animal, his knee suddenly raising
between Hawks's legs. Hawks's entire body shuddered, but he held firm, baring down harder on the
ax handle. The lumberjack kicked upward again, and
Hawks was weakened.

"Stop them!" Maggie cried.

The lumberjack summoned all of his strength and
kicked a third time; the impact was crippling and
Hawks spun away. He struggled to regain his footing,
but the lumberjack kicked out, his boot sinking into
Hawks's stomach. Hawks doubled up and the lumberjack kicked him in the face. The impact sent him
sprawling backward and the lumberjack leaped for
him. Hawks rolled and sparks flew as the chain saw
hit rock where, a moment ago, Hawks's neck was.
They rolled on the ground now, Hawks trying to fend
off the chain saw with the ax handle. But the handle

splintered into matchsticks, and suddenly all movement stopped. Hawks lay immobile, his eyes wide
and staring up into the lumberjack's as the chain saw
lowered to just inches from his Adam's apple.

"Call it!" the lumberjack snarled. "Your head or
those trees!"

"You destroy this forest, and this forest will destroy
*you!*"

"You *got* it!" the lumberjack shouted. The chain
saw lowered until it skimmed flesh.

"Stop!" Rob cried as he ran forward. "Stop it!
Get off him!"

"Get up, Kelso!" Isely shouted.

"Tell him to open the chain!" the lumberjack
yelled.

"Open it, Hawks!" Isely demanded.

"No!" Hawks bellowed to his people. "Don't open
it!"

"I want to *kill* him!" screamed the lumberjack.

"Open it!" Rob shouted.

"No!" Hawks cried.

Rob turned to Romona. Her eyes were wide with
fear.

"Open it!" Rob shouted at her. "Open it, goddammit! What the hell does this prove?"

"That they are murderers!"

"Don't open it!" Hawks screamed.

"Murderers!" Romona shrieked at Isely.

"No!" Rob shouted to Romona. "It doesn't prove a
damn thing! This blockade is against the *law!* These
people have a right to go in there! You stopped
them! You raised a *weapon!* This man will die here
and it won't prove a goddamn *thing!*"

The buzz saw skimmed a line of red on Hawks's
neck. Romona's eyes were swept with fear.

"Whoever has that key," Rob declared in a near
sob, "is guilty of murder!"

"Don't open it!" Hawks cried as a stream of blood
trickled from his neck.

"I'm *killing* him!" the lumberjack shouted.

In a sudden movement, Romona ran to one of the other Indians, ripped a key chain from his belt, and raced to the padlock.

"No!" Hawks yelled.

She unlocked the chain, throwing up her hands to show she had done it. Suddenly there was silence. The chain saw went quiet. No one moved. The forest was filled with an awesome hush.

The lumberjack still lay atop Hawks, glaring into his eyes. Then he spat on him. Hawks lay unmoving. Then the lumberjack slowly stood, straddling him in triumph.

"If there wasn't a white lady here," he snarled through his teeth, "I'd piss on you."

Then he turned and walked back to his car, the other lumberjacks following him. Their car doors slammed one at a time.

"I'm sorry about this, Hawks," Isely said quietly. "Truly, I am." Then Isely walked to his car. "Mr. Vern?" he said, looking to Rob. Rob stood close to Hawks, gazing down at him. He could feel what the man was going through.

"Are you all right?" he asked Hawks quietly.

Hawks did not reply. Nor did he move. The lumberjack's spittle was still on his face; there was a rip in the skin on his neck where blood was quickly clotting. Rob also saw something else. There was moisture at the corners of Hawks's eyes.

"There's nothing to be done here," Isely said to Rob.

Rob slowly nodded and walked to the car. He moved in beside Maggie, whose eyes were fixed on the Indian woman. She had her back to them, her forehead bowed against a tree. Maggie knew she was crying.

"I'd have given anything for that not to have happened," Isely said to Rob. "I just . . . didn't really think he'd fight."

"Let's go," Rob mumbled.

The two yellow cars of the Pitney Paper Mill pulled slowly forward, over the chain, and drove into the forest.

# 7

THE DRIVE FROM the blockade to Mary's Lake passed
in silence; Rob, Maggie, and Isely were numbed by
the sudden and unexpected violence that had occurred. Isely had made a weak attempt to justify his
persistence in running through the blockade—something about the Indians being willful children, needing
to be disciplined. It fell on unreceptive ears. Rob and
Maggie refused to respond.

They reached the lakeshore near evening. There
was a fine mist on the surface of the water; swallows
swooped low in silent aerobatics. The glass-smooth
water was dappled by the mouths of hungry fish as
they, too, sought what the birds were after. Mayflies,
an insect delicacy that was served up only once a year.

Rob had read of the mayfly when he was a first-year
biology student, and it had had a lasting impact on
him. For the life cycle of the mayfly was unique in
the evolutionary plan. After incubating for twelve
months in the mud on the lake floor, these tiny,
gossamer insects had just one night to live. On that
night they hatched from their eggs and swam upward,
preyed upon by the fish as they sought the safety of
the water's surface. Those that made it quickly
sprouted wings and took to the skies, devoured by
the birds as they struggled up toward the light of the
moon. The few that survived would meet high in
the sky, their bodies touching, male to female, and
in the moment of touch, fertilization would occur. By

morning they would fall dead upon the water's surface, the convulsions of their death agony expelling
their eggs. The eggs would slowly drift downward,
sinking into the mud on the lake floor. There they
would sleep for twelve months, waiting for their one
brief night of awareness.

When Rob had first read of this life cycle, it
had raised speculation that he had never been able
to resolve. The mayfly came and went, asking nothing, taking nothing, living and dying in the brief moment
that nature had intended. Were there, in the course
of those twelve hours, youth and old age? Was knowledge gained? Could it be that, because of their size,
their minutes were like hours, their hours like years?
Could man himself, seen through the eyes of some
greater creature, perhaps be perceived as living and
dying in the blinking of an eye?

As Rob stood beside Maggie at the shore of the
lake, he was reminded of these questions. Perhaps it
was man's need to question that was the source of his
torment. Were there no questions, nothing would go
unanswered. Perhaps his own life was the same as the
mayfly's, with no more purpose, beyond that which
he invented, than to perpetuate life itself.

"Look at the birds," Maggie whispered.

"Mayflies," Rob answered. Then he took her hand
and they stepped into the small rowboat that Isely had
left for them. He had left a car as well, so they could
be free to move from the cabin to town or throughout
the forest at any time they wished. Were it not for
the violence at the blockade, it all would have been
ideal. But Rob and Maggie felt wounded now. Perhaps
irreparably so.

Their small outboard motor hummed as the boat cut
a wedge in the unbroken surface of the water; the
birds dove around them, and fish jumped from the
water, unaffected by their intrusion. Before them, in
the middle of the lake, stood a small island, the pinnacle of an aquatic mountain that barely broke the
surface and supported a small grove of pine trees. On

the island stood a single cabin. It was small, made of logs and mortar, with a front porch that led onto a dock, which was illuminated by a flickering signal light.

"Looks nice," Maggie said as their boat inched through the water. But, in fact, it did not. It looked isolated and foreboding. The cabin was silent and dark, as though it had been uninhabited for years.

"Hold out that oar, okay?"

She followed Rob's directions, keeping the boat from bumping the dock. They tied the boat and sat for a moment in silence. It was so quiet, they could hear each other breathe.

"We've got to snap out of this," Rob said quietly.

"I know."

They stepped out of the boat; the shuffling of their feet on the dock resounded in the air around them.

The sky was streaked with orange; a pale blue backdrop was sneaking into gray. The moon was faint and almost full, hazed behind a tangle of mayflies, rising in a cloud above the lake. Rob paused and looked up at them before entering the cabin.

"Well. This isn't bad," Maggie said with relief. Rob quickly moved to a kerosene lantern. It lit with a hiss and they gazed at each other across its stark, white light.

"Look at the fireplace," Rob said.

It was made of stone and occupied one entire wall.

"Wow," was all Maggie could say.

"It's not bad, Maggie. The place is really nice."

She forced a brave smile. "It really is, isn't it?"

"It's beautiful."

Rob explored the cupboards and found that someone had taken great pains to see that the cabin was well stocked and comfortable for their arrival. There was everything there that they could possibly need. Canned goods, hammer and nails, an ax, candles and matches, a first-aid kit, even a game of Scrabble. There was a new couch and chair in front of the fireplace, a freshly cleaned gas stove, an old-fashioned icebox with a block of ice in it, and large jugs of bottled water standing on the sink in the kitchen area.

The entire cabin was just one large room, but the kitchen area was lower than the living room, and the sleeping loft above it created a half ceiling. Maggie climbed the narrow, stairwell to the loft and found a double bed with a down comforter, tucked just beneath the eaves. It looked welcoming, and calmed her apprehension. She walked to the loft railing and looked down at Rob.

"No bathroom?" she asked.

"Guess not."

"Yoiks."

"Too rugged?"

"Nah," Maggie responded bravely.

"No light switches up there, are there?"

"I'm afraid not."

"Guess we go native."

"Guess we do."

"You up to it?"

"You bet."

They paused.

"Margaret?"

"Yes, sir?"

"It's going to be nice."

"I know it will."

They both set to work; Maggie unpacked while Rob lighted another kerosene lantern, then started a fire in the gargantuan fireplace. There were two canoe paddles, mounted like crossed swords above the fireplace; Rob took them down, fearful that the flames might lick upward at them. With his experience as a Public Health inspector, he knew this place could go up like tinder.

"What about dinner?" Maggie called from upstairs.

"Well . . . we've got canned goods, and Mrs. Isely's cherry pie."

"I don't think I feel like eating Mrs. Isely's cherry pie."

Rob paused, catching sight of a fishing pole standing in the corner. "How 'bout fresh trout for dinner?"

"Don't I wish."

"Want some?"

"You bet. And some baked potatoes."

"Will you clean them?"

"The baked potatoes?"

"The fish."

"What fish?"

"The fish I'm going to catch."

Her face appeared over the loft railing. He held up the fishing pole and disappeared out the front door.

Maggie spent a long moment gazing down into the main room of the cabin. The fire was blazing now, the thick logs hissing and crackling, filling the air with the scent of pine. She went downstairs and unpacked her cello, bringing a chair to the center of the room where she would be warmed by the fire's glow. While Rob found peace in his way, she would find it in hers. She tightened her bow and tuned the instrument with light finger picks on the uppermost parts of the strings. Then she began to play. The sound filled the small cabin, its gentle mood edging out the tension of the day.

Standing outside on the dock in twilight, Rob could hear her music, and it filled him, too, with a sense of peace. It wafted from the open cabin door and floated out across the lake, seeming to stretch to the very peaks of the distant mountains. He knew he was a fortunate man. Privileged in every way. He wondered why he took so little time to appreciate it.

Far across the lake, along the shallows of the distant shore, the silhouetted figure of a large, four-legged animal moved silently as it grazed. It paused and raised its head, as though listening to the music. Rob could see that it was a moose. There was a calf beside it; it, too, gazed toward the source of the odd, musical sound. Rob wished that Maggie could see it, and was about to call her when suddenly a fish hit the end of his line. It was a small salmon, surging and leaping, quickly tiring as Rob brought it in and raised it to the dock. Hooking a finger beneath its gill, he held it up to examine it, admiring its shiny silhouette against the darkening sky. It was a moment of consummate beauty; Rob wanted to savor it.

He took off his belt and tied the fish to it, then lay down on the dock, gazing up into the sky. The stars were beginning to appear, brighter than he had ever seen them, and the sky had a kind of depth to it that made him feel he was gazing into eternity. But the moment was suddenly shattered. There was a resounding crash in the water, as though a huge boulder had been dropped. Rob sat bolt upright, his head spinning in the direction of the sound. Just twenty feet from him, the water had been disturbed; circles widened outward and melted into calm.

Rob's eyes traveled to the shoreline, the only possible place from which a boulder could have been thrown. There was nothing there. Just shadows and silence. The water was smooth again. A light breeze drifted across the lake, bringing with it the smell of night in the wilderness. Dark and damp, and mysterious. Rob scanned the water's surface and detected a tiny dark shadow moving toward him through the mist. It was a small black duck, chortling to itself as it paddled shoreward to bed down for the night. It was apparently unaware of Rob's presence; it headed directly for the dock. Rob sat stock-still. He could see the glint of its eyes as it moved forward. But suddenly it shrieked. Its wings flapped in a spastic attempt to fly as something dragged it down. In a split second it was gone. The chop in the water that gave evidence of its brief struggle quickly faded to calm.

Rob sat immobile. Stunned. Then he saw it. Just a foot from where the duck had disappeared. A swelling in the water that indicated something large had flashed just beneath the surface. The water had become engulfed in darkness, and Rob was relying on the light of the moon as his eyes followed the reflective swells and swirls. Whatever they were, there were several of them, probably fighting over the remains of the duck. Then suddenly something rose in a spray.

It was a fish. A salmon. Gargantuan in size. At least
four feet long, with a girth as thick as a man's body.
It sailed upward into the air, its body vibrating as it
crossed the circle of the moon. It crashed back into
the water with a resounding smack, like the sound of
a boulder being dropped from high altitude.

Then everything went silent. All traces of movement
were gone.

Rob watched the water as mist gathered on its
surface, and became so thick that everything was obscured. In moonlight, the lake had come to look
unearthly, like a crater of steam.

He picked up the fish he had caught, rose on trembling legs, and headed slowly back to the cabin.

On a far shore of the lake, John Hawks sat alone,
in darkness, gazing across at the island. Tiny spots of
light showed in the windows of the cabin there. He
remembered, when he was a boy, the sense of mystery
attached to that island. There had been no cabin there
then; the Indian children used the island as a test of
their courage. When any one among them could swim
back and forth to it without stopping, particularly at
night, they had taken a major step toward joining the
ranks of their elders.

There was said to be a spirit living on the island.
An angry spirit whose face and form were uncom-
monly beautiful. According to legend, the spirit had
been banished to the island by jealous siblings, and
in its loneliness it had become demented. The sounds
of dawn and dusk were attributed to this spirit; the
cry of the loon, the moanlike call of the moose. The
spirit was called *N'ayh'an'tak'tah*. Literally translated,
it meant Crazy Beautiful. It was also the name of the
island.

The cabin on the island was built by Morris Pitney,
and thereafter the island was declared off limits to the
Indians. Many believed that that was why the Pitneys
had suddenly, within two months of each other, died.
Crazy Beautiful had killed them. Her methods had

been bizarre. They had slept with their mouths open, as whites commonly did. The spirit *N'ayh'an'tak'tah* was a woman; her breasts were filled with poison. As they slept, she dripped her poison into their mouths.

When Hawks recalled legends such as these, he understood why the whites looked upon the Indians as children. The whites did not understand that an unbridled imagination was a gift to be cherished, given only to man. Those Indians who became absorbed into the white world lost it quickly. It took careful nurturing to maintain. The old man, M'rai, had nurtured the gift well. His imaginary visions were crystal clear, and he could describe them in such detail that it seemed as though they were real.

After the confrontation at the roadblock, Romona had taken Hawks to the old man's encampment, where she treated his wounds with valerian root and peat moss. It had taken the sting from the flesh, but not from the spirit. In the hours that elapsed. Hawks had sat in silence, staring into the fire at the old man's encampment while M'rai spun tales of the creatures of the forest. He spoke of *K'hrah'nitah,* his secret lagoon, where the tadpoles grew so large that they could be eaten like fish. Where the inchworms spanned half the length of a man's hand.

The old man urged them both to come to the pond and see, but they refused. They would not trespass into the sacred lagoon. They would not disappoint him by failing to see the things he saw.

After M'rai retired, Hawks and Romona sat without speaking, their eyes fixed on the glowing coals of the fire. When she whispered his name, Hawks had risen and walked alone into the forest.

As he sat now at the shore of the lake, he replayed the events of the roadblock in his mind, trying to slow it down from the blur in which it had happened. He wondered if he'd known when it began that he was prepared to give his life. He wondered if others who had died fighting for what they believed in had had that knowledge.

John Hawks did not envision himself as ever growing old. Not that he would remain young. There was simply a void in his imagination, as though the future did not exist.

From the darkened foliage behind him, Hawks heard the sound of movement. But he instinctively knew there was nothing to fear. The crickets continued to chirp, indicating there was no menace afoot. Their chorus at night meant that there was good will in the air. When there was bad feeling—if a man walked in anger or a predator stalked—the crickets fell silent.

"John . . . ?"

It was Romona. She emerged gracefully, like a moving shadow, and slipped down beside him. In the darkness he could sense the whole of her. Her scent was like leather and pine. Though their bodies were not touching, it felt to him as though they were. His skin responded to the proximity with a vague, tingling sensation on the side where she was close. He turned and could see only her eyes. They shone like an animal's as she gazed out at the island that seemed to float suspended in the mist.

"Do you suppose they'll sleep with their mouth's open?" she whispered. Hawks smiled. They sat for a time in silence, both staring out at the lake.

"Your pride will kill you, John," she said softly. "You learned it from the white man. It doesn't serve you."

Hawks turned to her, his mood hardening with the insult.

"I learned pride from the Indians," he said.

"There is a difference between dignity and pride."

"Is there?"

She nodded. When she spoke, her tone was soft and caring. "Dignity comes from knowing what you cannot accomplish. Pride is the opposite." Hawks turned away.

"You've been going to the dictionaries again," he said.

"Yes."

She moved closer to him, hoping he would turn to her. But he did not.

"We don't need you to die for us, John," she said. "We need you to *live* for us. We need you to heal our wounds, not deepen them. I was wrong in saying I would fight beside you. I didn't know that you meant to die."

"I didn't mean to die," he responded quietly. "I was willing to die."

"You're angry at me because I didn't let you?"

As her words sunk in, Hawks remembered what it was like to be with Romona. She had a wisdom that penetrated his facade. In response to her question, he could only shake his head. "I don't know," he finally whispered.

"If you died today, it would have been the death of a willful child. If you are intent on dying to help your people, don't die before you've helped them."

Hawks watched small waves lap up against the shore. The body of a crawfish glistened in the moonlight as it picked through shining pebbles just beneath the surface.

"I have little to give except my life."

"There is much you don't know. Much that is happening in this forest that you don't know."

"The *katahnas,* you mean?"

"You know of them?"

"Yes."

"Do you know of the stillbirths?"

Hawks gazed at her in confusion. "No."

"Our bodies are going bad. And our minds are going bad. Our insides are as sour as the milk in *N'ayh'an'tak'tah's* breasts." She leveled her eyes with his, and spoke with quiet intensity. "Our women are giving birth to badly formed children. In this year there have been eight. Six were born dead. Two were put to death." She paused, feeling revulsion at the image that flashed through her mind. "These babies are . . . unfinished. They look much like animals."

Hawks could see the pain in her eyes. He shook his head, unable to fathom it.

"We're dying," she said. Her voice was trembling now. "Our people are dying in here."

"Who knows about this?"

"No one. Just me. The women are ashamed to tell."

"Why haven't you told anyone?"

"I was afraid."

Hawks rose and looked toward the island. He could see shadows moving in the windows of the small cabin, and he could hear music wafting out across the water. While he stood here listening to the death knell of his people, they were listening to music. His jaw clenched with anger.

"The people in town are angry at us," Romona said. "They say we've killed their people. I was afraid to go and tell them what I know."

Hawks looked down at her. "Who *did* kill their people?"

"No Indians killed their people."

"Who did?"

"No one knows."

Romona looked up at him, her eyes vulnerable and helpless. "Who can we trust, John?"

Hawks's fists clenched at his sides. At a time when they most needed to defy the white world, they found themselves *dependent* on them. With their health failing, there was nowhere else to turn.

"What about the government people?" Romona asked.

Hawks's mouth turned into a sneer. "The last people to trust are government people."

"He looked like a good man. I could see he was a good man."

"We need a doctor. Not a politician."

"Then come with me to town," she urged.

Hawks looked down at her. "Dr. Pope?"

"Yes."

"He won't do us any good."

Hawks knew Winston Pope well. He was the only

local practitioner of medicine, and he was on the pay-
roll of the lumber company. His main service was to
provide emergency care for the lumberjacks, and to
treat their families. Once a year he made an obligatory
tour of the Indian villages to give them inoculations,
but he did it with resentment, as if he were inoculating
so many head of cattle for hoof-and-mouth disease.
Now that the Indians were in head-to-head combat
with the lumber company, it was unlikely that Dr.
Pope would have any sympathy for them.

"How many pregnant women in the village?" Hawks
asked.

"Just two right now."

"We'll take them to Portland."

"They won't go."

"You'll have to convince them."

"They're ashamed . . ."

"A white doctor won't come eighty miles from
Portland to examine two pregnant Indian women!"

The crickets suddenly went quiet. Romona, too,
recoiled at the harshness in Hawks's voice.

"I'll do what I can," she whispered. Then she rose
to go.

"Mona."

She paused, looking back at him. He walked slowly
toward her, his face coming into the moonlight. It was
etched with anguish.

"Don't go away now."

"There's nothing more to say."

"I know," he whispered.

She looked at him with uncertainty, and he lowered
his head, not knowing how to express himself.

"You know what my grandfather says, John? About
words?"

He shook his head.

"That man invented them to hide his feelings."

When Hawks looked up at her, his eyes were misted.

"I'm glad you can still be frightened, John," she
whispered. "I was afraid the human part of you was
gone."

From the darkness that surrounded them, the crickets slowly resumed their chorus.

"I'm telling you, Mag. It was a world's record. It was *more* than a world's record. I've never *heard* of a salmon that big!"

Rob paced the main room of the cabin as Maggie stood in the kitchen, cooking the small salmon that he had caught. He was agitated and bewildered, filled with disbelief that he had actually seen what he saw.

"It was at least four feet long!" he exclaimed.

"Well," Maggie replied, as she sprinkled salt on the sizzling salmon steaks, "this *was* the land of Paul Bunyan, wasn't it? And his giant ox, Babe?"

"Was that Maine?"

"Sure was."

"I'll tell you, there might have been something to it. Maybe Paul Bunyan *did* exist."

She laughed, somehow enjoying his bewilderment. It was refreshing to see him so puzzled. It brought out the child in him.

"That fish was a *giant*. I mean a *freak*. And it looked like there was more than one of them."

"Maybe you'll go home with a trophy."

"You don't believe me."

"I always believe fishermen."

"You think I don't know what I saw?"

"It got away, didn't it?"

"Maggie." He moved into the kitchen and gestured for her to look at him. "I'm a sane man. More than sane. I'm a scientific man."

"You're a *brilliant* man," she cooed.

"You're not taking me seriously."

"Yes I am. Would you hand me that fork?"

"I'm telling you, I saw the biggest fish I've ever seen in my life."

"By the light of the moon . . ."

"Yes, it was dark out."

She flashed him a playful look as she dug into the

frying fish. "Your Honor, my client says he saw the biggest fish he ever saw. Now, the fact that it was pitch-dark out has no bearing whatsoever on his testimony."

Rob was stopped, realizing she could be right. "You think I didn't see it?"

"I'm your defense lawyer. I believe everything you say."

"Maybe it looked bigger in the dark, huh?"

"Your Honor, we plead temporary insanity."

"But it ate a duck, Maggie!"

"Your Honor, it ate a duck."

"I *saw* it."

"Tomorrow, try to catch it. Maybe it'll taste like duck."

He threw up his hands in surrender. Maggie giggled as she blew on a forkful of hot fish, gently putting it in her mouth.

"Might have been a duckling, I suppose," Rob mumbled. Then he shook it off, reaching for some paper napkins and putting them on the table.

"Mmmmmmmm!" Maggie moaned ecstatically as she mouthed the hot fish. "Taste it!"

She held out a forkful to Rob and fed it to him. His eyes rolled with approval.

"Ambrosia . . ." he groaned.

"This is all I want to eat as long as we're here. I want fish for breakfast, lunch, and dinner."

"No problem." Rob grabbed for some plates, putting them on the table. "I do happen to be one of the world's greatest fishermen."

"You fish and I'll eat," Maggie replied as she wrapped a towel around her hand to pick up the skillet.

"Now, that's a *relationship*."

As she put the skillet on the table, he bent over her and planted a kiss on her neck. It stopped her in mid-movement.

"How very nice," she whispered.

She turned and their eyes met, both of them filled with profound appreciation of each other.

"I'd forgotten it could be like this," she said.

"So did I."

She felt tearful, and was embarrassed for it.

"Like to see our wine list?" Rob asked.

"Just have my usual."

"Château Lafitte?"

"Mogen David."

"Mogen David coming up."

He spun around to an ice chest, producing a bottle of wine.

"Where'd you get that?" she laughed.

"It was here."

"Someone left it?"

"Compliments of Mr. Isely, no doubt."

"Ah. Wine and cherry pie."

"Other bureaucrats are bribed with Rolls-Royces for Christmas, all-expense-paid vacations. Me, I get wine and cherry pie."

"Well, hell," said Maggie, sitting down, "I don't like Rolls-Royces."

"I don't, either."

"Then again, I don't like Mr. Isely."

"I don't either."

"Pour the wine and bring on the pie."

"Corruption, corruption . . ."

Maggie giggled, and so did Rob. They had successfully shaken off the frightening events of the day, and no matter what lay behind them or ahead, for this moment they were high on being together; determined to savor every moment of it.

The dinner passed with more banter about Rob's fish story, and a lot of silences as they gazed across the table at each other and drank wine. The fire had faded to embers now; the sounds of the forest could be heard from outside: a chorus of night insects, the cry of a hawk circling high overhead.

Rob sat back, watching Maggie, basking in the peacefulness of the moment. She poured what was left of the wine into her glass and drank it down, closing her eyes as she listened to the sounds of the forest.

"The woods . . . are lovely, dark, and deep . . ." she whispered, reciting the lines of her favorite poem. "And I have promises to keep . . ."

Rob smiled. Her three glasses of wine had had an effect.

"My little horse gives his harness bells a shake," she continued, "as if to ask if there's some mistake . . ." She couldn't remember the rest, her eyes opening and roaming as she searched for the missing words.

"To harnesses," Rob said as he raised his glass.

"To mistakes," she mused.

"To the woods."

"Mustn't forget the woods."

"Dark and deep . . ."

She raised her empty glass to his and smiled sadly. "And to promises . . . we must keep."

Maggie closed her eyes again; slightly dizzy, slightly euphoric, slightly melancholic. Rob rose and slipped a cassette into the tape recorder; it filled the cabin with gentle music. He moved to Maggie, whose eyes were closed, her head resting on her hands, and he touched her hair. She made a noise that sounded like purring. Taking her hand, he led her to the couch. They eased down together, she moving her head onto his lap, basking in the warmth of the fire.

"Want to know something?" she whispered.

"Mmmmmmm."

"I was proud of you today."

He nodded, recalling the events at the blockade. "Wasn't that . . . crazy?" he whispered.

"You were so brave."

"I was scared."

"You didn't show it."

"Didn't dare."

"Wouldn't life be so much easier," she said, her voice lilting slightly, "if we weren't afraid to show we were afraid . . ."

"Had too much wine?" Rob whispered.

"Not enough."

"No?"

"Still afraid to be afraid . . ."

Rob smiled, She was drifting. And she was absolutely beautiful. He reached down and stroked her forehead, then swept his hand gently along her eyelids. She breathed deeply and nestled close to him.

"That Indian woman?" Maggie whispered.

"Mmmmmmm?"

"I was jealous of her."

"Really?"

"She had real courage. . . . To be strong when she was frightened . . . to demand her own way. It's the kind of courage that I don't seem to have."

"Oh, I think it takes a lot of courage to put up with me."

"I love you," she answered.

Rob leaned down and kissed her. She accepted it without moving, then smiled as she savored it. "Sometimes . . . I love you so much," she said, ". . . that I wish there were more of you."

"\       uld gain twenty pounds."

"I mean . . . I wish there were more of *us*."

Within the darkness behind her closed eyes, she realized what she had said. She hadn't planned it, it had just come out. She opened her eyes and saw it had had its effect. Rob's expression had turned somber.

"Could we talk about it?" she asked in a whisper.

"Now?"

"Why not now?"

"Everything's so perfect now."

"I see."

She could feel the wall coming up between them. The intimacy was so transient, so fragile, it took only a few words to shatter it. Maggie struggled in her mind for clarity; she tried to force that haziness away.

"Either we're too far apart . . . or too close together. Is that it?"

Rob's posture sagged with fatigue, his head sinking back against the couch. Maggie slowly sat up, a sense of loneliness sweeping through her.

"Just . . . talk?" she whispered. "Is that going to spoil everything?"

"You know how I feel about it," he answered sadly.

"About the state of the world, you mean."

"Yes."

She reached up and rubbed her forehead. She was losing heart. She hated that she was groggy; she wanted more than anything to be articulate. There were so many ways she had rehearsed this conversation, and now she was so unprepared.

"Listen," she whispered. "When I was a child, my mother told me to finish everything on my plate because there were starving children in the world. And it didn't make any sense to me." She looked up, trying to catch his eye, but he was staring at the fire. "And now . . . you tell me I shouldn't get pregnant, because there are starving children in the world. And that doesn't make any sense to me, either."

"It does to me."

"What is it, Rob?" she asked gently. "Are you afraid?"

He rose from the couch and walked to the fire, gazing into the smoldering embers.

"Is that it?" she asked. "You're afraid?"

"I don't know, Maggie," he whispered. Then he shook his head in mute reiteration. "I don't know about a lot of things any more."

Maggie's sobriety was returning. She realized that she had never heard Rob admit confusion before. In all the years that they had been together, she had never known him to be uncertain. It gave her hope. She watched and waited, wanting him to say more.

"I feel like . . ." His eyes searched the air as though looking for words. ". . . like I've been going around a race track at a hundred miles an hour . . . and I wound up where I started." He gazed back into the fire. "And no one else was even in the race."

She was deeply moved. She knew she'd heard a confession that he would share with no one else in the world.

"Can I *help* you?" she asked on a trembling breath. Their eyes met and held.

"I need some time," he answered.

He slowly approached, kneeling in front of her and gazing directly into her eyes. "I've felt so close to you tonight."

She nodded, raising a hand to touch his cheek gently.

"Can't we just be like this for a while?" he asked. "Just be close?"

His tenderness was so compelling that she couldn't help believing that some small step had been taken. "Yes," she whispered. His lips moved to hers and she came into his arms, their bodies melding into a close, almost desperate embrace. She slid her face onto his shoulder and closed her eyes as if in prayer. She, as much as he, wanted to cherish this closeness. They had two weeks here. She would wait until the end.

"Should we go upstairs?" she whispered.

He nodded and took her hand, leading her up the narrow stairwell to the sleeping loft, where they undressed and slipped beneath the soft brown comforter. The lights from the fire flickered on the rafters above them, and the cassette that played symphony music ran to its finish, leaving just the sound of their breathing as they made love. It was intense and passionate, both swept into a single movement, Maggie whimpering as she felt herself being pulled upward by an overwhelming force to a peak that caused her to cry out and burst into tears. Then she clung to Rob. He stroked her hair, as if to console her.

They fell silent, Maggie watching shadows from the firelight play on the ceiling as Rob slept in her arms.

It was Maggie who heard it first. A faint, barely audible scraping sound coming from the floorboards of the porch outside. It stopped; replaced by a rapid thumping, which rose in intensity, then ended abruptly. Feeling Maggie's body tense, Rob stirred. And the noise came again. It was as rapid as a jackhammer now, a muffled vibration just outside the downstairs door. They sat up and listened to it, their eyes wide with apprehension.

"What is it?" Maggie whispered.

Rob shook his head. "Did you unpack the flashlight?"

"It's downstairs."

Rob rose from the bed, wrapped a blanket around himself, and quickly descended the stairwell. He found the flashlight and moved to the door. The sound was increasing in intensity, growing louder and faster with each passing moment. Maggie rose and stood looking down from the loft, her face illuminated by the firelight below, casting shadows that accentuated her fear.

"What is it?" she whispered.

"I don't know."

Rob unbolted the door and grabbed the handle. He paused, summoning his courage.

"Don't open it," Maggie hissed.

He glanced up at her, then back at the door. He could literally see the loose floorboards vibrating beneath his feet. Then, in a sudden movement, he pulled open the door; his breath sucked in with shock.

"What is it?" Maggie cried.

At Rob's feet lay a raccoon, face up, convulsing. Its eyes were glazed and froth poured from its mouth, its talons quivered at the end of limbs that shook in every fiber.

Rob looked up at Maggie.

"What is it?" she cried again.

"It's a . . ."

"Watch out!" she screamed.

In a sudden blur of fur, the animal spun to its feet and leaped for Rob, latching on to his back.

"God! God!" Maggie shrieked.

"Jesus!" Rob cried out. He spun and lurched, dancing grotesquely in the firelight, but the animal held firm, sinking its teeth into Rob's side, its vicious snarl rising above Rob's cry of pain.

"Rob!"

He managed to rip the blanket off him and the animal fell, dazed for a moment, but quickly focused on Rob and darted after him again. It lunged at Rob's feet as he sought to escape, catching his knee and clinging tight, sinking its teeth in just below the thigh.

"Oh, God," Maggie sobbed. "Someone help us!"

"Knife!"

Maggie ran down the stairs as Rob pulled the snarling animal off him, hurling it across the room where it hit a wall and fell with a resounding thud. But it wasn't finished. Foam and blood poured from its mouth; it focused on Maggie as she raced toward the kitchen.

"No!" Rob screamed. The animal streaked across the room as Maggie ripped open a drawer, knives and forks splattering on the floor around her.

*"Watch* it!" Rob shouted. Maggie spotted it just in time. She jumped up on the table, the animal smashing into a cabinet beneath her. The raccoon was staggering now, wobbling as it once again searched for a target. Rob shouted at it, trying to get its attention away from Maggie, and the animal turned on him, shooting forward with full fury. Rob ran to a far wall, his body colliding with a canoe paddle that clattered to the floor beside him. As the animal bore down on him, he grabbed the paddle and swung. It caught the raccoon directly in the stomach; a puff of dust rose from the impact, but the raccoon clung hard to the canoe paddle, climbing toward Rob as he swung it around to the fire. Rob smacked it hard against the edge of the stone fireplace and the animal took flight, hurtling directly into the flames.

It went up in a ball of fire. Maggie screamed.

Suddenly it was over. The animal lay stiffened, face up, smoldering in the flames.

Rob stood, naked, his body streaked with blood. Maggie lay, curled up and sobbing, on the small kitchen table.

# 8

WITH THE ONSET of spring, the overture to dawn started early. The eerie voices of the loons began in darkness, bridging the hour when night gave way to morning.

Within the silence of his cabin, Rob heard the voices of the loons, and it chilled him. His palms were sweating; the handle of the butcher knife stuck to his fingers as he studied the brain tissue of the dead raccoon, smeared, in bits and pieces, all over the kitchen table.

He had seen plenty of rabies, observed at least a hundred brain histologies performed on rats, cats, and dogs taken from the slums. He had no microscopes here or surgical knives, only a butcher knife and a magnifying glass. But the signs he was looking for could have been observed with the naked eye.

What he saw was at once a relief and a mystery. Whatever the disease was, it was not rabies. But it was something that Rob had never seen before. The brain tissue had lost its substance. It had simply turned to mush.

He wrapped the remains of the raccoon in newspaper, saving a small chunk, the size of a quarter, which he sealed tightly in a mason jar. Then he went outside with his blood-soaked parcel and deposited it in a trash can that stood near the porch, using a section of firewood to weight the lid. He'd bury it in the morning. He knew the odor of flesh could attract bears.

He gazed out at the lake; it was gradually gaining definition as the sky began to lighten. The haze was lifting, creating a veil of steam that obscured the shore. He rubbed his eyes and moved back into the cabin, closing the door softly behind him and gazing up toward the sleeping loft.

All was quiet. In the hours after the attack, Maggie had been so overwrought that Rob had insisted she take Valium in order to sleep. He had sat with her on the bed until she drifted into slumber. Just before she did, she mumbled to him that she wanted to leave there.

"It's against us," she had said.

Rob felt it, too. The atmosphere was alien. The violence at the blockade, the sight of the enormous fish, the raccoon attack. In the short time that they had been here, they had suffered an assault on all their civilized senses.

Though he shared her uneasiness, Rob fought down the impulse to leave. He had a job to do. He would try to do it as quickly as possible. The survey involved taking soil samples and photographs, and visiting the lumber mill. If he worked steadily at it, it was possible to finish in five or six days.

He moved to the tape recorder and slipped in a blank cassette, then carried the machine to the couch, where he sat back, bringing the microphone close to his mouth so he could whisper into it and not awaken Maggie.

"May thirtieth . . ." he began. Then he paused to check his watch. "Five A.M. Brain histology. Raccoon." He played it back to himself to make sure it was recording, then continued. "Cortical atrophy at the anterior end of the calcarine tissue . . . going into the depths of the sulci of the lateral lobes . . . involving the hypothalamus, midbrain, and basal ganglia. Gennari striation completely gone . . . total declive of the cerebellum." He stopped and switched off the

machine, then switched it on again. "Cause of damage
. . . unknown."

He turned off the tape recorder and closed his eyes.
As he drifted beyond awareness, he heard the demented
cry of the loons.

At the same moment Robert Vern was drifting into
slumber, a family of campers was awakening. A ten-
year-old boy and a twelve-year-old girl stirred in their
sleeping bags, their father was already moving about,
lighting a small fire over which he would cook breakfast.

Travis Nelson was at home in the forest. He had
been born and raised in New Hampshire; his own
father had been a great outdoorsman who tutored his
son in everything from which mushrooms to pick to
how to set rabbit snares. It was the most valuable train-
ing he'd ever had. Even though his own life's course
had taken him far from the wilderness, he'd always had
a sense of security in the knowledge that he could
survive under primitive conditions. He wanted, now,
to pass that on to his own children.

By profession, Travis Nelson was a history teacher,
employed by the public school system in Newton,
Massachusetts. By hobby, he was a licensed pilot who
for years had stashed away small savings from his
teacher's salary to finally buy his own single-engine
Cherokee. Its maiden flight was from Boston to Manatee just yesterday. This was the first real vacation
that he had ever taken with his family. He had
waited until he could afford it, and until his two
children were old enough to absorb the things he
wanted to teach them. Ten-year-old Paul was a born
adventurer, twelve-year-old Kathleen was determined
to be as rugged as her brother; Travis's wife, Jeanine,
was game for anything. The only thing that had disturbed her were the words of a forest ranger who
warned them, as they entered the forest, that they
were going into the Manatee Wilderness Area at their

own risk. People had gotten lost in there, he said, and the authorities were "investigating."

Travis recalled the sight of the "flying bloodhound" when they had arrived at the Manatee airport; it was no doubt part of the "investigation." He himself had no fears. He knew how to blaze a trail and follow a compass, and he knew that a fire was ample discouragement for bears foraging in the night. But he was troubled by the word "investigation." It sounded so policelike.

"Dad?"

The face of his son, Paul, appeared from a narrow opening in the zipper at the top of his sleeping bag. He had slept completely enclosed within it, like a caterpillar in a cocoon, to protect himself from mosquitoes.

"I think I can hear it," the boy whispered. "The waterfall."

Travis smiled. "It's still two days away."

"What do I hear?"

"The wind in the trees."

The boy rolled onto his back, the entire sleeping bag rolling with him.

"Is it gonna rain?" he asked, gazing up at the sky.

"Better not."

"Are we gonna do like you said? Sleep by ourselves one night?"

"Think you're up to it?"

"Sounds scary."

"Nothing to be scared of."

"Is Kathleen gonna do it?"

"I don't know."

"If *she* can do it, *I* can do it."

The face of Kathleen appeared from her sleeping bag. "I can do it."

"I can do it, too," Paul rejoined.

"I guess we're going to do it, then." Travis smiled.

"What if we roll off the cliff?" Kathleen asked.

"We won't sleep close to the cliff."

"Maybe we should sleep at the *bottom* of the waterfall instead of the top," Kathleen said.

"Maybe. We'll see."

Paul got to his knees within the sleeping bag and inched toward the fire. "I can't get this unstuck," he said, pulling at the zipper from the inside. His father reached in under the boy's chin and, with a yank, got the zipper down.

"I think we ought to live like the Indians lived," Paul said as he stepped out of the sleeping bag. "Just eat what we can catch."

"I think that's a good idea," his father answered. "I just happened to catch a little bacon during the night."

"How'd you catch it?" Kathleen asked.

"That's a joke, dummy," Paul said.

"I know, dummy," she answered wearily. "What I said was a joke, too."

"Oh."

Travis chuckled as he laid the strips of bacon on the fire. He had planned this vacation for over a year; he felt it was going to fulfill every expectation.


By noon, Robert Vern had awakened, and, without delay, began his survey. Maggie was still jittery, afraid of being left alone in the cabin; she accompanied him through the forest and watched as he collected soil samples, which he put in small vials that rattled within the pockets of his jacket as he walked. It was the only sound to be heard as they moved through the trees. The day was overcast; the morning fog had lingered, creating oppressive humidity and a hushed atmosphere around them. Moisture clung to the thick carpet of ferns on the forest floor; Rob's and Maggie's pant legs were soaked to the thigh.

"Look there," Rob said, pointing upward through the trees.

Maggie followed his gesture and saw something that looked like a wood-shingled roof, about a half a mile away, protruding above the tops of the trees.

"Looks like a tree house," she said.

"It's a ranger station. I could probably get some good photographs from up there."

He held out his hand to her and she took it; he could feel a sudden tension in her fingers.

"What's wrong?"

Her eyes turned toward the forest.

"What's wrong?" He repeated.

"I don't know . . ."

He gave her a reassuring smile and started forward. Then he froze, his eyes also turning toward the forest. They both remained stock-still.

"You hear something?" he asked.

"There's something in there," Maggie answered on a trembling breath.

A twig snapped in the foliage just in front of them; Maggie closed her eyes. Her breath shuddered as the sound came again.

"Open your eyes," Rob whispered. His voice was filled with awe.

Twenty yards ahead of them, the stately form of a deer emerged from the trees. It stood as still as statuary, its antlers held high, conveying a power and dignity that was overwhelming.

"Just look at that . . ." Rob hissed under his breath.

Maggie clutched his hand, weakened by the immensity of it. She had seen deer before, from a distance or in cages at a zoo. But seeing one this close, with nothing separating her from it, made her appreciate, for the first time, the meaning of the word "wild." She felt small and vulnerable, like a trespasser in a king's domain.

"Never . . . ever," whispered Rob, "have I seen anything so beautiful."

The animal swung its head with regal aplomb, then turned and began moving away. But the power and dignity quickly faded. It staggered forward on its front legs, a limp hindquarter dragging in the dirt. One of the rear legs had been nearly severed, but had somehow healed, leaving the animal a permanent cripple.

As the deer disappeared into the foliage, Rob and Maggie watched with anguished eyes. They began to walk again, silent and somber, trudging through the thick growth of ferns.

"Nothing's as it seems, is it, Rob?" Maggie said. "Nothing's as pretty as you want it to be."

He gripped her hand tightly, and they continued plodding forward. Within a half hour they had reached the base of the ranger station.

The station stood in a small clearing, on a rise that overlooked the lake. It was a small redwood shack built atop fifty feet of crisscrossed scaffolding; a narrow, ladderlike stairwell stretched almost straight up from the ground to the top.

There was a sense of isolation to it that went beyond the physical. It was somehow alien, as though it existed in exile, separate and apart from everything that surrounded it.

"Anybody *up* there?" Rob called.

There was no answer.

"Hello?" Rob shouted.

Still there was no response. Rob spotted a cord hanging down from the door at the top, weighted with a rock.. He pulled it and a bell sounded. It was a light sound, like a dinner bell. He pulled it a second time and waited in silence.

"Guess nobody's home," Maggie said.

"These towers are never supposed to be empty. They keep watch for forest fires."

"Maybe he's asleep."

"I want to get some pictures from up there."

He mounted the narrow stairwell and began climbing upward, Maggie following. It was higher than it looked; as they ascended, Maggie began to feel queasy. Midway she paused, closing her eyes.

"Rob . . . ?"

He stopped and looked back at her.

"I'm getting dizzy," she said.

He descended a few steps and took her hand. "Is

this the lady who one year ago wanted to climb Mount McKinley?"

"This year's different."

"Just out of shape, that's all."

She looked directly into his eyes. "I think it's more than that." She was about to say more when they were suddenly interrupted by a voice from above.

"You people go back down! You aren't allowed up here!"

The face of the forest ranger thrust itself from a small window above. He was a man of about sixty, his face heavily lined and thick-skinned, set in a bull-doglike scowl.

"Go on, get down!"

"Uh . . . excuse me, we're from—"

"I don't give a goddamn where you're from. I'm not going to tell you where *I'm* from, so don't tell where *you're* from."

Rob and Maggie exchanged a long glance.

"He looks like that bloodhound," Maggie whispered.

"Go on! Get off!"

"I'm from the government," Rob called up.

The forest ranger was visibly jolted.

"The government?"

"Yes, sir."

"I work for the government."

"I'd like to take some photographs. Just take a few minutes of your time."

The ranger smiled, the force of gravity causing tobacco spittle to form on his lips. "Come on up, pardner!"

"I think he's daffy," Maggie whispered.

"Can you make it?" Rob asked her.

"Hold my hand."

They climbed up with effort and stepped onto a narrow porch where the ranger awaited them at his open door.

"I'm glad you came," he said. "It's about time. Laiken is my name."

"Thank you," Rob mumbled as he crossed the threshold, bringing Maggie in with him.

"You government workers hold hands all the time?" Laiken smiled as he closed the door behind them.

"This is my wife."

"She's a beauty."

"Thank you," Maggie said.

"My wife was a beauty, too. More beautiful even than you, present company included."

Maggie laughed, not knowing what to say.

"Want to see her picture?"

"Yes," Maggie said.

They were both taken off guard by his sudden familiarity, and sensed that there was something wrong. A quick glance at his living conditions told Rob more. The small glass and redwood enclosure was littered with rumpled clothes and overused magazines; empty food tins and discarded liquor bottles were stacked in a corner on the floor. And the air was thick with an overwhelming stench. It was an odor that Rob had smelled before. Uremia. An aroma that exudes from the skin pores of alcoholics who have consumed so much liquor that their livers are no longer filtering out bodily toxins. The man's eyes were discolored, too. Another sign of liver ailment and alcoholism. The forest ranger was, mentally and physically, in a state of alcoholic deterioration.

As he rummaged through a littered bookshelf for the photograph, both Rob and Maggie saw that one of the ranger's hands was wrapped with a makeshift bandage of rags and blood-soaked cotton. The color of the blood told Rob that the wound was fresh and, because of the unsanitary bandage, would soon be infected.

"What do you think?" the ranger asked as he found the photograph and held it out to them. It was aged and blurred, the woman in it hardly visible.

"That's your wife?" Maggie asked.

"God bless her dead soul."

"Very pretty."

"Not any more."

Maggie couldn't help laughing. "Probably not," she said.

"No . . . not any more," he said as he gazed at the picture.

A moment of silence passed, the man sadly replacing the photograph on the bookshelf.

"Mind if I get some pictures?" Rob asked.

"No, help yourself. You want me to smile?"

"Beg pardon?"

"For the pictures."

Rob almost laughed. "Oh, uh . . . no, I just want to get some pictures of the trees."

The ranger smiled, as though sharing some secret.

"I'll just sit and wait here," he said, moving to a rocking chair, "until you're ready to question me."

Rob glanced at him with uncertainty, then began to snap photos while Maggie browsed through the littered bookshelf, trying to find some way to keep herself occupied.

"So you people are from Washington," the ranger said.

"Um-hm," Rob replied. "Is that the Espee River over there?"

"Wouldn't be no other."

"So I guess that smokestack is the pulp mill."

"You with the FBI?"

"The FBI?" Rob answered with surprise.

"Yeah. You with the FBI?"

"EPA."

"FBI, EPA, it's all the same."

Rob smiled and shook his head, then attached a long-distance lens onto his camera and focused on the smokestack that rose above the trees on the shores of the distant Espee River. The pulp mill was much bigger than he'd expected. It looked like a huge factory. The metal pipes and holding tanks that snaked around it were all glistening and new.

"I figured you'd be up here soon," the ranger said.

"Is that right?" Rob replied.

"Gotta find out the facts, don't we?"

"I guess we do."

"Yes, sir. When people get murdered, that's what we gotta do."

Rob turned and looked at him; he saw that Maggie was doing the same.

"*Don't* we?" the ranger said.

"What do you mean?" Rob asked.

"Them lumberjacks. The ones that got killed, I'm innocent, and I'm ready to answer anything you want to ask me."

Rob and Maggie exchanged a glance. They had finally gotten the drift of the man's confusing conversation.

"Whenever you're ready to ask me something," the ranger said, "I'll be happy to answer. Already told the sheriff everything I know, but he didn't seem to want to believe me."

"No?"

"Said I was drunk. You think I'm drunk?"

"I don't know," Rob answered. "Are you?"

"I drink some, but I know what I saw."

Maggie took an interest and sat on the arm of a chair near him. "What did you see?" she asked.

"I told him I'd take a lie detector, I'll tell you the same damn thing."

"I'll believe you," Maggie reassured. "What did you see?"

The ranger looked at her and smiled. "My voice sound strange to you?" he asked.

"No."

"Does to me. Rattles in my head. Maybe it's my ears, not my voice."

Maggie was completely baffled.

"Maybe it's my hand," he said, holding up his bandaged hand.

"What happened to your hand?" she asked.

"Didn't even know I was bit till I saw the blood."

"Something bit you?"

The ranger nodded and pulled a crumpled piece of

paper from his pocket. "You like poetry?" he asked. "I wrote me a poem."

Maggie looked at Rob. The conversation had gotten totally beyond her.

"What *did* bite your hand?" Rob asked as he packed up his camera.

The ranger ignored him, gesturing toward Maggie with the tattered piece of paper. "Go on. Take it. It all rhymes up. Everything rhymes." Maggie hesitantly took it.

"Maybe you can put it out in *Playboy* magazine," he said. Then he suddenly gasped with laughter, wheezing and coughing as he slapped his thigh. Maggie watched him with compassion. The man was plainly out of his mind.

"Mind if I look at that hand?" Rob asked. "I'm a doctor."

"You are?" the ranger said with surprise.

"Uh-hm."

"Well, I'll be damned." He burst into laughter again.

Rob pulled up a stiff-backed chair in front of him, and opened the dressing on his wounded hand. It was an animal bite, the marks of sharp incisors clearly visible in the puffy flesh.

"What did this?" Rob asked.

"Him," the ranger answered, nodding toward the corner. There, amid a pile of rubbish, lay the body of a dead cat. Maggie gasped at the sight of it and quickly shut her eyes.

"Died just last night," the ranger said. "Bit me and then he died. Didn't even know I was bit till I saw the blood."

Rob rose and walked to the body of the dead cat. There was dried saliva around its mouth.

"Can we go?" Maggie asked quietly.

Rob knelt and picked up the dead cat. It was stiff, its body arched grotesquely, as though it had died in a back bend.

"Can I take this away for you?" Rob asked the ranger.

"I don't know why he turned on me," the ranger said. There was sadness in his voice now. "I was always good to him."

"I'd like to examine it."

"We always ate dinner together," the ranger continued. "He liked fish the best. Liked it cooked. Now, that's some unusual cat . . . don't you think?" His eyes began to glisten and he quickly turned away. Maggie watched him in silence, her eyes filled with sympathy.

"You ought to soak your hand in warm water," Rob said.

The ranger nodded and began to weep. It was a pathetic sound, as though the act of crying caused him physical pain.

Rob gestured toward the door, but Maggie was reluctant to leave the man like this. Finally, she rose.

"We'll be back, all right?" Maggie said to the ranger. "We'll be back here before we leave."

"Bury it deep, will you?" the ranger replied through his tears. "I don't want that thing to eat it."

Rob and Maggie exchanged a puzzled glance, then stepped outside.

They stood in momentary silence on the narrow porch, saddened by the misery that existed here.

A breeze had begun to blow, rippling the surface of the lake; the tattered piece of paper the forest ranger had given Maggie fluttered in her hand as she opened it and tried to decipher the childlike scrawl.

"Three . . . little . . . searchlines," she said, reading quietly aloud.

"Searchlights," Rob corrected as he gazed over her shoulder.

"Searchlights," she continued, "burning bright. All went out in a turrible fight." She paused, looking at Rob, then went on. "See him by the lake next day . . . big as a dragon . . . with wings that was . . . gray."

The breeze came stronger; Maggie's hair wafted into her face as she stared at the note, trying to make out the rest.

"That's it?" Rob asked.

"The rest is crossed out."

Their eyes met, and neither spoke.

"Does it sound like something you've heard before?" Maggie asked.

Rob thought about it and shrugged.

"Big as a dragon?"

He slowly shook his head.

"It's this man's job to sit and stare out at this forest," Maggie said. "You said so yourself. He's supposed to be here night and day."

Rob looked at her and smiled.

"This poem is about what he *saw*."

"He's blind drunk, Maggie. What he sees are hallucinations."

"As big as a dragon? That's what Isely said at the airport."

"If you were that drunk, you'd see dragons, too."

She thought about it and nodded. Then she grimaced with embarrassment, suddenly feeling foolish.

"This place is getting to you," Rob said as he took her hand and started down.

"I'm afraid it is."

"Let's go fishing, huh? Let's just mind our own business for a while."

They climbed carefully down the narrow stairs, Rob securing Maggie with one hand, holding the stiffened carcass of the dead cat in the other. As they walked back through the forest, they smelled rain in the air. There was a rumble of thunder from a cloud bank hovering dark and low over the peaks of the distant mountains.

The family of campers, Travis Nelson and his wife and children, felt the first drops of rain and decided to pitch their tents and wait it out. It would delay their climb to the waterfall, but the uphill journey would be too difficult on saturated ground. They set up camp by the shores of Mary's Lake, in the hope that the downpour would end by morning.

But it did not. The cloud bank that had moved in hung over the wilderness basin like a permanent lid, sending down a seemingly inexhaustible supply of rain. Within two days, new buds had broken through the ground; the once bare branches of trees were lined with the light green felt of spring. The forest animals took shelter for the duration, accepting hunger with the instinctive knowledge that when the deluge ended, the ground would swell with plenty. The rain that was absorbed into a thirsty earth would hydrate dormant seeds, bringing sustenance to the small creatures that thrived on vegetation; they, in turn, would provide a food source for the meat eaters. The food chain that began with microscopic fungus ended with the largest predator; a bear that consumed a deer was eating acres of vegetation that had brought the deer to adulthood.

In the rain- and wind-whipped trees, the only figure that moved was that of Robert Vern. Maggie had became increasingly nervous with the confinement caused by the rain; he was eager to complete his work as soon as possible.

The brain histology he had conducted on the dead cat had been inconclusive. There was damage there, not unlike that of the raccoon, but the hours that had passed between the time the animal had died and when it was examined, had caused the brain cells to atrophy. It would require sophisticated equipment for proper analysis; as soon as the rain stopped, Rob would send some tissue samples, along with some from the raccoon, to the laboratory in Washington.

For now, there was little to do but trudge through the mud on the island, which was quickly becoming a swamp, and examine the changes caused by the rain.

As far as Rob's ecological survey was concerned, the rain itself was providing important answers. The soil was clay-based and therefore absorbed an enormous amount of rain. If the trees were to come down, denying the soil the root system that hungrily sucked up excess water, the soil would become oversaturated.

It would cause new seedlings to drown, and in ten years' time the entire forest would become an ecological wasteland.

There were, of course, artificial ways to save the new seedlings. They could be cultivated separately, in a controlled environment, and replanted once they had become stable. If the Pitney Paper Mill were willing to make this kind of costly and time-consuming commitment, it could override the immediate effects. But promises were easy to make and impossible to police. The lumber company could agree, then fail to meet its obligation. The Environmental Protection Agency did not have the funds to undertake a constant watch.

Rob had read of the duplicity of the lumber companies. The publicity budget of a single lumber company was probably equal to what the Environmental Protection Agency survived on, and supported a full staff with, for an entire fiscal year. In terms of their respective messages reaching the public, the lumber companies had a clear edge. In television advertisements and brochures, they convinced the public that they were refoliating as fast as they were *de*foliating, but the simple mathematics would tell even a schoolchild that that was impossible. It takes fifty seconds to cut a tree. Fifty years or more to grow one.

As Rob trudged knee-deep in mud through the turbulent forest, he was awed by the power of the elements around him. It was little wonder that the Indians had assumed that lightning and thunder were sent down by the gods. Rob wondered if his own explanations were any better. Surely the perfection of the environmental system, from the respiration of the smallest insect to the motion of the planet itself, left a gap that scientific logic could not fill. Man himself was physically among the weakest and most vulnerable of the earth's creatures; perhaps his analytical mind was no more than a defense mechanism, a bully that rose up to compensate.

Rob's isolation in this new world had opened up

resources in his mind that he was eager to probe. He wondered if man, in his most primitive condition, was not the predator but the prey. In prehistoric times, when saber-toothed tigers roamed the American forests, men must have been like rabbits, cowering in silence and fear. It was an established fact that the evidence of man's cultural development, his cave paintings, his written language, began with the evidence of his campfires. Perhaps there was an important relationship there. If fire provided protection from the animals at night, it would have given primitive man the first opportunity to speak with his fellow man without the fear that the sounds he made would attract predators. If he hunted by day and hid by night, the fact of fire might have given him the first comfort to speculate, to dream, to let his mind roam. On the complicated and hazardous road to survival, perhaps it was something as sudden as the first controlled fire that allowed man's mind to begin developing into the abstract and, ultimately, self-defeating mechanism that it was today.

The speculation led in a circle of defeat. If indeed there were a master plan, if the creation of the planet were more than chemical accident, was man designed as the tool for destruction? Or did the master builder go too far? Perhaps man *was* created in God's image. Perhaps they both were prone to developing one machine too many . . .

To find himself speculating in this way was a revelation to Rob. He was a man of science, not easily given to thoughts of mysticism or God. It was, perhaps, because he felt so small here, so vulnerable compared with the size and power of everything around him. Also, there was the cello music coming from the cabin, its haunting sound rising and falling on the wind, enhancing the sense of mystery.

Maggie had become claustrophobic; music provided her only relief. In Rob's efforts to complete his job as quickly as possible, he had become consumed with his research, walking the island by day, burying himself in reading material and writing his report by night. Maggie had read every magazine in the cabin, all outdated periodicals, played Scrabble by herself until she had become sick of it, and experimented with how many ways there were to prepare the salmon that Rob easily caught in the lake and brought home for dinner every night. Their supply of canned goods was running low, and they were subsisting mainly on fish. The diet was as monotonous as the rest of their existence.

On the third day of rain, they hazarded the boat ride from the island to the shore, but found that the road into town had been damaged by the rain. It was ten miles long, and even though they were eager for supplies, they were fearful of getting stuck in a pothole. They returned to the cabin, hoping that in the morning the sun would shine.

For John Hawks and Romona Peters, the rain was a welcome relief. They had pitched camp together deep in the forest and for three days and nights lain in each other's arms, forgetting the torture and frustration of their lives on the outside. In the deluge, the lumbering activities had come to a halt; Hawks did not have to deal with the fearful spectre of the roadblock. It was as though nature had intervened to halt the catastrophic momentum of events.

Romona had spoken with the two pregnant women in the Indian village, and they had flatly refused to accompany her to see a doctor in Portland. There was nothing to do now but wait. If either of the two children these women gave birth to were deformed, Romona would take them, living or dead, to be examined by someone who could give her some answers. For now, all she could do was push the troubling thoughts from her mind and allow herself to be soothed by the sounds of rumbling thunder.

The only troubling aspect of the rain was that it had somehow given rise to a renewed epidemic of the *katahnas.* The Indian villagers had used the first day of rain to empty their heavily laden salmon nets and smoke the carcasses of the fish in their smokehouse. For two weeks prior, they had been living on canned goods, reluctant to go to the river for fear of being confronted by villagers or lumberjacks.

Now, three men were felled with seizures, trembling with fever as the chill wind swept through the silent Indian encampment.

Word of the new onset of *katahnas* reached Romona and Hawks on the third night of rain; they went to the village to investigate. There they visited each of the three men, all delusional and frightened. Hawks was bewildered and, for the first time, understood the severity of the mysterious illness. The *katahnas* struck without warning, and there seemed no explanation for why, or when, they hit.

As he and Romona walked back toward their encampment, they were swept with a sense of defeat. It was as though the forest itself had turned on them.

In the quiet of the night, an owl hooted above them and took flight; they stood and watched it as its powerful wings propelled it toward the glowing circle of the moon. The clouds had parted and the rain had stopped. The downpour that had provided respite from the problems that beseiged them had passed as quickly as it had come. The trees glistened in moonlight, and Hawks and Romona knew that in the morning their battle would resume.

But it did not hold until sunrise. They were awakened at night by the sound of an approaching landcar, its motor groaning as it lurched toward them, cross-country, through the forest.

Hawks stepped out of their tent and his eyes were hit with a spotlight. He could see the silhouettes of three men approaching him in the glare, rifles held loosely at their sides.

"You John Hawks?"

"Yes."

Hawks shielded his eyes and saw that they were garbed in the attire of lumberjacks; the man in the middle was apparently in charge. He held a plastic drinking cup in his hand.

"Someone in that tent?" he asked.

"No."

"Then you won't mind if we fire some buckshot in there."

One of them quickly cocked his rifle.

"Wait."

"Tell him to come out."

Romona emerged from the tent, three flashlights turning on her frightened eyes.

"Well, well . . ." one of them muttered.

"My name is Romona Peters. I am the granddaughter of Hector M'rai."

She stood stiffly, with her head erect, a slight tremble of her chin betraying her fear.

"What do you want?" Hawks demanded.

"Turn around."

Hawks remained still.

"I said turn around."

"Why?"

"I want to check for concealed weapons. I hear you carry a mean ax."

"I won't turn around."

One of the rifles slowly lifted.

"Turn *around*."

"Do as he says," Romona urged.

"Better listen to your squaw."

"I won't turn around."

"*I'll* turn around," Romona quickly said. She turned her back, and one of the men approached her from behind. Hawks made a move for him, and a rifle barrel swerved close to his face; the sound of a hammer clicking back echoed in the night.

"Did you come here to kill us?" Hawks gasped.

"Why don't you just wait and see."

The man behind Romona reached around her and

cupped her breasts; Hawks tensed and two rifle barrels jammed into his head, stopping him.

"Let them do this, John," she whispered in a trembling breath.

"See there? She likes it."

"Get him off her," Hawks growled through his teeth.

"Just checking for weapons—"

"Get him off her!" Hawks shouted.

Romona whimpered and Hawks lunged for the man; the man grabbed Hawks by the collar, spinning him against a tree, the two rifle barrels poking hard into his neck.

"You'll have to kill me," Hawks gasped.

"We'd rather you watched."

"Please let us alone," Romona implored. "We've done nothing to you."

"You're trespassing."

"We'll leave!" she cried.

"We're *not* trespassing," Hawks hissed.

"This land is owned by the Pitney Paper Mill."

"This land belongs to my people."

"Now, that's just not true, Indian."

"What do you want from us?" Romona moaned.

"We want you out."

"We're not leaving."

"I think you are."

The man in charge raised the plastic cup he'd been holding, as if to toast Hawks, then suddenly threw its contents onto the crotch of Hawks's pants. Hawks could smell gasoline. He tried to run, but the other two pinned his arms against the tree, overpowering him.

The man in charge moved slowly forward, putting a pipe in his mouth and lighting it with a butane lighter. His eyes were on Hawks as he turned the flame up high. Then he slowly lowered the lighter until the dagger of flame was just out of reach of Hawks's gasoline-soaked pants.

"You have twenty-four hours to leave this forest,"

the man with the lighter said. "If you aren't gone by tomorrow night, we'll be back for you."

Then he switched off his lighter and the threesome backed away. Hawks stood, unmoving, as he watched their car turn and lurch away into the night.

# 9

ROB AND MAGGIE responded to the sight of the morning sun like prisoners who had been in solitary confinement seeing the first light of day. It was a tonic to them, filling them with energy and refreshing their spirits. They quickly organized for a trip into town.

The lake sparkled in sunlight as they crossed it in their small boat; when they reached shore, they saw that the road to town had already begun to dry. They put down the canvas top of the car that Isely had left for them, and let the fresh air wash over them as they drove through a glistening green forest. Rob had a momentary concern that they might be stopped again by Indians because they were in a lumber-company car, but when they passed the place where the roadblock had been, there was no one there.

"Think they gave up?" Maggie asked.

"Doubt it. I'd like to get rid of this car."

They turned onto the main highway and drove into town, parking in front of the library, which was Maggie's first priority. She would look for some books, then shop while Rob went to the bank and cashed some traveler's checks; then they would rendezvous at the post office, where Rob was planning to send soil and tissue samples back to Washington.

They were so exhilarated to be out of the confines of their cabin, to be walking on cement instead of mud, to be rubbing shoulders with other human beings who nodded and said good morning, that they failed to notice they were being watched. John Hawks and Romona Peters had also journeyed to town and spotted the lumber-company vehicle, recognizing it as one of the two that had run through the blockade. In the small, one-street town, they waited quietly for the opportunity to confront them.

Hawks had come to demand that the sheriff provide protection from the men who had threatened them the night before. The sheriff of Manatee County had listened without sympathy, not even making the gesture of a lie that he would look into it. It was his customary way of dealing with the Indians; simply to nod until they were tired of talking. Romona had tried to dissuade Hawks from wasting his time, for she knew this sheriff well. He was the same man she had tried to appeal to when she had been raped as a twelve-year-old girl. Now, sixteen years later, she saw the same hint of amusement glinting behind his eyes.

The sheriff's name was Bartholomew Pilgrim; a heavyset man, fifty years of age, he was allowed to continue as head of local law enforcement over the years, more out of public lethargy than from support. There was little crime in the town of Manatee, little need for effective personalities in public office. He, the president of the local bank, the mayor, the three pastors of the churches, the board of the Chamber of Commerce, were all of a generation that grew up together, supported one another and, once seated, held firmly to their jobs. Recently, the chief operating officer of the Pitney Paper Mill, Bethel Isely, had joined their ranks. In its small-town way, it was a ruling junta; each defended the other for the good of the whole.

Bartholomew Pilgrim had been alerted to the presence of John Hawks in the Manatee forest; the news of the events at the blockade had been brought to him by Bethel Isely. But he could not deal with Hawks in the way that he would have liked to. He had been cautioned by his superiors in Portland that the

Indian spokesman for the O.P.'s was known in Washington and had to be dealt with, on an official basis, delicately.

On an unofficial level, it was different. As long as no law enforcement personnel could be accused of harassment or violation of civil rights, Pilgrim could close his eyes to events like those that happened to Romona and Hawks the night before.

As Hawks spoke to the sheriff, he could see in his eyes that he knew what had happened to them, and had likely sanctioned it.

"Gee, I'd sure like to help you, my friend—"

"Don't call me your friend."

"I'd sure like to help you, pal, but there's nothin' much I can do."

"It's your job to protect me."

"It's my job to protect the citizens of this county."

"I *am* a citizen of this county."

"No, no, you're from out of town."

"I was born here and I'm *living* here."

"I wouldn't advise that. If I were you, I'd move on down the road."

"I'm not moving anywhere."

The sheriff sat back in his wooden swivel chair; it creaked beneath the weight of his massive body.

"I'm gonna tell you somethin', old pal," he said. "I'm not against you people, and neither is Mr. Isely. Matter of fact, he's a very generous man. After I heard about the blockade, I was all for bringin' you into this jail. I'd have been perfectly within my rights to put you under arrest. But Mr. Isely, he said no. He said that John Hawks is a good old boy, and we just got to give him a little time to move on down the road."

"I'm going nowhere."

"I'm sorry to hear that."

"If anything happens to me, people will find out about it."

"I'm sure they will."

"You will be held responsible."

"I hope you take care of yourself, then."

It was after this exchange that Hawks and Romona exited the police station and spotted the lumber-company vehicle parked in front of the library. Now, with his life threatened, Hawks knew that he had nowhere to turn except to the man from the government.

"This is a hell of a vacation you sent me on, Victor." Rob pressed one hand to his free ear and spoke loudly into the telephone as he stood in a phone booth on the corner next to the post office. "I get away from the rats, and the raccoons attack me. The Indians are out for blood, and the lumberjacks are only too happy to give it to them. I'll tell you, it makes the tenements look like a rest home." Rob paused and nodded. "I'm going to get this done as quick as I can. I'll finish up the report when I get back to Washington."

Victor Shusette sat in his office in Washington, listening with concern. His choice of Robert Vern to conduct the field survey in Manatee had backfired on him, and the last thing he wanted to hear was that Rob was going to make fast work of it. The timber lobby had learned that Vern had no experience as an environmentalist; the fact that he was qualified by virtue of his having been tutored by veteran field workers, and by reason of his own native intelligence, meant little to them. They now had a possible cause with which to discredit his report. It was too late for Shusette to reverse his choice; if he did so, it would further damage the Agency's credibility. Credibility was all they had to sell, and credibility was a fragile commodity. In many ways, people looked upon the Environmental Protection Agency as they would look upon a police force. Even though it could function perfectly for years, a single questionable incident or the transgression of one individual could bring out all the hidden resentment toward it and collapse the entire structure. Whatever report Robert Vern brought back had to be airtight, documented with an overkill of thoroughness to make up for any doubt about his abilities or experience.

"I hate to tell you this, Rob, but I want you to stay there as long as possible."

Eight hundred miles away from Shusette, Rob stood in the phone booth and listened, his expression turning more sober as Shusette explained the situation they were in.

"Victor," Rob broke in, "I want to explain something. I was a little glib a minute ago. When I said the Indians are out for blood, I meant it. They say they've killed a couple of people up here."

"What are you talking about?"

"That's what people say. And from what I saw, I can see why they say that. I saw real violence."

"You're saying you think you're in danger?"

"I'm saying I'm not terribly comfortable up here. And neither is Maggie."

"You want protection? I can arrange that."

"No, that's not what I want."

"Tell me what you want. What can I do?"

"I want to leave here, Victor. I want to do the job I came to do, and leave here as soon as I can."

"If you come back too fast, it's not going to look good. If you're not in any real danger, I'd like you to stay there as long as you can."

Rob didn't answer.

"Rob?"

"I'm here."

"Look, if you *have* to come back, then come back. I'm just telling you that appearances are important right now. If you want, I'll take over for you."

"No," Rob answered with fatigue.

"If you can, give it another ten days. I'll be satisfied with that."

"Yeah."

"Check in with me, huh?"

"Right."

Rob hung up and leaned against the wall of the small glass cubicle, his eyes set with despair. More than anything, he hated failure; he had never before so unwittingly set himself up for it. The field survey had been a mistake from the start; he cursed himself for allowing Shusette to talk him into it. It was the appeal to his ego that had made him grab for it; the promise that he could do something that could make a real and permanent difference. Now, by virtue of his inexperience, it was earmarked for failure.

He had promised Maggie that they would leave as soon as possible, but if he did that, he'd be throwing the whole thing away.

As he gazed out toward the street, he spotted Maggie heading into the grocery store. She was wearing boots and a riding jacket, the wind gently lifting her hair. Her arms were loaded with books, and she walked with energy, looking like a girl crossing the street of some small-town college campus. He rarely saw her at this distance; it reminded him of the mornings he used to watch her from the window of their New York apartment. It filled him with sadness at how complicated their lives had become.

The conversation he'd had with Shusette had swept him with fatigue. It made him feel like surrendering. The obsessive treadmill he'd been on for the last four years was suddenly slowing beneath him. There was nothing he could do to alter the course of the planet; he sensed that here more than anywhere. Walking among the towering trees, he had gotten a true perspective of his own size and strength. He was no more than an ant. And he was trying to push over skyscrapers. This job had been a last-ditch, desperate attempt to make his mark, and he was being defeated. They knew in Washington what he had sensed from the start. He had no business here.

"Mr. Vern?"

Rob was jolted by the intrusion; he turned to see John Hawks waiting for him outside the pay phone. The woman, Romona, was there, too. Their expres-

sions were intense, no more gentle now than they had
been at the blockade.

Rob stepped out into the street, feeling apprehensive.

"My name is John Hawks."

"I remember."

"We want you to come with us."

"What for?"

"We want to speak to you."

"Right here will be fine."

Hawks saw the fear in Rob's eyes and was surprised by it. It was rare that a white man gave him
credit for equal strength.

"Are you afraid of us?"

Rob paused. "Yes."

"Because of what you've heard?"

"I haven't heard anything."

Hawks knew it was a lie. "You haven't heard we're
drunks? We're violent? We're murderers?"

Rob studied Hawks, uncertain of his attitude. He
didn't know if he was trying to reassure or frighten.

"That's what they say about us, Mr. Vern. They
discount our rights by telling these lies." He moved
closer; Rob could smell the dampness of his leather
jacket. "We are not drunks. And we are not violent.
My people are fishermen, and their lives are clean."

Rob was uncertain of how to respond. Hawks
stiffened, misreading the silence as a threat of dis-
missal.

"I tell you this not out of choice, but from neces-
sity."

"Why is that?" Rob asked.

"They're going to kill me."

"Who is?"

"The lumber company."

"Why would they do that?"

"Isn't it obvious?"

"They have a right to enter the forest—"

"I'm not speaking of the *blockade*."

The sharpness of Hawks's voice created a silence; the men assessed each other as adversaries.

"Please," Romona said quietly. "We want you to come with us."

"Why?"

"No one from the government has come here before. We want you to see who our people are so you can go back and tell them."

"Look," Rob said. "I can understand how you feel, but my work here has nothing to do with—"

"Are you deaf like the rest?" Hawks interrupted. He was bristling now, fighting to control his anger. "I was educated at your schools, Mr. Vern. I'm a well-educated man. I've studied your laws and I've perfected your language, but it did me no good. Your laws do not apply to Indians, and your language is wasted in an Indian's mouth because you refuse to hear!" He came close to Rob, his face taut with rage. "Why is it you refuse to hear!"

The words hit Rob at the wrong time. He was fed up.

"Perhaps you don't even hear what I'm saying *now*," Hawks goaded.

"Oh, I can hear," Rob shot back. "But I can also see. You're surprised that people call you violent . . ."

"The violence you saw was provoked."

"By whom?"

"It was necessary."

"It was *suicidal*."

"Hawks's eyes bore into Rob's. "Tell me. For what you believe in, are you willing to *die*?"

Rob backed off, unwilling to escalate any further. "Look, I'm here to study the environment?"

"And what is your concept of the environment? I want to know. Is it dirt? Is it trees? Rocks?"

"Come on, this is—"

"The environment is *us!*" Hawks declared. "It's what we're *made* of! It's being torn and mangled, and so are we!"

"My people are sick, Mr. Vern," Romona said.

"Their minds are confused. They tremble and fall, and it has nothing to do with *alcohol,* as the townspeople claim."

"Tell him," Hawks commanded.

"I've acted as midwife, Mr. Vern. I've seen the results of this chaos."

Rob looked from one to the other, unable to comprehend what they were saying.

"Tell him all of it," Hawks said.

"Children born dead, Mr. Vern. Born deformed. So badly. . . ." She faltered. "They must be put to death."

"What?"

"Children that look more like animals than men."

Rob was stunned. It was plain by the woman's intensity that she was telling the truth. But he was unable to make any sense of it.

"We need help, Mr. Vern. Desperately. And no one will help us."

"The end of our forest is the end of our people," Hawks proclaimed. "So don't talk about the 'environment' as though it had nothing to do with *us!*"

In the silence that followed, Rob saw Maggie approaching. As she came close, she hesitated, sensing the tension in the air. Rob held out his hand to her.

"These people want us to go with them, Maggie. There are things they want to show us."

As they drove through the forest, Romona described to Rob the history and details of the seizures, the stillbirths, and the deformed fetuses. And she told of her own futile quest at the public library to find some explanations. Maggie listened in silence, her heart going out to the young Indian woman. She thanked God that the fetus within her own womb was slumbering safely, and secretly, protected from the tragedies that had befallen these people.

Rob questioned Romona with professional thoroughness, then revealed to her that he was a doctor.

It caused her to raise her hands to her eyes, conceal-ing tears of gratitude. Maggie reached out to touch her, but Romona withdrew. The gap between their two worlds was too wide to be bridged with a single gesture.

"Have you done experiments with animals?" Hawks asked.

"Some."

"Of what sort?"

"Routine things. Drug effects."

"I've seen caged animals become sick and die. I've seen them turn sick and abort their young. I've seen them become crazy and eat their young. This is what happens to a natural creature when it discovers it's become imprisoned."

"I've seen that, too. But it doesn't explain what you're describing. Stress can play a big part, but it can't cause all this."

"My grandfather says that when men turn against the forest, the forest turns against men. He says we will all suffer from this profanity."

They passed a fork in the road and Hawks touched Rob's arm. "Stop here."

"Why?" Romona asked.

"They'll never be back. I want them to see every-thing."

Rob pulled the car off the road and they all got out, following a narrow footpath toward the encampment of Hector M'rai.

The trail was a gauntlet of thornbushes that tore into their clothing and scratched their faces. A cloud of blackflies buzzed about their eyes and whined in their ears; Hawks broke through spider webs as he led the way. All of these things were indications to Rob that few people used this trail.

A chilling thought came suddenly into Rob's mind. A glance at Maggie told him that she was thinking the same. The Indians had been accused of murder, and both Rob and Maggie had witnessed the violence that John Hawks was capable of. They had allowed

themselves to be brought deep into the forest, where
they were defenseless.

"Where are we going?" Rob asked.

"Just ahead," Hawks replied.

Rob stopped.

"I want to know where we're going."

Hawks pointed ahead. "You can see."

Maggie took Rob's arm and they moved tentatively
forward, stepping into the sudden oasis of beauty,
known to the Indians as *M'ay-an-dan'ta*. The Garden
of Eden. Three large tepees stood in a circular compound, surrounding a large fire pit rimmed with
stones. A line strung on poles held drying animal
skins; an elegant archer's bow leaned against a tree.
In the midst of this embattled forest, it was like an
artist's rendering of Early American history. An oasis
where time stood still.

"It's . . . beautiful," Maggie whispered.

"What is this place?" asked Rob. "Is this the village?"

"No," Romona replied.

"It's all that's left of what we once were," Hawks
said. "I wanted you to see this before you see what
we've become."

"My grandfather built it. To him, this place is
sacred. He lets no one come here."

Rob moved to the center of the encampment,
gazing up at the trees. He could feel the sense of peace
that existed here. "I can see what you're fighting for."

"We're not fighting to live in the past any more
than you are," Hawks replied. "We're fighting for our
share of the present. We're fighting to have the same
choices that you have. We're fighting for everything
that you would fight for."

Rob accepted the words in silence. He recognized
in John Hawks the same kind of man that he himself
was. The zeal was the same, the rhetoric was the same,
the frustration was the same. The only difference was
that John Hawks, as an Indian, was denied the right

to be angry. "What I meant to say was," Rob said softly, "that this place is very beautiful."

Romona turned to one of the tents. *"A'hns-pahni'- tah,* M'rai?" she called. "My grandfather is not well," she said to Rob. "He, too, has suffered from the *katahnas."*

*"Y'ahn'ta'tha?"* a voice called back.

*"A'han-pahni'tah Ki'ythi."*

A tent flap pulled back, and M'rai emerged. He was dressed in buckskin, but also wore a necktie, and his hair was slicked back in a way that Romona had never seen it before.

*"N'iyhn-tah?"* Romona asked quizically.

*"N'ahn-mohn'i'ka,"* the old man replied as he smiled. *"A'yah'al-mah'nitah."* He moved with diffi- culty, pulling himself into an erect posture, his head trembling slightly as he attempted to arch it with dignity. His eyes turned to Maggie, and she returned his smile.

"He says he knew he had visitors coming," Romona translated.

"How did he know?" Maggie asked.

"M'rai knows such things," Romona replied. It was plain from the way Romona looked at the old man how deeply affectionate she felt toward him. Maggie, too, had an instant feeling for him. There was a gentleness in his smile that made her feel as if she were being embraced.

"Would you tell him," Maggie asked, "that we're pleased to be here?"

"He speaks some English," Romona replied. "I taught him myself."

"Welcome," the old man said.

Rob, too, was captivated. But he was assessing the old man with a professional eye. He saw that M'rai's eyes were dimmed with cataracts, and that the knuckles of his fingers were scorched and burned, possibly from cigarettes.

"These people are from the government," Romona said to M'rai. "We're hoping they will help us."

"How many?" the old man asked.

"There are two of us, sir," Rob answered.

"Is that enough?"

Rob chuckled. "Well, we're working hard."

"That's good."

M'rai extended his hand toward Maggie, and she came forward.

"A soft woman," he said as he felt her hand.

"Too soft," Maggie replied.

"Just right."

"Your home is very beautiful," Rob said.

"Thank you."

"Don't mistake these tents for his home," Hawks interjected. "His home is this whole forest."

"You know," Rob mused as he turned to Hawks, "I visited a place just one week ago where eleven people were living in a single room."

"Yes?"

Rob sensed Hawks's defensive tone. "I just wanted you to know—"

"That we're asking too much?"

"That some people are fighting for a single inch of living space—"

"Because they fought too late!" Hawks declared. Then he grabbed up the archer's bow, glaring into the forest.

"This camp is all as the old people did it," Romona said, trying to restore calm. "M'rai is teaching us so someone here will remember. There are underground tunnels beneath the frost line to store perishables . . . one can move from one tent to the other without showing himself."

Hawks threaded an arrow into the archer's bow and angrily released it; it hit with a resounding thud into the bark of a tree. "He taught me this as well."

Romona was becoming visibly uneasy. She again tried to distract Hawks's anger. "When he had his eyesight, M'rai was a great archer," she said. "They say he could hit a hummingbird by the light of the moon."

"Is that right?" Rob replied.

"We have big hummingbirds," the old man said.

Rob laughed, but then realized that M'rai hadn't intended it to be funny.

"It's true," M'rai said. "Here, everything grows big. Very big. Bigger than you can imagine."

"Well," Rob replied, "I did see a salmon that took my breath away."

"It is the Garden of Eden," M'rai said. "Would you like to see?"

"Yes."

"Come, then."

"Where?" Romona asked.

"The pond."

Romona reacted with disbelief. "You'd take them to the pond?"

"Yes."

"What's the pond?" Rob asked.

"No one is allowed at the pond," Romona replied. "Not even other Indians. It's the private sanctuary of the oldest man in the tribe."

"I can do as I wish," M'rai said.

"Don't expect them to see what you see, old man," Hawks cautioned M'rai.

To this, M'rai smiled. "I expect nothing. That's why I see everything."

He moved into the forest and they all followed, traveling another narrow foot trail, this one well-worn, which led to the secret lagoon. In all the years that Romona had been with the old man, she had never walked this trail. And she felt that it was wrong to do so now. She sensed they were trespassing and knew that if M'rai was not losing control of his faculties, he would never have allowed it to happen.

"No one has come here before," M'rai said as they walked. "No one who has seen this is alive. Except me."

Hawks smiled to himself, recalling the time, as a boy, when he had sneaked in here. He still remem-

bered his disappointment on finding that there was
nothing unusual about it.

"One time some hippies came," the old man said,
"to grow bad seeds."

"Marijuana," Hawks explained.

"But they were chased away before they saw anything," M'rai added.

"What is there to see?" Maggie asked.

The old man pointed into a clearing. They all
stopped, absorbing the wonder of what they saw there.

Nestled in the midst of towering trees was a still
pond, a shimmering circle of pale blue water, surrounded by lush foliage and twisting vines. The trees
were bent forward, as though paying homage, and
the leaves of the bushes were larger and greener here
than anywhere else in the forest. It was an though in
this single spot it were midsummer instead of spring.
And the differences did not end there. As Rob walked
slowly forward, he noticed a profusion of fungus;
every tree trunk was covered with it, tendrils reaching
out at odd angles into the air. And there were mush-
roomlike growths attached to the bark of the trees;
some of them were the size of an elephant's ear.

Rob approached the water's edge and saw, through
the shimmering pale blue surface, images that were
difficult to discern. They looked like thick packages
of logs that had been tied together and then apparently
sunk into the pond.

Hawks, too, was carefully assessing the environment. The pond was different than when he had seen
it as a boy. It did indeed have a mystical feeling
now. A near physical sensation that made him uneasy.
He walked to the water's edge and stood beside Rob,
and saw that Rob's eyes were troubled, as though
searching for some kind of answer.

"It *is* like the Garden of Eden," Maggie whispered
behind them. "It's *magical*."

"We were once a magical people," M'rai said.

"It's true," Romona added on a hushed breath.
"And this was the most magical place of all." She

walked slowly forward, overawed that she was actually standing here. She turned to Maggie, wondering if she could possibly understand her feeling. "This lagoon is the setting for many Indian legends."

"We heard about one of them," Maggie replied with a smile.

"Yes?"

"Katydid . . . dadin . . . or something?"

"Katahdin," Romona corrected.

"Katahdin is no legend," the old man interjected.

M'rai's words caught Rob's attention. He glanced his way with troubled eyes.

"My grandfather is the oldest person in our tribe," Romona said with embarrassment. "It is his duty to foster these beliefs."

"I've *seen* him," the old man protested. "Here on these very shores."

Hawks stepped forward to silence him. "This is what makes people think the Indians are drunk, old man. Our legends are best kept to ourselves."

"He's *real*," M'rai implored.

"What does he look like?" Maggie asked.

"Are you humoring him?" Hawks snapped.

Maggie was taken aback. "No."

The old man turned to Maggie, calming her with his smile. "He is a part of everything created," he said quietly. "From clay to man. And he bears the mark of each of God's creatures." He spoke slowly and distinctly, as though teaching a child. "When he sleeps he looks like a mountain. When he stands, he is the size of a tree."

"You say that with affection," Maggie answered softly.

"He has awakened to protect us."

"Nothing will protect us," Hawks sneered. "They say we killed those people. That will be their excuse for killing us."

"Mr. M'rai?" Rob called from the shoreline. "Are those *logs* in there?"

M'rai walked to the edge of the pond, his eyes straining to see where Rob was pointing.

"There, toward the middle. Under the surface.."

"They come twice each year," the old man replied. "By magic. Then they move into the lake."

"This pond leads into the lake?"

"Beyond the trees there. Water comes from the river and leads into the lake."

Following the old man's gesture, Rob could make out a shimmering avenue of water snaking through the distant trees. The pond was not self-contained, as it appeared; it was a small pocket formed by an offshoot of the river.

"Does the water have the same color over there?" Rob asked. "The same light blue?"

"Coming in, it does not. Going out, it does."

"So this color begins here in the pond and then goes out into the lake."

"It disappears in the lake. It returns to dark blue. The color is from the magic in the water. It is only here, in this secret place."

Rob exchanged a glance with Hawks. Hawks was beginning to get the message.

"Look!" Maggie called out. They all turned toward the water and saw a V-shaped ripple, created by something swimming just beneath the surface.

"What is it?" Rob asked.

The old man turned to Hawks, gesturing as he spoke. *"A'han'tka'Prodai th'ay'andan'tah."* He picked up a small hand net made of twigs that was resting beside a tree. *"N'hoan'thaiy'do'e,"* M'rai instructed.

"He says he will show you why he calls this place the Garden of Eden," Romona explained.

Hawks took the hand net and waded into the water, making a swipe at the swimming creature, missing it.

"Stay there," M'rai said. "He must come up again."

At that moment Rob caught sight of an exposed root system at the base of a tree. The roots had literally risen out of the ground, as though seeking sustenance from the sky.

Maggie noticed his expression change. "What's wrong?"

"Those are feeder roots. They're supposed to be *under* the ground."

There was a splash from beside them; Hawks grunted with satisfaction, wading to shore with a large object flapping in his net. He approached them and dumped it out onto the ground. All stared down with revulsion and shock.

"Is it a fish?" Maggie gasped.

"No."

Wriggling at their feet was the outsized form of a polywog. Its head was lumpy and misshapen, and it was fully ten inches long. And there was more wrong with it still. One of its eyes protruded bulbously from the socket, as though forced out by some pressure from behind, and one of its partially developed legs was much longer than the other, almost as long as the tail.

The old man surveyed their faces and smiled. "I told you, things grow big here," he said.

Rob quickly looked up and riveted into Hawks's eyes. "You've seen this before?" he asked.

"No."

"No one has seen them," M'rai said proudly. "They are only in this pond."

Rob was shaken. It had all come together. The sunken logs, the coloration of the water, the profusion of fungus . . .

"This pond feeds into the lake?"

"Yes."

"And it comes from the Espee River?"

"Yes."

"And that's where the paper mill is?"

"Yes."

Rob's fists clenched. He paced quickly, then stopped, addressing the old man.

"Don't eat anything from this water. Don't eat anything from this ground." His voice was trembling. "Don't eat *anything* from here."

"Why?" the old man asked.

"This ground is poisoned. This water is poisoned."

The old man was shocked. Then he suddenly laughed. It was beyond his understanding.

"How far is the paper mill?" Rob demanded.

"Three miles upriver," Hawks answered. "It's best to go by boat."

"Wait here for us," Rob ordered.

"What about the village?" Romona asked.

"I'm going to the paper mill first," Rob seethed. He turned on his heel, heading for the trail.

"Mr. Vern," Hawks called after him. "I'm in danger in this forest tonight. I can't stay here."

"Where can I find you?"

"Your cabin at sunup."


The point where the Espee River entered Mary's Lake was easy to find. It was a wide avenue of churning water, lined with salmon nets that were strung across the mouth of it on poles.

As Rob sat at the motor of their outboard boat, he glared straight ahead, too angry to speak. He knew from the massive amount of reading he had done that there were certain life forms that were extremely susceptible to chemical change. The most susceptible were those that went through two or more stages before they reached the adult form, such as salamanders and frogs. He remembered specifically of reading about a pond in New Jersey that had produced six-legged frogs after the trees around it had been sprayed with a chemical pesticide called Deldrin. There were no pesticides being used here in the Manatee forest; it was all too obvious that toxic chemicals were being used by the lumber company. The aberrated color of the foliation around M'rai's pond, the exposed root system, and the deformed polywog were all clear barometers of a dangerously toxic environment.

As their small boat cut through the churning water,

the roar of industry began to fill the air. The river separated into two channels; Rob followed the narrower of the two, guided by the growing sound. It led to a bend where the landscape suddenly changed. The surface of the water became oil-slicked and pockmarked with Pepsi cans and the belly-up bodies of dead fish; the huge edifice of the Pitney Paper Mill loomed like a giant, its smokestack spouting brown fumes that muted the sun. The shoreline was littered with tree stumps; huge tractors hauled logs across ground that had been mulched to mud. And there was an overwhelming stench in the air.

Rob and Maggie found each other's eyes, their disgust expressed in silence. The outboard motor began to groan and Rob realized that the water had suddenly become shallow. The waterway had narrowed to a single avenue directly down the middle of the river, flanked by mountains of sludge that had accumulated on either side. In fact, there was no way to get the boat to shore.

"Over *there!*" a voice called from the shoreline. Rob looked up and saw a group of lumberjacks waving him in a direction upriver toward the far side of the factory. But it was too late. The stern of his boat hit a silt drift and the motor quit on him. He was stuck a good fifteen feet from the shore.

"Got a rope?" a lumberjack shouted.

Rob had a docking rope, but it was too short.

"Won't reach!" he called back.

"Hang on!" Rob and Maggie waited as the man ran to a truck and returned with a long coil of rope, which he threw out to them. Rob tied it to the bow; four men on the shore pulled the boat across the silt until they could pull it no farther.

"I'm looking for Mr. Isely," Rob said.

"His office is upstairs."

"Can you get me any closer here?"

"You'll have to wade. But watch it; you can really sink into this stuff."

Rob took Maggie's hand and they eased over the

side, sinking almost knee-deep into the mud. Two of the lumberjacks waded in to help them, one of them lifting Maggie onto the shore.

"You want Mr. Isely?"

"Yes," Rob replied as he climbed to the shore.

"This way."

Rob and Maggie followed the men toward the factory, the noise growing louder as they approached. Just outside the doors, they were stopped by a uniformed guard who phoned upstairs to get permission for them to proceed.

"Name?"

"Robert Vern."

The guard repeated the name into the phone, then nodded, handing each of them a set of earphones and a hard hat.

"There's a self-service elevator just inside the door. Take it up to four."

As Rob and Maggie entered the building, a barrage of heat and noise overwhelmed them. It was like a huge warehouse, filled with gargantuan, roaring machines that ̄warfed their human masters. Men could barely be s ̲ ̲ ̲vithin the maze of twisting tubes and gleaming tanks tha ̄ shot steam and glowed with heat as they processed crude timber. The temperature was easily a hundred degrees; Maggie was struck with nausea as they waited for the freight elevator to arrive.

"You okay?"

She nodded. "How do people *work* in here?"

The elevator arrived and they stepped in, the doors clanging shut around them. As they ascended, their eyes fell upon a row of gas masks. A sign beneath them read: "Use in the event of warning bell. Proceed immediately to the outside."

The elevator jolted to a stop and the doors opened, revealing Bethel Isely. He was dressed in a suit and tie, wearing a hard hat and a genuinely welcoming smile.

"You can take the earphones off!" he shouted as

he extended his hand to them. "It's nice and quiet up here!" Then he took them to his office where a secretary offered coffee. Both Rob and Maggie refused; Rob was eager to survey the plant.

"I want to know how everything works here," Rob said firmly. "From start to finish. I want to know about the entire procedure."

"No problem. It's real simple. You want to follow me?"

The tour began on the roof of the factory, where they stood at a handrailing, gazing down at stacks of cut timber piled as high as mountains. Men below fed the timber into a conveyor belt that ran up the side of the building, bringing the short sections of barkless logs onto the roof, where they splashed into a tank of water, then floated across the length of the roof in an artificial stream.

"This stream is called the flume," Isely explained as they walked along the length of it. "All the wood that's unfit for lumberyards is cut into four-foot sections and fed down this channel toward the grinding machines. We use stone grinders to turn the logs into pulp. Once we've got pulp, we bleach it so the color will turn from brown to white. Then we press the pulp into paper. That's really all there is to it. It's a very simple process and a very conventional industry. With the exception of volume, it's no different today than it was sixty years ago."

"What *is* the volume?"

"At the moment?"

"Peak capacity. How many logs can you process in a day?"

"Five acres, maybe."

The answer fairly knocked the wind out of Rob; Isely was quick to lighten the blow. "That's if we wanted to rush. But we're in no hurry.."

"How long in terms of a single tree? How long does it take for it to turn into paper?"

Isely could see that Rob was upset. "I never timed it."

"An estimate."

"You know, the primary goal of any industry is to be efficient . . ."

"You must know, then."

"What I'm trying to say is, it's something we're proud of."

"I asked you a simple question."

"Ten minutes."

Rob was staggered. The trees that were being fed down this stream toward the grinders had been standing on the earth for perhaps ten centuries. Now, within ten minutes they would be rendered into a condition where they could be written on, or wrapped around something, or used for someone to blow their nose on and then thrown into a trash basket. Man's powers to *undo* were mind-boggling.

"I want to see the rest of it," Rob demanded. "All of it."

"You can see whatever you like. We've got nothing to hide."

Rob took Maggie's hand and they descended a narrow metal stairwell to the third floor, where massive grinding machines chewed the logs into pulp. The noise level was thunderous. Isely had to shout directly into Rob's ear to be heard.

"The logs are crushed mechanically in there! No chemicals! We break them down with heavy stones!"

"Then you bleach it?"

"What?"

"Do you bleach it next?"

"We *bleach* it!"

"I want to see!"

They descended another stairwell to the second floor, where the dark brown pulp spilled into steaming vats and emerged on a conveyor belt, its color transformed to white. It was from here that the acrid stench emanated; the air was barely breatheable. Maggie held her hand over her nose and mouth; she was beginning to feel woozy again.

"You all right, Mrs. Vern? You can sit over there by the door."

Maggie nodded gratefully and went to a fire exit, where she sat on the stairs and gasped for breath. Rob watched her for a long moment and determined that she was all right. Then he turned back to Isely.

"Why do you bleach it?" Rob shouted over the din.

"With the exception of grocery bags, no one likes paper that isn't white. Don't ask me why. Just a *quirk* that people have. I wish they didn't. It would save us a lot of money."

"What do you bleach it *with?*"

"Chlorine. But it stays right here in the plant. It's a hazard for us, because the chlorine can turn into gas. It would be a lot safer for us if we could pump it out into the water, but we know it would play hell with the environment. And the last thing we want to do is disturb the environment."

"It doesn't go into the water?"

"Not a drop. It's easy to test for. You're welcome to test the water. We do nothing here that isn't recommended by the EPA. We follow your rules religiously."

"I want to see *more.*"

"This way."

Maggie followed as they descended the last stairwell down to the main floor, where they had initially entered. The heat level was more intense here than anywhere else in the factory. It was here that the white pulp was put into pressers that looked like steamrollers, and emerged as a huge, continuous sheet of paper.

"That's the whole of it!" Isely said. "Once the pulp gets down here, it's pressed into sheets and dried into paper."

"How does it turn into paper?"

"The pulp is fibrous. When it's pressed, the fibers entwine, creating a solid."

Rob looked around at the huge machines, his face

betraying frustration. "And the only chemical you use here is chlorine?"

"Yes. No, excuse me. There's a caustic agent mixed with the chlorine. It's biodegradable, recommended by the EPA, and stays with the chlorine. It does *not* go into the watershed."

"Just as clean as a whistle, huh?"

"Beg pardon?"

Rob turned to him, assessing him with a wary eye.

"Something wrong?" Isely asked.

"What happens to the logs before they get here?"

There was something in Rob's voice that alerted Isely. It was more an accusation than a question.

"They get floated down the river to the plant."

"That's it? You just float them directly to the plant?"

"That's right."

"You don't *hold* them anywhere? They don't stop anywhere along the line?"

"Sometimes. If we get stacked up . . ."

"Where do they stop?"

"They normally *don't*."

"But sometimes they do. Isn't that what you just said?"

"Yes."

"Where do you hold them?"

"Various places."

"Ponds? Do you hold them in ponds?"

"Probably. It softens them up to soak them."

"So soaking is part of the process."

"They get soaked coming down the river."

"But *extra* soaking is more desirable."

Isely was beginning to take offense at the interrogation. "As a matter of fact, it's *not*. If they soak too long, they sink and get algae on them, and the algae goes into the pulp."

"All right, let's back up a minute."

"What is this? The third degree?"

"I'm just asking you some questions."

"I'm happy to answer your questions."

"I'm glad to hear that, because I have a few *more*."

Maggie looked at Rob in an effort to calm him. She was becoming uneasy with his anger.

"You say that 'sometimes' the logs are held in ponds?" Rob challenged.

"Yes. When we've got too much surplus to process."

"I saw *mountains* of cut logs out there. Would you say you have a surplus right now?"

"Yes."

"And how often is that the case?"

Isely didn't respond.

"This is easy for me to find out," Rob warned.

"What are you getting at?"

"How often do you have too much surplus?"

"Fairly often."

"Maybe all the time?"

"I don't know."

"But more than occasionally."

Isely was beginning to bristle. "I don't know."

"Aren't you in charge here?"

"I'm in charge here, but I don't know everything."

"It's your *job* to know everything!"

Isely leveled his eyes into Rob's. "I'm new to this, Mr. Vern. Just like *you* are."

Rob stiffened with anger; Maggie touched his arm to calm him.

"Do you soak the logs in chemicals?" Rob demanded.

"Not to my knowledge."

"What does that mean?"

"You're out of my area on this. The transport is handled by a private contractor. We have no jurisdiction over what he does."

"I asked you a question!"

"And I answered it!"

"You are responsible for whatever effluent comes out of this process!" Rob shouted. "You hire the contractor, you sell the product, *you* are accountable for *whatever* goes on here!" He pushed his face close to

Isely's. "Now, I want to know what *chemicals* you're using."

"I want to ask *you* something!" Isely shouted back. "How many pages in that report you're going to write?"

"Answer my question!"

"How many pages? A hundred? A thousand? And how many copies? Five hundred, maybe?"

"I want to know what *chemicals* you're using!"

"We're talking about five hundred thousand sheets of paper just for your report. Am I far off?"

"I asked you—"

"And how many sheets in the *rest* of the filing cabinets in Washington?"

"You're not answering—"

"I *am* answering. I supply, and you demand! *You're* responsible, too! Unless you want to start filling your filing cabinets with rocks, and wiping your nose with cactus—"

"What chemicals are the logs soaked in?" Rob shouted over him.

"None!" Isely snapped.

"I don't believe you."

"Then test the water!" Isely raged. "That's what *we* do! If the logs were soaked in chemicals, it would squeeze out in the pulping process right into the watershed in front of this plant!" He was fuming; his face reddened with anger. "We take samples out there every tenth day, and there's not a damn thing floating in that water that we don't know about, and that isn't perfectly safe for this environment!"

"Why are there dead fish out there?"

"If you knew more about your work, Mr. Vern, you'd know the answer to that! The water's overused in this section of the river. There's not enough oxygen to support aquatic life within a half-mile radius, and that's perfectly acceptable to the EPA and has no effect on the rest of the water. And it has nothing to do with chemicals."

The tirade silenced Rob. It was plain that Isely knew what he was talking about.

"Do you know how to test water, 'Dr.' Vern?"

"I know how to test water."

"Then test it! We've got nothing to hide!"

Isely turned on his heel and entered the freight elevator, the doors clanging shut on his angry scowl. Rob sagged with fatigue and took Maggie's hand; they exited into the cool outdoors.

Outside the factory, the muted sun was hovering low against the horizon. Rob and Maggie walked to their boat in silence, wading into the deep mud and crawling with effort over its side. Rob used an oar to push the boat out of the silt drift and into the narrow channel, then started the motor and headed back down the river. Within minutes they had reached the mouth of the Espee River, where it spilled into Mary's Lake. Rob noticed the body of a dead beaver tangled in one of the nets.

The sun was beginning to set; the bats had come out to feed on the profusion of insects given birth by the rain. They dove and swooped against an orange-streaked sky as silently as butterflies in a field of flowers.

The irony of this land was that it looked so unconquerable. Regardless of what havoc was churning beneath the surface, it maintained a calm and implacable face. It was the sum of all of its parts and had a kind of collective courage; all the more difficult to dissect because everything was so inextricably entwined.

As their small boat cut across the calm surface of the lake toward the island, they sat in silence, inhaling the tranquilizing fragrance of pine trees. In the heat and noise of the paper mill, Maggie had experienced a stirring in her stomach that was unlike any feeling she had ever had before. It felt like movement. But not the kind of pleasant movement she had heard described by other pregnant women. It felt sharp and rebellious, as though her insides were in conflict. It was subsiding now, the tonic of fresh air and quiet soothing her nerves.

From her position in the stern of the boat, she turned and faced Rob, noting the despair in his eyes. She knew he was unaccustomed to defeat, and she wished there were some way she could help him.

"Isn't it possible that tadpoles can sometimes grow big?" she asked meekly.

"The roots were coming out of the ground, Maggie. The foliage there was different from anywhere else in the forest. The color of the water was wrong."

"Does it have to be from the lumber mill? Couldn't it be something else?"

He shook his head in despair. "I don't know."

Maggie noticed that her boots were covered with a thick layer of grayish-brown ooze. It had gone all the way to her boot-tops and leaked down to her toes. She dug her fingers into the narrow space at her boot top and grimaced at how slimy the mud felt as she rolled it between her fingers. "Ick." Then she washed it off her hand by trailing it in the water. She repeated the motion, scraping mud, then washing her hand, ritualizing it with a kind of unconscious rhythm.

"I believe him," she said as she continued scraping the mud away. "Isely, I mean."

"Why?"

"I don't know. He makes too many mistakes to be a liar."

"Makes too many mistakes to be a *good* liar."

"I don't think he was lying."

As Rob watched her cleaning the mud from her boots, he began to take an interest. As the grayish-brown slime trailed off her hand into the water, he detected glints of reflection in it, as though it contained tiny grains of something metallic.

"Besides," Maggie continued, "if he were lying, how could he have offered to let you test the water? I mean, if there were something *in* it. How could he let you test the water?"

Rob's eyes traveled to Maggie's boots as she scraped

away more mud, and he saw there, with chilling
certainty, a faint streak of silver in the imprint left
by her fingers. His expression suddenly went cold.

"Maybe it wasn't in the water," he answered.

Maggie caught his tone and quickly looked up at
him.

"Maybe it was heavier than that," he said.

The look on his face frightened her. "What do you
mean?"

"Look at your boots."

She did, and saw what he saw. She pulled a large
clod of mud from the instep of her boot and separated
it in her hands, uncovering a tiny nugget of a soft,
metallic substance.

"It looks like silver," she said. "It looks like a
filling from a tooth or something."

"Is it soft?"

She squeezed it. "Yes."

"Silver is hard."

"What *is* it, then?"

"Wipe your hands and touch it."

She quickly dried her free hand on her wool scarf,
then delicately touched the puttylike blob.

"Is it dry?"

"Yes," she answered with amazement.

Rob's face hardened with anger. But there was
triumph in his expression, too.

"What is it?" Maggie repeated.

"They used to give us a trick question in medical
school. I remember it because I got it wrong."

"What was it?"

"What's the only liquid that isn't wet?"

"What's the answer?"

Rob's face was flushed with excitement. He now
had something to go on.

*"Mercury."*

# 10

AS THE NIGHT creatures foraged beneath gentle moonlight in Manatee Forest, Robert Vern toiled intensely within his cabin, his face illuminated in an island of harsh white light from a kerosene lantern that stood on the kitchen table beside him. The thick stack of books that Victor Shusette had given him were slowly and grudgingly giving up their answers. For five continuous hours Rob had devoured one text after the other, feverishly jotting notes and checking cross-references, until now, at one o'clock in the morning, the enormity of what he had discovered began to take hold.

Maggie was in the loft, asleep; the pin-drop silence within the cabin accentuated the awesome clarity with which the discovery was unfolding.

An index at the back of a book on industrial poisons had supplied over a hundred symbols for chemical compounds containing mercury that were used in industry. One by one, Rob had set about narrowing them down. His own knowledge of chemistry was both an asset and a liability. Though it enabled him to understand the language, it prevented him from taking the direct route that someone more naïve might have taken.

He knew that for a chemical to have such a profound effect on living organisms, the chemical itself had to contain living organisms. He therefore dismissed the laboratory-created synthetics and concen-

trated on the biochemicals—the living cultures, made
from mold, viruses and bacteria. But two hours of
searching ended in frustration. After tracing each one
of them down, he found that their uses were primarily
pharmaceutical and agricultural. None of them had
any possible application to the lumber industry.

Starting fresh, he began to work with the synthetics, the *in*organic chemical compounds, more commonly used in industry: the caustics and antiseptics
used for hygenic purposes and to keep machinery parts
clean. One among them began to stand out. It was
called PMT. It was used for vegetation control,
to keep algae from forming on machines such as oil
rigs and sewer pumps that had to function under
water. Rob recalled Isely's telling him that if the logs
soaked in water for too long, aglae formed on them,
and this was undesirable. It was possible that they
were using this or a similar compound in the ponds
where they soaked their surplus logs, to keep them
clean.

But it still didn't make perfect sense. PMT was not
organic. It was synthetic. Inorganic. Inorganic sub-
stances could only cause external harm, that of pol-
lution. What Rob was looking for was something that
could cause internal, biological chaos. He was looking
for an organic substance.

Turning to a book on chemical analysis, he broke
down the elements of PMT, and in so doing, found
the key. PMT was the symbol for inorganic methyl-
mercury. The "methyl" stood for methyl-nitrate.
Methyl-nitrate, when ingested by a living organism,
could turn *organically viable* as it was absorbed into
the body. In other words, inorganic methyl-mercury
could become an *organic* substance, the kind he was
looking for.

Rob quickly drew a diagram to fix in his mind how
the chemical chain-reaction worked. PMT is spilled
into the water. The microscopic grains of mercury
within it act like magnets with each other, each grain
slowly finding another and collecting into small balls.

The same magnetic attraction that draws the mercury together also collects plankton, the microscopic vegetable components of algae. Instead of fixing itself to the submerged logs, the algae grows on the small balls of *mercury*, which become heavy as they grow larger and sink down to the mud. The tadpoles, the minnows, the aquatic insects that eat algae, consume the green furry balls of mercury, and, as it goes through their bodies, it becomes *organic*. Those smaller creatures are eaten by larger ones. The concentration of methylmercury begins to escalate as it travels up the food chain. A single minnow will carry a minuscule amount of toxin in his body, a salmon will eat a thousand minnows. A bear with eat a thousand salmon. By the time the mercury has reached the top level of the food chain, the creatures that have ingested it are filled with toxin. Their waste products go into the ground, fertilizing the foliage that is eaten by the herbivores: the deer, the rabbits, the mice, the vermin. The entire environment becomes toxic.

But this was not all that Robert Vern was to discover on this night. He turned, finally, to a book called *Legal Precedent with Regard to Industrial Decisions*, which detailed case histories of the most catastrophic industrial accidents of the technological age. Listed in the table of contents was something called "MMT." The symbol was different from PMT, but he quickly determined that the difference was only semantic, reflecting a change in the language of chemistry over the last twenty years. MMT and PMT were one and the same. Inorganic methyl-mercury.

What Rob found within the pages of this book made his blood run cold. The chapter on MMT was a detailed account, with photographs, of the most devastating industrial accident known to man. The pictures looked as if they might have been taken in a war zone: hospital photographs of maimed and disfigured people, deformed children, old men with glazed eyes and demented smiles. They were photographs taken in 1956, in Minamata, Japan. In that year, in that place, an entire community of one hundred thousand people had become diseased and disfigured and had died from methyl-mercury poisoning. A paper mill on the shores of Lake Minamata had been pumping methyl-mercury for fifty years into a watershed that was used as a source of drinking water for the entire population. Not one man, woman, or child had escaped its distastrous effects. When the symptoms first became evident, it had been called the "Drunk Sickness" or the "Grinning Sickness" or the "Cat Sickness," so named because the population of pet cats, who ate only fish from the lake, were the first of the animal species to go insane and die.

It was discovered then and there that inorganic methyl-mercury, when converted by the digestive process to *organic* methyl-mercury, became a neurotoxin and a mutagen. As a neurotoxin, it attacked the brain cells, causing loss of sensation, disorientation, eventually paralysis and death. As a mutagen, it attacked the developing fetus. Unlike any other mutagen known to man, it had the capability of jumping the placental barrier, traveling *through* the blood-purifying organ which normally protected a developing fetus from impurities and poisons ingested by it's mother. PMT actually *concentrated* in the fetal blood cells; a thirty-percent-higher concentration than in the blood cells of the mother. After extensive laboratory tests, methyl-mercury had been pronounced by scientists the most potent toxin to come of the post–World War II age. Its wide-scale use in industry was forever after outlawed by the World Court in The Hague, Holland.

The last page in the chapter was eloquent testimony to the power of PMT. It was a full-page photograph of a woman, crippled and bent, carrying in her arms, the body of a disfigured child.

Robert Vern closed the book and sat immobile in the silence of his cabin. He was too overwhelmed to move; numbed by the proportions of what he had uncovered. He struggled in his mind to get a grip on it, to somehow lock in the last pieces of understanding.

The poison in Minamata had had fifty years to accumulate. Here, in the Manatee forest, the paper mill had been operating only for twenty.

Perhaps it could be stopped before it was too late. The unknown factor was the strength of the chemical used in Minamata compared with that used here. It was possible that fifty years could be shortened to half that time, if the strength of the chemical were doubled.

The last question that formulated in Rob's mind was one that began to stir his emotions. How could they be using it here? How *could* they? Was it possible that they were ignorant of its effects? Was it possible that the change in chemical language that now labeled it PMT instead of MMT, made them think that it was not the same? Or did it give them an excuse, a reason to plead innocence.

How *could* they? his inner voice repeated. How COULD they? In a sudden explosion of rage, Rob smashed his fist down on the table, causing everything on it to jump. He rose quickly and threw open the cabin door, stalking out into the night. There he stood with fists clenched, gazing helplessly at the stars.

"Rob . . . ?"

He turned and saw Maggie descending from the loft in her nightgown. Her eyes were frightened as she came and stood in the open doorway.

"What is it?" she whispered.

"Inorganic methyl-mercury," Rob said on a trembling breath. "PMT. It's a de-sliming agent. It collects algae and keeps it off the logs. That's what they soak the logs in."

He could see that she did not understand. "It's a neurotoxin. In 1956 it wiped out a community of a hundred thousand people in Minamata, Japan."

Maggie absorbed his words with confusion. "Why would they use it here?"

"Because it's cheap and effective. Isn't that what Isely said? They're proud of their efficiency?" Rob was beginning to tremble with rage.

"You're sure of this?"

"The Indians eat the fish and behave like they're drunk when they haven't had a drop of liquor. Isn't that what Hawks said? People think the Indians are drunk? 'My people are fishermen.'—isn't that what he said? In Minamata it was called the drunk sickness!" With his breathing accelerating, Rob began to pace, frustrated that there was no outlet for his rage. "A raccoon turns vicious and dies, its brain has turned to mush! A cat, the same! The forest ranger's cat that ate fish? He *told* us that! And that old man. That Indian. Did you see the burns on his fingers?"

"That's from mercury?"

"It's from cigarettes! The reason he didn't *feel* it is mercury. He has no feeling in his hands! He eats what comes out of that pond! It's a chemical-soaking pond! That's why there was a tadpole the size of what a frog should be!"

"The mercury did that?"

"The mercury *did that!* It's a mutagen! And for twenty years it's been spilling into this water!"

"A mutagen . . ."

"It's a *disaster,* Maggie!!"

Maggie moved onto the porch, her expression becoming fearful as she watched Rob pace in front of her. "You man . . . it mutates . . . ?"

"It mutates. And *how*, it mutates. It's the only mutagen that jumps the placental barrier. It concentrates in the fetal blood cells thirty percent higher than—"

"Rob," she said softly, "I want to understand this . . ."

"*You* want to understand it? *I* want to understand it! I want to know why the hell it's being *used* here!"

"It's in the fish. Is that it?"

"Anything that eats the plankton. Anything that eats the algae. Anything that eats *anything* that eats the algae! That means *everything!*"

Maggie tried to keep her voice calm and not betray

her fear. "What does it mean . . . jumps the placental barrier?"

"It adheres to the chromosomes just like it adheres to the algae—"

"I'm not understanding you. What does it *mean?*"

"Freakism!" he shouted. "Freakism!"

Maggie recoiled, as though hit with a body blow.

"That's what's going on out there!" Rob raged. "That's why there was a goddamn salmon five feet long! You thought I didn't see it? I *saw* it! Why the hell didn't I *know?*"

Maggie felt a sudden pang of nausea and closed her eyes, trying to keep herself from crumbling.

"And *stillbirths!*"

"What?" Maggie gasped.

"That's what that Indian woman said. Stillbirths. And deformed children. Grotesquely deformed children. Children that looked like animals, she said! And God knows what *else* is going on out there!"

Maggie felt herself trembling in every fiber, her mind beginning to spin. But she clung hard to reality, needing to be strong, needing to know more. "So if a pregnant . . . animal ate the fish it could . . ."

"It *would.*"

She shuddered and Rob turned, seeing the fear in her eyes. It hit him like a thunderbolt. "My God."

"Rob?"

"Is it possible?"

"Yes."

Their eyes locked in terror. But their terror was not the same.

"The size of a dragon," Rob whispered.

"What?"

"That poem. The forest ranger. The size of a dragon. Isn't that what it said?"

Maggie stood in a daze. But Rob was unaware of her torment, swept up in his own.

"And that old man. That Indian. Didn't he describe that creature as being a part of 'everything in God's creation'? Isn't that what he said?"

Maggie eased herself down on trembling legs and sat on the porch stairs.

"The eyes of a cat," Rob hissed. "That's what Isely said at the airport."

Maggie lowered her head into her hands. The words kept coming and she was powerless to stop them.

"Listen to me, Maggie," he whispered intensely, "listen to me."

But she was trying to shut it out.

"A developing fetus goes through certain, distinct phases. Each phase represents a specific stage of evolution. A human fetus. At one stage, it's like a fish. It his fins and gills. At another, it looks feline. The face looks like a cat. It develops upward in the shapes and phases of the evolutionary scale."

Maggie's eyes were glazed. The words that fell on her ears echoed as though coming from a great distance.

"This chemical, clings to the DNA. DNA is a chromosomal fixative. It could 'freeze' certain parts at one evolutionary stage, while other parts continue growing." He paused. "Are you listening?"

"Yes," she responded numbly.

"A pregnant animal—a bear, maybe, ingests the fish . . . and it corrupts the fetus to the point where it gives birth to a monst—" He turned to Maggie, who sat unreacting, with deadened eyes. "Maggie?"

"Yes?" she whispered.

Rob gazed into the night, finding it hard to believe the words that he was about to utter. "There could be a monster out there. A literal *monster*."

In the silence that followed, a loon began its unearthly cry. It echoed across the darkened lake, filling the entire forest with its wail.

"How much fish, Rob," Maggie uttered haltingly, "would it take . . . to give birth to a . . . ?"

"It concentrates in the fetal blood cells."

"How . . . much?"

"Very little."

Maggie knew she was going to vomit. She rose and started for the cabin.

"I'll need proof," Rob said in a deadened tone as he glared toward the lake.

"You're not sure?"

"I'll have to take blood samples. My first priority is the people."

She turned to him, fighting down the nausea long enough to get her question out. "How long? Before you'll know for sure?"

"If they have a laboratory at the hospital here . . . tomorrow."

Maggie entered the cabin, closing the door behind her. Rob remained outside, listening to the demented call of the loon.


As Travis Nelson lay beside his campfire reading, he, too, heard the call of the loon. Checking his watch, he noted that it was too early for the loons to call. He smiled to himself as he listened, wondering what had prompted it to waken so early. Perhaps it had responsibilities on this night, as he did.

The three-day rains had severely hampered his and his family's progress to the waterfall. They were waiting until the ground was dry before they attempted the uphill climb. It had been an exciting idea to the children to scale a mountain and camp out by a roaring waterfall; to assuage their disappointment, Travis had suggested that they explore the shores of the lake and learn survival techniques on the way. After walking all day, they had found themselves at a remote offshoot of the Espee River, one of three outlets where the rushing water found its way down from the mountains and merged with the lake. It was a sheltered area, surrounded by high cliffs, a natural inlet, listed on the Forest Service Map as Mary's Bend. They had walked a quarter mile upriver and pitched camp in the trees where they could hear the sound of the rushing water. Travis had noted several beaver traps and

salmon nets along the way, and he had dismantled
most of them. The Forest Service Map listed this
area as "protected." It was a spawning ground; there
was no hunting or fishing allowed here. The nets were
set by poachers, probably Indians, who did not heed
the boundaries and limits set by those whom they
considered outsiders.

The nets and traps did, however, give Travis the
opportunity to teach his children a lesson on primitive
hunting techniques. It had led to a conversation, as
night fell and they sat around their campfire, of what
it must be like to have to rely on one's own courage
and resources to survive in a primitive environment.
The children had dared each other to face the night
alone; Travis and his wife, Jeanine, had watched with
amusement as the challenge escalated to a point where
neither of the children was willing to back down. They
had each taken their sleeping bags and a flashlight
and moved off separately into the trees to prove that
they had the courage to do it.

Travis had expected them to return within minutes.
When they didn't, he went looking for them. To his
relief he found that they were no more than a hundred
yards away, and they had decided to camp out *to-gether*. He built them a fire, which they promised to
maintain during the night to discourage any wandering
bears; then they bedded down, side by side. Paul had
zipped his sleeping bag up over his head, as was his
custom, to keep the mosquitoes away; Kathleen opted
for a liberal dousing of insect repellent all over her
face so she could breathe the cool night air.

Travis had returned to his own campsite and then,
at his wife's urging, gone back to check on the children at midnight. He found that all was peaceful. The
fire was still going; Kathleen's alarm clock was on
the ground beside her, set for 2:00 A.M., no doubt to
awaken her for the purpose of refueling the fire.

Travis had lingered there, moved by the sight of his
two children asleep beside their campfire in the darkened wilderness. They were at once vulnerable and

courageous, beautiful in their innocence, endearing in their effort to prove that they were brave. The everyday problems and frustrations of raising children were, for this moment, washed away. It was a scene of unparalleled peacefulness, and he wanted to remember it.

An owl hooted from the trees above, and Travis saw Paul stir, pulling the zipper down to nose level and peering out into the night. His eyes slowly closed again, then he returned to slumber.

Travis stayed as long as he dared without causing Jeanine any concern. Then he returned to his own encampment a hundred yards away. His wife, too, had fallen asleep. Curled in her sleeping bag, she looked every bit as vulnerable and beautiful as the children did. There was something very special to Travis about being awake in this environment while his loved ones were asleep. It made him realize how much they depended on him for protection; how safe they felt in closing their eyes, even in unfamiliar surroundings, when they knew he was there to defend them. The feeling of self-worth was so delicious that he was unwilling to give way to slumber. He remained awake, reading a book of poetry by Thoreau that he had always loved.

At 2:00 A.M. he heard Kathleen's alarm clock sound. It ran clear to the end without being turned off. Then he heard the sound of movement through the trees, and felt satisfied that she had awakened to fuel the fire. She was the responsible one, Paul was the impulsive one. They were good for each other, and Travis hoped they would always be close friends.

He closed his book and rolled onto his back, gazing into the heavens. He had never in his life seen so many stars. He started counting them as he listened to the sound of Kathleen rummaging among the trees in search of dry twigs.

As she lay in her sleeping bag, twelve-year-old Kathleen also heard the sound in the trees. She had been awakened by the alarm clock but felt so snug in her sleeping bag that she didn't want to reach out into the chill night air to turn it off. She had let it dwindle to silence, then debated the relative merits of remaining warm and snug or getting up to refuel the fire. Paul was asleep beside her, his nose protruding from the narrow opening at the top of his sleeping bag. There was a mosquito on his nose; she reached out to wave it away. Paul responded with a snort, then rolled over, away from her, and began to snore. The sound irritated her; she knew she'd have to awaken him. But just as she was about to, she heard the sound in the trees. It was a heavy, crunching sound, as though something large were moving toward her.

"Daddy?"

In response, the sound stopped. The crickets stopped, too, the entire environment falling into a vacuum. Then the sound came again. It was barely audible this time, a rustle of leaves as though something heavy had shifted weight in the foliage just beyond the glow of the campfire.

"Daddy?" she whispered.

The atmosphere returned to pin-drop silence. Kathleen forced her eyes in the direction of the trees. It was a wall of darkness. But she could hear something breathing in there. And she could smell it. An odor of dampness, like a basement after a rain. Feeling herself begin to tremble, she looked at the smoldering fire. It had gotten too low to discourage the bears. She wanted to cry out to her father, but when she opened her mouth, no sound would come. She struggled with her shuddering breath to form words, but they came only as a whisper.

"Daddy . . . ?"

Then the sound moved closer. She could feel it now as well as hear it; the ground vibrated beneath her as the lurking presence came into the clearing and hovered near.

Kathleen began to whimper and closed her eyes, her silent tears tracing a path toward the ground. "Don't eat me, Mister Bear . . ."

Paul heard her voice and his eyes slowly opened.

The next sound he heard was a heavy thud, followed by a groan. He rolled over to where Kathleen was. There was nothing there. The ground was empty where her sleeping bag had lain. There was something leaking down, splattering on the ground like heavy rain. But the raindrops were red.

Paul lay immobile, as if in a dream. The red raindrops were followed by snowflakes; a cloud of soft goosedown drifting groundward from Kathleen's sleeping bag, sticking in the growing pool of red. There was a crunching sound from overhead. Like a dog breaking chicken bones. Paul's eyes slowly traveled upward and froze in terror. The gargantuan shadow that towered over him ate silently, almost lazily. The bloody rain and feathered snow fell harder, the wetness hitting Paul's forehead as he lay in a daze, gazing up through the narrow opening in his sleeping bag through which only his nose and eyes protruded. Then he saw the eyes staring down from above. They were saucerlike. Flat and reflective. And they made contact with his own.

Paul rose and tried to run, but he could not. He was trapped within the cocoonlike confines of his sleeping bag. He fumbled with the zipper, but it was stuck. It would not budge from beneath his chin. He heard the thud of Kathleen's sleeping bag hitting the ground; her outstretched arm sprawled in the dirt in front of him. He screamed and began hopping toward the trees, crying out in desperation as the lumbering shadow swept down on him.

From his campfire a hundred yards away, Travis Nelson heard the desperate cries and bolted to his feet, racing through the forest. "Paul! Paulie!"

The child's screams continued, growing more frantic. Then they suddenly stopped.

Travis Nelson raced into the campsite and saw the silhouetted form of his son's body, flying upward with the weightlessness of a rag doll, consumed in a billowing cloud of goose feathers, against the light of the full moon. Then he saw the gargantuan form emerging from the trees.

"Oh, my God!" he sobbed.

They were the last words he would ever utter.

John Hawks had spent the night in the safety of the tunnel-like storage areas dug into the ground beneath M'rai's tents. As the lumberjacks had promised, they came looking for him. They had questioned M'rai and Romona then left, satisfied that Hawks was gone. The old man had been upset by the intrusion into his encampment, and withdrew into isolation. From Hawks's hiding place beneath the ground, he had heard M'rai chanting mournfully within his tent.

At dawn Romona and Hawks moved swiftly through the forest to the water's edge and rafted to the island where Rob and Maggie were awake and waiting for them. In the cabin, Rob recounted to them his discoveries of the night before. They listened with rapt attention, their eyes filled with incredulity and outrage. As evidence of what they were up against, Rob showed them the photographs of Minamata. If the blood samples Rob was intending to take from the Indian villagers were positive, they might be facing a disaster of the same proportions here.

Maggie forced herself to listen this time and concentrate on every detail. She was on the verge of hysteria and knew that she must face and understand all of it, or else slip into the irresponsible safety of emotional collapse. No matter how awful the reality was, she was determined to cling to it.

Rob had dumped his soil samples from the glass vials, and sterilized them to hold blood samples instead. He felt that if he got a cross section of ten men, ten women, and ten children, he would have all the samples he needed. Hawks was unable to tell him whether or not the Manatee hospital had laboratory facilities; Rob and Maggie hurriedly packed some overnight things in the event they had to take the blood samples to the Portland hospital eighty miles away.

At 8:00 A.M. they left for the village. The sky had become thick with cloud cover, the air was again oppressive. The mosquitoes, gnats, and blackflies swarmed about their faces as the small boat cut across the water; the insects were stimulated into aggressiveness by the humidity, attempting to fill their bellies in the event of another rain. As they crossed the lake, Rob told Hawks and Romona of his speculation that the mutative effects of the chemicals might have reached the higher forms of animal life. He carefully couched his language, not wanting to sound overly dramatic or appear foolish. In the light of the day, with the forest around them looking peaceful and benevolent, it seemed more a flight of fancy than scientific reality to talk of a "monster" lurking there. But Romona and Hawks did not find it fanciful. They accepted it in silence.

From the boat landing where Rob's car was parked, they drove along a narrow, little used road through the forest toward the Indian village. It was overgrown with foliage and mined with jagged boulders; the ten miles they traveled took well over an hour.

When they arrived at the outskirts of the village, the leaves on the surrounding trees were rippling with a light wind that brought the smell of rain from the mountains. Rob hurriedly unpacked his medical gear and allowed Romona and Hawks to precede him into the village to explain to their people what was going to take place. Rob could not hear their words, but from their gestures and the reactions of the people they spoke to, he saw that it was not going to be easy to convince them. Hawks returned and summoned Rob forward.

"We'll visit the sick men first. They will not resist."

"They're afraid?"

"They have known only one doctor. He treats them as though they are animals."

Rob and Maggie followed Hawks and Romona into

the center of the village. It did not look like anything that could be called an Indian village. It was more like a slum on the outskirts of a major city; poorly built shacks, made from cast-off materials, that stood at odd angles, surrounded by rusted machinery parts that littered the ground. The opened carcasses of drying salmon were spread out on canvas platforms, the flies buzzing about them in profusion. There were skeletons of defunct automobiles, a dozen or more, scattered throughout the surrounding trees.

To Rob, it all had a familiar feel. The people followed him in a horde, and crowded around him as he entered the first dwelling and examined a man felled with what they called the *katahnas*.

Rob made sure that his actions were smooth, efficient, and without hesitation. He used Maggie as he would use a nurse, calling for instruments that she pulled from his kit. The man they examined was raging with fever and suffering febrile tremors. His pupils were dilated and his sensory reflexes were almost nil. And on his face was a muscle contortion that looked like a grin, the same kind of demented grin that Rob had seen in the photographs of the methyl-mercury victims in Minamata.

Rob gave him an injection of phenobarbital to reduce the fever, then strapped his arm with rubber tubing and drew the first blood sample. In the tenements in Washington, this procedure would have drawn *oohs* and *ahhhs* from the crowd of onlookers. Here he was watched in stoic silence. Even the children remained expressionless.

They next visited the two other men suffering the same symptoms. Rob repeated the procedures, then moved outdoors, instructing Romona and Hawks to bring a table into the center of the clearing and select ten men, ten women, and ten children to have their blood drawn. He especially wanted the two women who he saw were pregnant. If their blood toxin level was lower than that of the nonpregnant women, it would be further proof that methyl-mercury was at work. If it acted here as it had in Minamata, the poison would be concentrated in the blood of the *fetus,* not in that of the mother.

But the villagers were still reluctant. Hawks and Romona had to submit to blood tests themselves before the others would begin to step forward. An old man came first, hobbling on bent legs; then a mother with an infant in her arms. Then they all came forward, holding out their arms and those of their children, realizing, from Rob's manner and gentle tone of voice, that he was there to help. In all of his experience, Rob had never seen such stoicism. They submitted, all of them, without wincing, without making a sound.

Rob was flanked by Romona and Hawks on one side, by Maggie on the other; they worked in an efficient routine. Hawks asked name and age; Romona wrote it down and labeled each vial. Maggie worked with the medical accessories, sterilizing alternating needles and storing the vials. An Indian girl of about twelve stood beside Maggie, watching her with unabashed admiration. She and Maggie exchanged smiles; Maggie reached out and held her hand. The human contact was as important to Maggie as it was to the little girl.

Romona looked on with approval. "You'll be a good mother." Maggie stifled a sudden impulse to cry.

Within twenty minutes Rob had filled his vials, but there were dozens of people still waiting, wanting to take part.

"Get the slides," Rob said to Maggie. "We'll do finger pricks."

She turned toward the bag.

"They're in the car," Rob said.

Maggie moved quickly, and as she did, she heard the sound of car motors approaching them from the forest. There were several of them, and they were converging fast from all sides, their machinery grinding as they bumped and lurched cross-country through the trees.

Romona exchanged a frightened look with Hawks.

Rob instinctively took a defensive stance in front of them. They were sheriff's cars, and they emerged with a rush, deputies jumping out with rifles drawn to quickly surround the village.

"What's happening?" Rob gasped.

"They're going to kill us," Hawks answered.

The sheriff stepped forward, holding a piece of paper that fluttered in the rising wind. "I want everybody out of the houses!" he called. "I want everybody right out here."

"What's going on?" Rob demanded. The sheriff was shocked to see a white man there.

"Who are you?" he asked.

"I asked you what's going on!"

"Just step back—"

"I want an explanation—"

"Step back!"

Another car pulled in. It was a car from the Pitney Paper Mill; Bethel Isely got out from behind the wheel and joined the sheriff in the center of the clearing. He caught sight of Rob and was plainly pained to see him here.

"I want the women to my right and the men to my left!" the sheriff ordered.

"I want to know what's going on here!" Rob shouted.

Isely quickly approached him. "You're at the wrong place at the wrong time, Mr. Vern," he said quietly. "I suggest you pack your things and get out."

"I demand to know what's happening."

"There were more killings in the forest last night. We're not waiting around for any more."

Hawks overheard, stiffening with the knowledge that the moment he most feared had finally come. The battle with the Pitney Paper Mill would end with the persecution of every man, woman, and child in his village.

"I've got a list of names, and I want the following people to step forward as their names are read," the sheriff shouted.

"Who was killed?" Rob demanded of Isely.

"A family up at Mary's Bend."

"You have some reason to think these people did it?"

"They're guilty as hell, Vern!"

"You have some evidence?"

"The evidence is at the hospital. It's in *baskets*."

"Russell Windraven, step forward!" the sheriff shouted.

The Indian villagers remained immobile, frightened and confused.

"I said step *forward!*" the sheriff commanded.

A man moved slowly from the crowd; Rob recognized him as one of the men who had stood with Hawks at the blockade. Rob turned to Hawks and saw that Hawks was no longer beside him. He was slowly fading back toward the trees.

"Chester Pinot!" the sheriff shouted, and another man came forward.

Four deputies converged on the two men, locking them into handcuffs. "Raphael Nightwalker!" the sheriff called. There was a hint of ridicule in his voice, as though he were announcing the winners of a contest. "Mr. John Hawks! Mr. Steven Sky!"

Hearing Hawks's name, Rob hurried to the center of the clearing in an effort to draw attention away from him. "I want to see your arrest warrants! Right now!"

The sheriff turned to him. "I told you to stay back."

"I demand to know by what right—"

"Somebody take this man away."

The entire circle of deputies converged, giving Hawks the moment he needed. He spun on his heel, bolting toward the trees.

"Stop that man!" the sheriff bellowed, and three deputies ran toward the forest to cut Hawks off. Hawks whirled, changing directions in mid-stride and charged into one of the cabins. A burst of splintering glass signaled his trajectory through a window at the rear. The deputies raced behind the cabin just a mo-

ment too late. Hawks had disappeared into the thick
tangle of trees.

"He'll outrun you on foot!" the sheriff called to
his men. "Go after him in the car."

Three deputies raced by Maggie and jumped into
their car; its motor whined as it bumped off through
the trees. From where she stood Maggie could see
that Hawks had not run into the forest but rolled
into a gully behind the cabin.

"Everybody stay where you are!" the sheriff
warned. "When you next see your friend Mr. Hawks,
you'll be very happy that you did!"

Rob turned to Romona, who stood in a state of
shock. "Mary's Bend," he said urgently. "Do you
know where that is?"

She nodded.

"Just follow me to the car," Rob said as he quickly
packed his things. "Don't look right or left, just stay
right beside me."

"They'll kill these men," Romona implored.

"Maggie?"

Maggie ran forward and Rob handed her the rack
of vials. "You and Romona get in the car."

"I've got two men here, I'm looking for five!"

Rob strode to the sheriff. "I want to tell you something," he warned. "You're not alone here. I'm a
witness to this. When you charge these men, you'd
better set bail, because I'm coming back and posting
it. And if they don't come out of that jail in exactly
the same condition they went in, you're going to be
very sorry about it. If there's one mark on *any* of
them! Do you undertsand me?" Then he turned on his
heel and went to the car. Its gears groaned as it
lurched away into the forest.

The place called Mary's Bend was inaccessible by
road; it could be reached only on foot along ten miles
of difficult wilderness trails. Burning with anger and
frustration, Rob headed for the airport, hoping to

requisition the Forest Service helicopter they'd seen carrying the bloodhound when they arrived. He was desperate to get to Mary's Bend by nightfall. It looked as if the rains were going to begin again, and if they did all evidence might be washed away by morning. If he could find some trace of the animal that he suspected was responsible for the killings, he would have the tools he needed to act swiftly and efficiently. Without such evidence, his theories would be no more than alarmist speculation that would be attacked because of its dramatic proportions. The word monster was not in the vocabulary of a credible man. Yet it was the word, Rob was becoming more and more convinced, that applied.

"Where's the hospital?" Rob asked hurriedly as they sped through town on their way to the airport.

"Where the main street ends," Romona replied.

Rob made a quick stop there to look at the so-called evidence Isely had talked about: the bodies of the family that had been killed at Mary's Bend. He wanted to make sure they would not be disposed of before he had a chance to examine them.

The "hospital" was not a hospital at all. It was a small emergency facility located among a cluster of houses at the edge of town, a one-story green stucco structure comprising seven rooms. One was an operating room, one was an office, four had beds, and the seventh room was for storage. It was in the storage room that the remains of the Travis Nelson family were being held. The larger pieces had been put in a deep-freeze, the smaller pieces had been packaged for incineration. Rob had gotten there just in time.

There was no doctor on duty, only a nurse; she summoned Dr. Pope, who lived two doors away.

Pope was a tall, gaunt man in his late sixties. He was bald and looked physically weak, and was instantly intimidated by Rob's urgent manner. Acceding to Rob's demands, he opened up the storeroom and spread out the remains on two long wooden tables. Some of the pieces had hardened from the freezing;

others were soft and mushy from being wrapped in plastic. It looked like a grotesque jigsaw puzzle in disarray. In all Rob's years of practicing medicine, he had never before been seized with such revulsion; the sight he faced now was beyond his tolerance. The bodies were broken and disemboweled, as if someone had opened the belly of a cow and dressed what spilled out in men's clothing.

"Will there be anything else?" Pope asked.

"What makes you think this was done by men?" Rob demanded.

"I don't know what else would have done it."

"Why not an animal?"

"Bears, you mean?"

"Could a bear do this?"

"A bear *wouldn't* do this. Not to four people at once. I've seen at least a dozen bear attacks. It never looks like this. When a bear attacks a group of people, it settles for one."

"These bodies are ripped and torn! *Men* wouldn't do this!"

"Unless they tried to make it look like an animal."

"You believe that?"

"Animals kill to protect themselves. Or to protect their young. Once that's accomplished, they don't have any interest in killing any further. This was an act of vengeance. This was the act of a sick mind."

"Men are going to be accused of murder based on your statements. You better know what you're talking about."

Pope didn't respond.

"I want everything frozen," Rob ordered. "Every piece there is. I'm going to have it autopsied. I've got blood samples I want frozen too. I'll be back to pick it up tonight."

Pope accompanied Rob to his car and took the blood samples; Rob, Romona, and Maggie headed fast for the airport. By the time they arrived, a light rain had begun to fall and the trees surrounding the landing strip were beginning to sway in the rising wind. Two helicopters were on the ground, both bearing the emblem of the Forestry Service. Rob's government credentials were sufficient to summon a pilot from his home ten miles away.

The pilot's name was Huntoon. He was a large and muscular man, with an abrasive manner and was clearly resentful about having been called out on such a bad day. He told them that the trip to Mary's Bend would take only thirty minutes but warned that if the wind rose any higher, he'd be unable to land. The shoreline at Mary's Bend was surrounded by high cliffs; a chopper could lift off in winds up to thirty miles an hour, but not if it ran the risk of being blown against a cliff side.

Before they boarded, Rob urged Maggie to stay behind, but she refused. Whatever there was to see, she wanted to see. And she expressed it with a forcefulness that Rob had never seen in her before. He reluctantly agreed, and they boarded. The winds swept them swiftly up and toward the distant mountains.

By the time they reached the lake, the wind had shifted and they were flying against it, the pellets of rain blurring the helicopter's windshield, so that their only view was out the side windows.

"If there were a large animal down there, could we see it from here?" Rob shouted to the pilot.

"How large?"

"Large."

"Like a moose, you mean?"

"Larger."

"There's nothing larger than a moose around here."

"Could we see it from here?"

"Oh, yeah. Moose, deer, bear. They start running when they hear the chopper. They're easy to spot."

"Keep your eyes open! I don't want to land if there's anything big down there!"

"We'll find out right now. There's the bend. I'll sweep a three-mile circle."

The helicopter tilted, circling low across the tops

of the trees while Rob, Maggie, and Romona studied the ground below.

"That's funny," the pilot said. "There's not a damn thing. Not even a deer."

Romona, too, was puzzled. "This is a protected area. It's usually *filled* with game."

"Protected?" The pilot laughed. "That's a joke. The Indians do all their poaching down there. They set bear traps, beaver traps . . . It looks like they finally wiped the place out."

"That's not true," Romona protested. "My people do hunt there, but the *reason* they hunt there is because there's so much game."

"Well, there's nothin' down there *now,* is there, little sister?"

"Where's the bend?" Rob asked.

"Right below us. See the crevice between the cliffs? Right there where the river comes out?"

Rob could see, far beneath him, the remains of a tent, torn and flapping in the wind. "Can we go down?"

"I'm not too crazy about the idea."

"The wind's too high?"

"Not yet, but these things can blow up fast."

"If it's at all possible, I'd like to go down."

The pilot checked his instruments, then radioed back to the airport, requesting a weather report. He received it and nodded his approval. "They say it's as bad as it's going to get."

"We can go down?"

"Yep." He spoke into his headset again. "XJ23Y to base. Breaking radio contact now." Then he turned to Rob. "Got to stay above the mountains to maintain radio contact. Once you get down in these gullies, the signal won't carry."

They descended in a swift verticle line and were suddenly buffeted by down drafts, the helicopter thrown off balance so suddenly that Maggie cried out in alarm. The small compartment swung around and stabilized, landing hard on the ground.

"Shit," the pilot muttered. "I didn't like that at all."

"Are we all right?"

"Yeah, but I'm not looking forward to that takeoff. You people take your time. Let's wait till it dies down a little."

Maggie was nauseated from the tumultuous landing and stayed behind with the pilot as Rob and Romona headed upriver into the crevice where Rob had spotted the remains of the tent. The environment was hissing with rain, and the force of the wind here at the base of the cliffs was double what it had been in the air. Maggie stepped out of the helicopter, hoping that the elements would refresh her and quiet the churning in her stomach. She pulled the hood of her parka over her head, wound her woolen scarf about her neck, and breathed deeply as she gazed off toward the mountainous horizon. The tips of the mountains were obscured by dark clouds, and there was lightning; the thunderheads pulsated and sent out a low rumble of thunder that slowly drifted across the lake.

"XJ23Y . . . is anybody reading?" the pilot called into his radio mike. "XJ23Y . . . can anybody read?" He switched it off and turned to Maggie. "I hope we haven't gotten ourselves into a mess here."

A quarter mile upriver, where the crevice narrowed to a tree-lined avenue of water, Rob and Romona stood in silence, gazing at the murder site. The signs of violence were awesome. Bushes were uprooted, tree limbs cracked, bits of clothing clung to the outstretched limbs of bushes and trees. The ground in front of the shredded tent was stained dark with blood. A child's tennis shoe dangled from a tree. There were huge divots in the ground, as though a backhoe had run rampant; Romona spotted a large mound of earth and walked to it. She lowered herself to her knees and began to dig.

"What is it?" Rob asked as she scraped the dirt away.

She turned to him with puzzled eyes. "Defecation." The rain fell on her face as she gazed up at Rob with confusion. "It's buried in the way a cat would bury it."

Rob turned and moved farther upriver into the trees. Romona paused for a long moment, then followed.

At the helicopter, the pilot had stepped out into the rain beside Maggie, and was watching the fomenting clouds with concern.

"It's moving in fast. Maybe it'll move *out* fast." He nodded as if to reassure himself. "Yeah, it'll probably blow over pretty quick." His eyes moved to the marshy shores where the lake curled inward to form Mary's Bend. There the cattails and high grasses swirled with increasing fury. "Remember what I said about poachers?" He pointed toward the marsh. "See those poles, over there? That's a beaver trap. Probably got some dead beavers in it. They catch their necks in it and drown."

Maggie's eyes followed his gesture and she spotted the poles, jutting stiffly upward among the pliable, bending cattails.

"I'll tell you," the pilot continued, "I'm as fair-minded as the next guy, but one of these days these Indians gotta be taught a lesson. Used to be when you caught an Indian poaching you just strung him up by the heels to the nearest tree. Can't do that any more. They gettin' like the blacks. You lay a hand on an Indian . . ."

Having heard all she cared to, Maggie walked away, heading toward the marsh. As the pilot watched her go, he snickered to himself, amused that he had offended her.

Upriver, within the deepening confines of the crevice, Rob and Romona found another place where violence had occurred. The tattered remains of two sleeping bags were scattered throughout the foliage, the smashed remnant of an alarm clock was flattened against the ground. Thunder rumbled overhead and Rob lifted his eyes. His gaze fastened on a gash about six feet above his head in the trunk of a tree. As he moved nearer, he could see within the whitened gash, the mark of three huge claws. "Romona?"

She hurried to him.

"What could have done that?" he asked.

"A bear perhaps."

"That high?"

"It could have climbed."

"Look higher."

Above the gash, caught in a section of splintered bark, was a swatch of thick black fur. Romona quickly broke a dried sapling about ten feet long and used it to dislodge the fur, which wafted down into her waiting hands. As she examined it, the expression on her face told Rob that it was unlike anything she had ever seen before.

"What is it?" he asked.

She handed it to him, and he spread it apart, revealing hardened fibers within, almost like the quills of a feather. The thunder rolled louder, and Rob was swept with a chill.

"It's not bear, is it?" he said quietly.

"No."

"What is it, then?"

Her eyes were distant, set somewhere deep within the forest. "It's Katahdin, Mr. Vern," she said darkly. "He's no longer a legend."

The foliage behind them suddenly erupted. Romona cried out. A figure rushed toward them.

It was John Hawks. His face was covered with dried blood that emanated from a gash in his forehead and his eyes were blank with shock. He stopped suddenly and held up a wad of the thick, black fur.

"You've seen this?" he cried.

"Yes," Rob answered.

"It's *here*. What you said is *here!*"

Romona ran to him and they clung to each other, their faces gripped with anguish.

"I want to find it," Rob said firmly. "I want the truth to be known."

"Truth?" Hawks shouted. "There is no truth here! This is the manifestation of *lies!*"

The thunder clapped loudly; as it faded, they heard something that sounded like a scream. It echoed off the cliff walls and melted into the whine of the rising wind that whistled through the crevice. Hawks, Romona, and Rob stood immobile. The scream came again. It was Maggie. Rob whirled, stumbling over boulders as he raced away. Hawks overtook him and Romona struggled behind. As they rounded a bend, they suddenly stopped. Maggie stood in the midst of the swirling cattails, her hands clasped to her head, her eyes wide with alarm. The pilot was near her, his posture frozen, as if he had become paralyzed in mid-step. Both were staring into the marsh. The sky burst with a flash of lightning and a sharp crackle of thunder. Maggie's eyes turned toward Rob, and he could see that she was in near shock. He ran toward her, Hawks and Romona following; when they reached her, she raised a trembling finger and pointed to the ground.

They all recoiled in horror.

There, in the marsh, at the water's edge, hanging from a poacher's net, were two grotesquely misshapen creatures. Their body surface was mottled pink and black; they were about eighteen inches long. One was dead and fully extended, hanging head down from the hooked claws of its stunted hind legs. Its body was long and thin, in the shape of a four-legged animal, but it had skin folds stretched between its clawed hand and its sides, like those of a bat. It was an evolutionary mockery. The head was long and furless, with an exocephalic brain that protruded in pink folds from the side of the skull; the snout was narrow, with sharp teeth jutting upward from an underslung jaw. And the eyes were huge, blank as fish eyes, dominating the surface of the face.

The rain began to drive harder, the wind rising in gale force as the group stood in stunned silence. Hawks's mouth was hard with bitterness. Romona was rigid, gazing down from the corners of her eyes.

"What the hell are they?" the pilot gasped.

No one answered.

"My people lived with this legend all their lives," Hawks said through his teeth. "Now this will be taken from them, too."

"One's alive," Romona said.

The second of the two creatures was bobbing on the gentle swell of the water, belly up, its teeth snarled in the net. Its eyes were half opened, and its small chest heaved in labored, pumping gasps.

"We've got to get it warm," Rob said. "It's dying of exposure."

"Leave it here," Hawks hissed. "Let it die."

Rob turned in sudden outrage. "Leave it here? Do you know what this is? This is *evidence!* This is what's going to save your *forest!*"

Hawks looked long at Rob, then turned to the pilot. "Your knife."

"No!" Rob shouted.

"I'm going to cut it free."

Hawks took the pilot's knife and waded into the water, Rob beside him. In an instant the creature was free. Rob lifted it into his arms. "Take the other one, too."

Following Rob's order, Hawks cut the dead one free, but he was reluctant to touch it.

"Take it."

"Why?"

"I want them both."

"Why?" Hawks challenged.

"I can open it up and find out what it's made of! I can find out what it feeds on! I can find out why it *exists.*"

"You've got that one!"

"I'm keeping this one alive," Rob vowed. "This one's going to stay alive. It's not going to go into a bottle of formaldehyde and be put on a shelf! If I can keep this alive, there's *nobody* who'll be able to ignore it!"

Hawks snatched up the dead creature by its hind leg; slime dripped from its nose and mouth as it rose from the water.

Maggie watched with glazed eyes.

"It's got to be wrapped," Rob ordered as he waded to the shore. "Maggie?"

She turned to him, blank-faced.

"Your scarf."

"What?" she asked weakly.

"Give it to me."

Numbly following orders, Maggie pulled out her woolen scarf and Rob wrapped the small creature in it. It looked like a child of the devil wrapped in swaddling cloth.

"Let's go," Rob commanded.

"Look at those trees!" the pilot shouted in the rising wind. "That's forty miles an hour! I can't lift off in this!"

Rob grimaced with frustration. The trees were being lashed by a wind that howled as it wound through the crevice. "We've got to get out of here!" he demanded.

"We'll get blown into the walls! You saw what happened coming down here. Its *worse* now."

"I've got to get somewhere warm! I've got to keep this alive."

"Take shelter. It'll blow over."

"How long?"

"Few hours, maybe less!"

"That's too long!"

"I can't *do* it!"

Rob turned to Hawks in desperation. "Where's your village?"

"Too far."

"Ten miles," Romona said.

"Isn't there somewhere closer?"

"Nothing," Hawks replied.

"My *grandfather!*" Romona exclaimed.

"Those are just tents."

"We can be there in two hours. If we follow the river . . ."

"In two hours the storm might blow over," Rob protested.

"It might not," the pilot contradicted.

Rob's eyes were desperate as he gazed into the angry sky.

"M'rai's camp," Hawks urged.

"Those tents aren't *warm* enough!" Rob insisted.

"We can make them warm."

"We can build fires within," Romona added.

"Can we go there, *please?*" Maggie asked with anguish.

"I think you better do it," advised the pilot.

"There's no other choice," Hawks said.

"We could wait here in the helicopter," Rob said.

"I don't want to wait here." Hawks's voice carried a warning that gave Rob pause. They were completely vulnerable out here, *in* the helicopter or *out* of it. They were possibly standing in the very lair of the animal that had caused the destruction. Judging by the height of the claw marks Rob had seen in the tree, it stood at least fifteen feet tall. He didn't know if it had reached up or reached down to make those marks. If they waited in the helicopter, they might find themselves trapped.

"Your grandfather's camp," Rob said to Romona. "Let's go."

The decision was punctuated with a spine-jolting clap of thunder; the rain fell in a deluge as they headed for the crevice. Rob raced back to the helicopter to retrieve his doctor's kit; the pilot grabbed his backpack. Then, bracing themselves against the rain and the wind, they re-entered the narrow opening between the cliffs and began an agonizing trek across slippery boulders, up the now-raging river. The pilot ran alongside Rob, straining to get a look at the grotesque parcel in Rob's arms.

"What *is* that thing?"

Rob shook his head and moved forward. He knew it would be impossible to explain.

Deep into the crevice, they headed toward the trees,

moving laterally away from the river along an upward slope that led to the interior of the forest.

Romona went first, followed by Hawks, who held the dead creature by a hind foot, its limp body dangling and swiveling before Maggie's eyes as she walked directly behind him. The slime-dripping snout scraped the ground, accumulating dirt, which gave the mouth the appearance of a smile.

Maggie trudged doggedly, her arms wrapped around her stomach as though to protect what lay sleeping within from seeing what she saw. She could feel the weight within her womb, and tried to force away the mental images of what might lie incubating there. She began counting the steps that she took, but the grotesque body of the creature that dangled in front of her kept thrusting itself into her consciousness and taunting her fantasies. She pushed her face down into her jacket and stifled an urge to weep. Her mind was swept with confusion, for she could not hate what was inside her. She had given life to it, and she had wounded it. It had not asked to be created, it had not asked to be crippled.

Yet the eyes, the underslung jaw of the face that hung before her filled her with fear and revulsion. A scene flitted through her mind that made her gasp and begin again to count her steps—she had seen herself plunging a knife into her stomach.

As darkness fell, the pilot switched on a flashlight, holding Maggie's arm as she stumbled forward. Rob had opened his jacket and stuffed his parcel inside. He felt a sudden, convulsive movement as the animal responded to the heat of his body. It was a good sign; Rob was determined to keep it alive.

Above their heads the canopy of trees hissed as the wind assaulted them; the rain was abating, but the wind continued to rise.

They had walked in silence all the way, Hawks's eyes scanning the trees as he followed Romona. Rob glanced often at Maggie, hoping she would not realize what it was that Hawks was keeping watch for. But she seemed oblivious to everything; the shock of discovering the creatures seemed to have affected her more deeply than the others. Her face was like a death mask, devoid of expression.

After three hours, they came to a shallow riverbed. Moving closely behind one another, they sank into water up to their ankles as they crossed to the other side.

They walked downhill now, their pace accelerating as they neared their destination.

"SShhhh!" Romona hissed. "Look there!"

They halted abruptly and gazed through the trees to where a distant, flickering campfire illuminated the contour of the tents at M'rai's camp.

"There are people there," Romona whispered.

Hawks and Romona crept forward until they could make out the figures of two men sitting by the fire with their backs to them.

"What's the problem?" the pilot called out.

Rob silenced him with a gesture. He knew that Hawks and Romona feared it might be the sheriff.

"What's going on?" the pilot asked.

Romona sprang from the foliage and ran into the camp; the men by the fire turned and stood, revealing that they were Indians. After exchanging a few words with them, Romona called out:

"John! It's all right! No one else is here!"

Rob grabbed Maggie's arm and they ran to the camp. With the fire blazing and with shelter from the rain, they felt protected here, grateful and relieved that the agonizing trek was over.

"The old man is gone," Romona said. "They don't know where."

"Can they help us?" Rob asked urgently.

"They can go to the village and send someone into town."

"Send them."

"Who for?"

"Anybody who can get us out of here."

Romona turned to the Indians and began speaking to them in their language.

"Wait a minute," Rob said. "Not just anybody. Everybody. I want people to *see* this. I want people to *know* about this. The Indians. The townspeople. I want them to get everybody down here that they can."

Romona again turned to the Indians. *"N'yah'yo-entra'ahsh . . ."*

"Is there a newspaper in this town?" Rob interrupted.

"Yes."

"I want *them* down here. With a camera. And I want people from the lumber company. And I want the sheriff. And I want—"

"Not the sheriff," Hawks interjected.

"I want people to see this!" Rob raged. "While we've got it! While it's *alive!* Your stake in this is greater than mine!"

The two Indians suddenly caught sight of what Rob held in his arms. Their faces went rigid.

"Please help us," Rob begged them. "Please hurry." Then he rushed toward one of the tents, barking orders as he went. "You said you could make these tents warm?"

"We'll bring coals in," Romona replied.

"Do it now. Steam some rags. Maggie, take my kit. I need some light in there. And I need a table. Something to work on."

Maggie and Romona swung into action; Hawks watched the activity for a long moment, then, with a nod of resignation, turned to the two Indians. He asked them to do everything that the man from the government wanted. He told them that the creatures they had with them had been poisoned with the same chemical that caused the *katahnas*; that they needed many people in their forest right now so their people could be cured.

The Indians answered that there was only one working automobile in the village; if it was not there, they would have to send people into town on foot. If that was necessary, they could not return here until after midnight.

Hawks nodded. They disappeared silently into the forest, their silhouetted forms seen for a brief moment against the horizon as it flickered with lightning.

Hawks walked to the body of the dead creature that he had left in the bushes on the outskirts of M'rai's camp. It lay on its back, stiffened now. The front legs were stretched upward, beckoning with talons as sharp as razors.

Hawks picked it up and tossed it close to the fire. Then he gazed into the forest, fearing what might be out there.

# 11

THE STORM HAD passed from overhead and now hung above the distant mountains, striking their peaks with daggers of finger-lightning and rumbling with thunder that sounded like cannon shot as it boomed across the lake. The forest surrounding M'rai's camp was becalmed, save for an occasional surge of wind that sent raindrops splattering down from the trees; the crickets were meekly attempting to start their belated night concert but were silenced each time the thunder rolled.

In the two hours that had passed since the Indians left the encampment, Hawks had foraged for firewood, stripping off the wet bark, and built up the fire in the center of M'rai's compound to a blazing inferno. He knew that nothing short of that would dissuade a beast the size of what he now came to think of as Katahdin.

He had also found M'rai's archer's bow and a quiver containing four arrows. He tested his marksmanship and found that the lessons of his youth were serving him well. Of the four arrows he fired, one stuck in the knothole of a tree. Its tip broke off as Hawks attempted to remove it. There were only three arrows now. There would be no more target practice.

Hawks knew that the bow and arrows were pathetically little to defend themselves with, but if they needed them, each arrow would count.

Behind Hawks, one of the three tents in M'rai's camp was brightly illuminated from within, casting shadows onto the thin tent walls and enabling him to see everything that was going on inside. The figures of Rob and Maggie stood motionless over a table; Romona knelt on the floor, fanning a bed of coals. The pilot was nowhere in sight; Hawks concluded that he was exploring the underground tunnels.

There was silence in the tent. The air was thick with smoke from the coals that Romona toiled over as she steamed wet rags; Rob's eyes burned from it as he gazed down at the weakened infant creature. It was sprawled out on a chopping block, limp and deathlike, its eyes closed, its chest heaving in labored gasps. Beneath the harsh white light of suspended kerosene lanterns, the details of its malformed body were clear. When the body had been wet, the skin appeared smooth, mottled pink and black. Now that it was dry, Rob could see that the black part was fur, soft and downy, like the skin covering of a newborn chick. The batlike skin folds that extended from the hips to the tiny clawed hands were extremely fragile, thin as an egg membrane, easily torn. The eyelids were transparent, so that the pupils seemed to stare out from them even when they were closed; the nose was no more than two holes at the end of a ligamentlike protrusion. The teeth were needle-sharp and even though the creature was unconscious, they occasionally snapped at Rob when his hands came too near the face.

But for all its grotesquery, the creature was somehow captivating. Perhaps because it was sick and vulnerable. Perhaps because it was small.

Rob knew that the internal organs might be as deviant as the external features, but he treated the creature in the only way he knew how: as though it were a human infant. He had given it five cc's of Adrenalin, and the heartbeat had responded. It was beating fast now. Almost too fast. Rob removed the warm rag from the body and fanned it with his hand. The skin crinkled where the breeze came across it, a sign that the creature was reviving.

"Will it die?" Maggie whispered from beside him.
"I don't think so."

Maggie could not help feeling relieved. In the hours
of keeping watch, her perception of the creature
had altered. The misshapen body was no longer ugly
but awesome, delicate and somehow beautiful in its
own unique way. The fact that it looked unlike anything she had ever seen before became easier to accept
as the hours wore on; regardless of its appearance, it
was a living, breathing, suffering thing. She felt pro-
tective of it. She imagined that it needed her to defend
it.

But deep within the recesses of her mind, she was
walking an emotional tightrope. The fall to one side
was the plunge into intolerable reality; to the other,
the abyss of insanity. To accept that this creature was
possibly a replica of what lay incubating inside of her
would have caused her to crumble. To deny it meant
to release her hold on reality. The hormones at work
within her body were in conflict with the logic of her
mind. She was trapped between the two, unable either
to accept or deny what was happening to her.

Rob had been aware of her torment but did not
recognize the depth of it. He knew of her compassion
for living things and that in recent weeks she had been
emotionally shaky. It was predictable that the shock
of finding the creature might cause her greater personal stress than the rest.

But as time passed, Rob was becoming more and
more concerned. She seemed to be withdrawing into
an isolated shell, focusing on the infant creature as
though nothing else existed.

"Do you want another rag?" asked Romona as she
approached Rob with a steaming cloth.

"No. It's getting too hot. Can we get some of the
smoke out of here?"

"I can widen the flaps."

The pilot emerged, covered with dust, from a narrow entranceway into the ground. "Nothin' down
there but dirt."

"No supplies?" Rob asked.

"Not that I could see. It's just crawl space."

"I need a sterile jar."

"I'll check the other tents," Romona answered.

"Just *any* jar. Anything that seals."

"I've got a jar of vitamins," the pilot said.

"Get it."

"It's in my pack—"

"Look!" Maggie gasped. Her voice was punctuated with a sharp squeal of pain. The creature was convulsing. Its eyelids had flown open and the pupils had flipped upward; its body was rigid and shaking in every fiber as froth poured from between its clattering teeth.

"Hurry with that jar!" Rob barked.

Maggie reached out to touch the creature, but Rob stopped her. "Don't touch it!"

"Can't you *stop* it?"

"I don't dare sedate it."

"Can't you do *something?*"

Maggie clapped her hands to her mouth to stifle a whimper as she watched with anguished eyes. The body of the small creature was back-bending, froth and vomit shooting from its nose and mouth.

"Oh, God . . . God . . ." Maggie moaned as she buried her face in her hands.

"Here's your jar," the pilot said.

Rob grabbed it, shook out the contents, and thrust it into Romona's hands. "Boil it! Steam it! I need something to puncture the cap!"

"My knife," the pilot said.

"In my bag, Maggie. Surgical tubing."

But Maggie did not respond. Her eyes were wide and staring, fixed on the infant creature that had suddenly gone limp and comatose on the table.

"*Maggie!*"

"Yes?"

"Surgical tubing. In my bag."

"Yes."

She fumbled in the kit and found the tubing, which

Rob grabbed from her and inserted into the small hole he'd punched in the bottle cap.

"It's steamed as best I could," Romona said, quickly handing the jar to Rob.

Maggie watched with glazed eyes as Rob quickly removed a hanging lantern and replaced it with the jar, then grabbed for a hypodermic syringe. He glanced at the comatose creature with uncertainty. He had sensed earlier that its body temperature was rising, which could have accounted for the convulsion. Were this a human infant, he would hydrate it intravenously to bring the temperature down. But it was not a human infant. He didn't know what the normal body temperature should be, or how it would respond. He touched the skin. It was dry as sandpaper and almost hot to the touch.

"Please help it," Maggie pleaded.

Rob nodded and began constructing the I.V. Within five minutes it was strapped to the creature's tiny arm and, as Rob listened to the heartbeat through his stethoscope, he nodded with relief. The respiration had returned to normal and the body temperature was coming down.

From outside, Hawks had watched the flurry of activity, and had a moment of alarm when he heard the creature squeal. Its voice was powerful and carried easily into the forest. It had silenced the crickets, and they had remained silent. The forest was hushed, as though holding its breath.

Hawks strained his eyes, searching the dark. He saw threatening shapes in every darkened configuration, frightening movements in the rustling of the trees, and realized that his imagination was beginning to stir. A sudden sound caused him to jump. It was a small toad plopping lazily out of the brush, attracted by the glow of the fire. It trundled forward and planted itself directly atop an anthill; the ants streamed all over it, biting into its eyes and face.

A sound came from behind Hawks, and he turned quickly to see the tent flaps parting as someone

emerged. It was the pilot. He shined his flashlight on
Hawks as he approached; the two assessed each other
in wary silence.

"Looks like the rain stopped, huh?" the pilot
mumbled.

Hawks nodded.

"Think your friends are coming back?"

"They said they would."

"Think they will?"

Hawks didn't like the question and was unwilling to
repeat his answer.

"If they don't show up pretty soon, I'm goin' back
to the chopper and fly outa here."

Hawks did not respond.

"You from around here?"

"Yes."

"You don't sound it."

"No?"

"You don't sound like an Indian."

Hawks glanced at him. "Neither do you."

"I'm not."

"Does that mean you're not from around here?"

The pilot was puzzled; Hawks moved away.

"That woman in there," the pilot said. "She your
squaw?"

Hawks glared at him with revulsion. "Which one?"

The pilot snorted with surprise and shook his head.
Then he walked away. Hawks could hear the sound
of his pants unzipping and his belt buckle rattling as
the pilot walked into the forest.


Within the tent, the hanging bottle had dripped its
last, and Rob refilled it. He used a pure saline solution
this time, leaving out the amenopheline additive he'd
used in the first bottle. The stimulant had done its
work. The creature had begun to move now, one of
its tiny arms waving in the air as though searching for
something to latch onto.

Standing beside Rob, her parched lips parted, her

downward stare vacant, as if she were barely main-
taining focus, Maggie responded to the creature's
gesture. She reached out, but her hand stopped,
trembling just above the outstretched claw.

Rob turned to her, his eyes filled with concern. Her
complexion was pallid, her expression dazed. He
realized that she was near collapse.

"Maggie . . . ?"

Her eyes traveled to his, as though finding him
across a great distance.

"Touch it," she whispered. "Let it know someone's
here."

He took her trembling hand and felt that it was
ice-cold.

"Come sit down," he said gently.

"How old is it?" she whispered.

"I don't know."

"Is it just born?"

"I don't know."

"It's a baby," she said, speaking so softly that he
could barely hear her. "It's just born."

Chilled by her tone of voice, Rob turned to his kit,
looking for a tranquilizer, but was interrupted by the
pilot, who strode in, picked up his backpack, and
addressed Rob with finality.

"It's all stopped out there. The rain, the wind,
everything. I say we go back to the plane and fly
outa here."

"We can't do that."

"Those Indians aren't coming back."

"They'll come," Romona said.

"You wait for an Indian to show up, you can wait
for three days."

"They'll be here," Rob said.

"You're wasting your time."

"We're waiting."

"I'm not." He started out.

"Wait a minute," Rob commanded.

"You want to come with me, that's fine."

Rob glanced at Maggie, reluctant to say what he

had to in front of her. But it seemed as though she weren't hearing.

"Do you see what's on that table?" Rob asked the pilot intensely.

"A freak."

"A mutation."

"If I found something like that, I'd kill it and bury it."

"It was given birth to by something that probably looks very much like it. Only a lot bigger. And it's probably close to where your helicopter is."

The pilot's expression sobered and he approached the table, gazing down at the creature with revulsion.

"I'm trying to keep it alive," Rob said, "to see that no more of them are born."

Though she seemed oblivious to the conversation, Maggie's fists clenched.

"We *need* you here," Rob continued. "If we can't make it out tonight, we'll have to try for the helicopter in the morning."

"You said I shouldn't go to the helicopter."

"I'm guessing that this animal is nocturnal. You can tell that by the size of the eyes."

The pilot looked unconvinced.

"You heard about the disappearances in the forest?" Rob asked.

"Yes."

"A night crew from the lumber company, a rescue team, a family of campers. They all disappeared at night. If we have to, we can risk going to the helicopter in the morning."

The pilot absorbed this in silence, then turned his eyes to Rob. "I've got a wife at home," he said quietly. "And a kid. They're gonna think I crashed somewhere. They're scared of my crashing somewhere."

"If you go near that helicopter in the dark, you might *never* get home."

The pilot gulped hard and nodded. "I'll wait," he said. Then he turned and disappeared through the tent flaps.

Rob looked at Maggie and was satisfied that the conversation had gone past her. She stood with exactly the same expression and posture that she had maintained from the beginning.

"Maggie?"

"Yes?"

"Let's go outside. Let's get some air."

She was reluctant.

"Romona's here."

"I'll watch it," Romona said.

Rob took Maggie's arm and led her out into the night. The air was clear and cold; the fire blazed high, illuminating the circle of trees. Rob could see both Hawks and the pilot, each at different points in the tree line, keeping watch. Hawks's archer's bow was beside him, resting against a tree trunk, the quiver on the ground beside it.

Maggie shivered within her parka and Rob brought her near the fire, taking the woolen shawl that hung loosely around her neck and wrapping it close beneath her chin. Her face was blank as she gazed beyond him into the flames. She seemed so withdrawn and unapproachable that Rob was hesitant to speak.

"Maggie?" He whispered.

She did not respond.

"I know it's a nightmare. But it'll be over soon."

She remained immobile, as though unhearing.

"We'll be out of here by morning," Rob said gently. "We'll go home. You don't ever have to think about it again."

She stiffened but made no reply.

"Maggie?"

She turned her head aside. Rob was becoming frightened that he was unable to reach her. He moved in front of her, but she stared right through him.

"Remember what the old man said?" Rob asked quietly. "About this creature awakening to protect them? In a strange way, it's true. What we found is going to stop what's going on here. No one can ignore this any more."

He waited for a response, but none came.

"Do you hear what I'm saying? There's a reason why this happened. And there's a reason why we're here."

He was becoming desperate now. He reached for her and she went rigid, as though warning him not to touch.

"I know it's ugly, Maggie. It's ugly because it wasn't meant to *be*."

Her eyes finally turned to him. They were hard, glinting in the firelight with anger.

"How do you know that, Rob?"

Rob shook his head with confusion.

"That it wasn't meant to be," she added.

"It's a sick and deformed . . . thing."

"It's a *living* thing. Who are you to say it wasn't meant to be?"

Her expression was harsh and taut; the muscles in her neck and face were tensed to the point of trembling.

"What is it they say?" she asked in a shaking breath. "That God works . . . in wondrous ways . . .?"

She shuddered and her breathing suddenly accelerated, hissing through clenched teeth as her face contorted into a mask of rage.

"Maggie?"

He reached out for her again and she raised both arms to ward him off. He stood paralyzed, held by her glaring eyes.

"What is it?"

"I'm pregnant!" she blurted. "I'm *pregnant!*"

Rob blanched, his eyes snapping wide with shock.

"I'm pregnant!" she screamed. "And I ate . . . what *they* ate! What the mother of those *creatures* ate, out there!"

"Dear God . . ." Rob breathed.

"The fish!" she sobbed. "For six days! Is that *enough*? Am I growing a monster, *too?*"

Hearing her cries, Romona hurried from the tent; Hawks and the pilot ran forward too.

"I'm *pregnant!*" she screamed at them. "I've got it, *too!* I've got one *inside* of me! I've got one, *too!*"

Rob grabbed for her and she spun, suddenly panicking, struggling to get away.

"No!" she screamed but he caught her sleeve and held firm, attempting to pull her into his arms. "Get *away!*" she shouted.

"Maggie!"

"Stop touching me!" she cried desperately. "Let me go!"

With a surge of energy she escaped his grip, backing away with wild and frightened eyes.

"Are you afraid of me?" she screamed. "I'm the mother of a monster! I'm the mother of a monster, *too!*"

"Maggie . . ."

"Don't get near me, don't get near me!"

"Please, Maggie . . ." Rob uttered as he moved toward her.

"You won't *kill* it! I won't *let* you!"

"Maggie . . ."

"You *did* this! You made this happen!"

"No . . ."

"You didn't want to know, you didn't want to *hear!*"

"Please . . ."

"You hated it! You *hated* it!"

"Maggie!"

"It's a *freak* now! It's a *monster* now!"

Rob stopped, his face etched with anguish as he watched her ranting in front of the flames.

"It wants to be born!" she screamed. "It wants to be born!"

Suddenly she groaned and slapped her hands to her mouth; vomit spewed out from between her fingers. Rob ran to her and held her, sinking with her to the ground, where she wretched and moaned, finally collapsing into his arms. She gasped and clung to him, her teeth beginning to chatter.

"Hold me . . ." she gasped.

"I will. I'm here."

"Don't let me go. Don't let me kill it. I can't kill it."

"No, no," he soothed, stroking her hair. And suddenly she inhaled sharply, her hands clutching at her stomach.

"It's hurting me!" she cried in panic.

"Lie back."

"It's eating me!"

"It's the vomiting, lie back. . . ."

"Don't let it *hurt* me!"

"Get my kit," Rob said to Romona. Romona whirled and rushed into the tent, reappearing instantly with Rob's bag.

"Don't hurt it," Maggie pleaded as Rob pulled her jacket off and rolled up her sweater sleeve. "Don't hurt my baby . . ."

Rob fumbled with trembling hands to prepare a syringe. He had nothing in his kit weaker than morphine; he drew a minuscule amount, injecting it directly into the crook of Maggie's elbow.

"Oh, God!" she shouted. Then she instantly became calm.

"Maggie."

"Yes."

"You're going to be all right . . ."

"No."

"We're going to get through it."

"No. I can't kill it."

"Just relax . . . relax . . ."

Her eyes closed and she sank back against him.

"Please . . . love me," she whimpered. Then she fell silent.

Hawks, Romona, and the pilot slowly disbursed, leaving Rob alone, cradling Maggie in his arms. His face contorted, and a sob of despair rose up from his gut. It had the sound of pain, as though it were breaking through a barrier of flesh and bone to escape from the depths in which, for an entire lifetime, the feeling of fear had been buried. Once it broke through, it would not be stopped. Rob's body shook with it as he rocked Maggie in his arms, the forest resounding with the sound of his tears.

Eventually he quieted, sensing the hush of the atmosphere around him. The forest was unmoving, as though suspended in a vacuum.

The he heard the movement in the trees. It was distant, a kind of shuffling sound. Almost inaudible at first, growing louder as he listened.

He roused Maggie and struggled to get her to her feet. The pilot came to help him with her, his eyes riveted on the forest. Hawks moved into the darkness of the tree line, straining to see.

Romona emerged from the tent, cocking her ear in the direction of the oncoming sound.

"It's people," she said with relief.

"Look," Hawks called.

Their eyes followed his gesture toward a line of tiny lights moving slowly toward them through the trees. They were lanterns and flashlights, strung closely together, seeming to float like an illuminated string of pearls in the surrounding darkness.

"They're from the village," Romona said.

"What good are they going to do?" the pilot asked grimly. "We needed cars."

Rob led Maggie into the tent, gathering some burlap for her to sit on beside the smoldering coals. As he eased her down, he could see that the effects of the morphine were waning. There was clarity in her eyes.

"Don't let them hurt it, Rob," she whispered.

He shook his head to reassure her. "Wait here."

As Rob stepped out of the tent, the procession of lantern-carrying Indians was emerging into the clearing. A few of them were young, but most were elderly, their faces deeply lined and somber. They assembled in silence, the glow of the fire casting their shadows high upon the trees.

Then the distant sound of a car motor broke the stillness. A beam of headlights stabbed through the darkness, and machinery rattled as a small vehicle wove its way through the forest toward them.

"All *right!*" the pilot exclaimed.

"It's the sheriff," Hawks said. Then he turned and headed for the tent. "I'll stay in the tunnels until you're gone."

The car squealed to a stop at the edge of the encampment, and four men got out—the sheriff and a deputy, both carrying rifles, Bethel Isely, and Kelso, the lumberjack who had fought with Hawks at the blockade.

"Put your guns away," Rob said as they approached him.

"What is this, Vern?" Isely asked.

"Leave those guns outside."

"I asked you what's going on."

"Put those guns away."

Isely glanced at the sheriff and nodded. The sheriff handed his rifle to the deputy.

"Just the two of you," Rob said to Isely and the sheriff. "The rest can come later."

Inside the tent, Maggie struggled to her feet, taking a defensive stance beside the table where the infant creature lay. Romona was there, too, and stood firmly beside her. Isely and the sheriff moved forward and recoiled, their faces contorting with revulsion.

The eyes of the infant creature stared up at them from behind transparent lids, and its body began to tremble, as though sensing danger was near. It whimpered, then went silent, its chest pumping in rapid gasps.

Rob came up beside Isely. "It's the result of methylmercury . . . spilling out of your plant. It's poisoned everything in this forest. It's given birth to this creature."

Isley did not answer.

"Did you know?" Rob asked.

Isely's eyes turned to Rob. They were filled with anguish.

"Did you know?" Rob repeated.

Isely's gaze returned to the creature. "I . . . didn't want to," he whispered.

They stood unmoving at the table, gazing down at the infant that was spotlighted beneath them in the glow of a kerosene lantern hanging overhead. The atmosphere was hazed with smoke from the coals and there was a sense of awe, almost reverence, in the air.

Outside, the Indians also stood in silence, their faces illuminated by the fire, the entire scene dwarfed by an enormous reddish moon that glowed brightly above them. One of the Indians stepped forward and entered the tent; others followed.

They filed quietly by the table; the atmosphere hushed, save for the sound of their shuffling feet as, one by one, they came and gazed down, then moved away. They expressed no disgust or surprise. Their faces were calm and accepting, even tender.

The creature had begun its pitiful squeaking sound again; it was struggling for consciousness. Its sounds came louder, permeating the thin walls of the tent and reaching into the forest.

Outside, from deep within the recesses of darkness, a sound came in response. It was an abrupt squeal. From their position beside the tent, Kelso and the sheriff's deputy heard it; the Indians heard it, too. The last of the Indians had exited the tent and gathered with the others in a small group near the fire, their eyes turning toward the forest as the sound grew louder. The infant squeaked, the squeal came in response. The tempo was increasing and the sound was coming closer.

Inside the tent, Romona heard it, and the sudden tilt of her head alerted Rob to listen, too. He left the tent, Romona following, the sheriff and Isely close behind them. The infant creature continued to squeak behind them but the squeal that came in response suddenly ceased. All stood immobile, listening to the silence.

Rob's eyes searched the darkened forest, but he could see nothing beyond the flickering shadows cast by the fire. Then he heard the sound of movement;

the foliage on the forest floor crunched as something moved in the darkness. It was coming toward them, the slow and deliberate rhythm growing louder with each footfall.

"What is it?" Isely whispered. Romona raised her hand to silence him.

The squeak of the infant became more desperate, suddenly rising in pitch, and the sound of crunching came faster upon them. It was at the edge of the encampment now, within moments of invading their sanctuary. Rob sucked in his breath and clenched his fists. Suddenly the foliage parted.

It revealed the figure of the old man, M'rai. He stepped into the clearing and gazed around in confusion, stunned to find so many people there.

"Welcome." He smiled. Rob and Romona sagged with relief.

Then the environment exploded. The trees behind M'rai shattered as they were ripped from the ground; an earsplitting squeal of rage rang through the air. A massive black form hurtled into the clearing, branches splintering and leaves flying as it lashed out at the men and women who ran and screamed beneath it. It was a gargantuan enlargement of the infant, its saucerlike eyes reflecting fire, its underslung jaw dripping saliva as it bellowed and swiped, throwing bodies into the trees like rag dolls. The deputy raised his rifle, but just as he did, was grabbed and hurled upward, his bones snapping as his body flew toward the sky. The air resounded with cries of panic; people ran everywhere, colliding with one another in their desperation to escape. Rob stood in shock, unable to move as the slaughter went on around him; he saw Kelso get slashed in half by the claws, the top half of his body landing in the fire.

A group of Indians attempted to escape in the car, but it toppled sideways as the beast attacked it. Men spilled out, screaming as the car rolled on top of them. Parts of bodies were flying everywhere. The scene turned to bloody chaos.

Inside the tent, Maggie grabbed up the infant, the I.V. bottle crashing behind her as she screamed and spun, not knowing where to go.

"The tunnel!" Hawks cried as he sprang from the narrow opening in the tent floor. He grabbed Maggie and threw her into it, then ran to the outside. "Mona!" he screamed. But Romona was nowhere in sight. The fire pit had erupted into a shower of sparks; people were wailing and running, some crawling, through pools of blood. "The tunnels!" Hawks cried out. "The tunnels! Get to the tents!"

The pilot raced forward, attempting to reach Hawks, but the talons caught him, yanking him upward and hurling him against a tree. The beast bellowed, whirling toward the sheriff, who was rolling on the ground, attempting to fire upward with his revolver. The beast's massive foot came down on his head, and juice squirted upward. Then the huge form turned on Rob; as its torso swung, Rob saw the pendulous breasts of a female.

"Watch out!" Hawks screamed.

Rob whirled and leaped away, hearing the tent poles crack behind him. "Maggie!" he cried.

"She's all right!" Hawks yelled. "Get to the tunnels!"

Rob scrambled on all fours as the beast turned its rage on the tent, ripping and tearing it as if it were tissue paper.

"John!" Romona screamed.

"The tunnels!"

She raced toward him, colliding with bodies that got snatched up and disappeared around her, spotting M'rai who stood near the fire pit in a state of shock, watching the massive form of the beast dancing violently around him.

"M'rai!" she screamed.

Hawks grabbed her, pulling her toward one of the tents, but before they could get there, it was ripped from its moorings; they changed directions, heading for the one tent that remained standing. Isely had

gotten there just ahead of them; he was weeping as
Hawks pushed him into the darkened hole, thrusting
Romona down behind him. Then Hawks ran to the
outside again. There was practically no one left alive.
The air resounded with the beast's howl of rage as
it shredded the remains of the tents. The only figure
left standing was M'rai, watching like an innocent
child; body parts, like broken toys, were strewn upon
the ground around him. Rob was out there, too,
desperately attempting to drag the pilot, whose face
was covered with blood, toward the last remaining
tent. But the beast spotted him, bellowing with anger
as it turned and lunged downward.

"Watch out!" Hawks screamed.

Rob leaped away and rolled fast. Talons slashed the
ground just behind his head as Hawks raced away
from him and screamed at the beast in an attempt to
distract it. The beast spun, and as Hawks hit the
ground, his eyes fell on the carcass of the dead infant
creature he had placed there while tending the fire.
He grabbed it and held it up, and as the beast rose to
its hindquarters preparing to charge, he flung it at her.
It hit her chest and fell to the ground. Suddenly all
movement stopped. The gargantuan form went silent,
its eyes fixed on the body of its dead infant. As Hawks
watched, the huge, hairless head tilted, blood and
saliva drooling from its open mouth. A small sound
emanated from within, almost like a question. Then
it lowered to all fours and nudged the tiny carcass
with its nose.

Hawks and Rob eased slowly backward toward the
one remaining tent and paused for a moment, watching.

"M'rai!" Hawks hissed.

But M'rai did not respond. He stood just beneath
the towering figure, his face turned upward.

"M'rai!"

The beast heard Hawks's voice and its large, saucerlike eyes slowly turned toward him. But it did not
move. It looked at the two men and whimpered. Then,

without warning, it suddenly charged. Rob and Hawks leaped into the tent and scrambled into the narrow floor opening, hearing the tent poles crack and the canvas rip behind them.

The noises gradually faded as they worked their way down into the subterranean darkness.

There, eight feet beneath the ground, three tunnels converged into a small earthern cubicle. Maggie was there, clutching the limp form of the living infant creature to her chest. Isely was crouched beside her, weeping, his face pressed close to the dirt wall. Rob wrested the creature away from Maggie and pulled her into his arms; Romona and Hawks stared at each other in the darkened silence.

On the ground above them, the beast's tirade had ended.

It turned away from the shredded tent and lumbered back toward the body of its dead offspring. It walked past M'rai without touching him and stood over the infant, rolling it over with its nose, then licking its chest in firm, upward movements, as though attempting to reinstill the life force within. It stopped and whimpered once more, then lifted the rigid carcass of the infant in its mouth and slowly moved back into the forest.

M'rai watched as it blended into the night shadows and disappeared into the trees. There was a smile on M'rai's face. His sanity was gone.

# 12

DAWN BROKE OVER M'rai's camp, revealing the grim aftermath in all its bloody detail. The once beautiful oasis looked like a battlefield. The tents were reduced to rubble and bodies were strewn everywhere, arms and legs protruding from the surrounding foliage, the ground torn and blotched with dark stains.

The fire had dwindled to a fine wisp of smoke; M'rai sat before it, chanting.

As the morning call of the loons sounded from the lake, a pile of torn animal hides that had once been a tent stirred, and the survivors emerged, one by one, from their hiding place beneath the ground. Hawks was first, followed by Romona. Then came Rob. He was bruised and caked with dirt, and he held the limp body of the still-living infant creature in his arms. Next came Maggie. Her face was scratched, her eyes dazed. Rob put his arm around her and turned her toward the forest so she would not see the nightmarish scene spread out before them. Isely was the last to emerge; he did not look like the same man. His eyes were hollow, his cheeks were sunken, as if he had suddenly aged.

Hawks and Romona spotted M'rai and slowly approached him. He turned to them and smiled.

"*A'haniy'aht* Katahdin," he said.

Romona knelt before him, gazing into his face. Then she reached up and gently pulled his opened jacket closely around him.

"Katahdin *Y'ho'w'atha*," the old man whispered.

"What's he saying?" asked Rob as he came up behind them.

"That Katahdin loves him," Hawks answered.

Romona turned away, concealing the tears in her eyes.

Rob surveyed the grim spectacle before them. The car was overturned and squashed. Arms and legs could be seen beneath it, but none of them moved. The corpse of the sheriff lay twisted and broken at the base of a tree; the body of the deputy was close beside it. He lay on the ground, face up, his skull flattened at the back from the impact.

Maggie stood shivering; Rob walked her to the fire, easing her down to a boulder at its edge.

"I'll stay with her," Romona said.

Maggie was holding her woolen shawl loosely in her hand. Rob gently removed it, wrapped the infant creature in it, and set it down near Maggie on the ground. Then he and Hawks walked to the edge of the trees, Isely following.

None of them spoke as they gazed into the misted forest.

"Do you think it's still here?" Isely asked in a faltering voice.

"It's nocturnal," Rob answered.

"Not any more," Hawks said. "It won't sleep until it collects its litter."

They looked to the infant creature, bundled in Maggie's shawl, lying motionless on the ground.

"We must destroy it," Hawks said. "We must burn it."

"No."

"Its mother will return."

"Not until night. It's nocturnal. It will sleep."

Hawks bristled. It was plain that the controversy was not over.

"John!" Romona called out with alarm.

They turned and saw her pointing toward the forest. There was movement there, the foliage swaying as something came toward them. It was the pilot, badly wounded and barely conscious, crawling on his belly toward the clearing.

Rob and Hawks ran to him and dragged him forward, propping him into a sitting position at the base of a tree.

His shirt hung about him in shreds, the strips of material meshed into streaks of clotted blood that ran from his chin to his belly. His front teeth were bent inward, and there was a discolored dent where his forehead used to be. He repeatedly mumbled something that they were unable to hear.

Rob gently touched the wound on his head; the flesh gave way beneath his fingers.

"Will he live?" Hawks asked.

Rob rose, moving out of earshot, Hawks following.

"Can he live?" Hawks repeated.

"I don't know."

"We'll have to leave him."

Rob gazed grimly back at the pilot.

"He can't *walk*," Hawks insisted.

"We could carry him."

"We're fifteen miles from town. We won't make half that distance by nightfall if we carry him."

"He wanted to leave. I wouldn't let him. I can't leave him here."

Hawks shook his head in warning.

"You go ahead of us," Rob said. "You can make it before nightfall. Send someone back for us. We'll be on the road."

"You can't carry him yourself."

"Isely's here."

"I can't carry him," Isely said quietly behind them. "I can barely stand."

They stood in frustrated silence, knowing that a decision had to be made.

"We'll go to my village," Hawks said. "It's only two miles. There's shelter there. My people can send for help."

"How long will it take them?" Rob asked.

"Last night it was six hours until a car came."

"They'd make it back by nightfall?"

"If we reached the village by noon."

"Wait," Isley said. "The plane you came in. It must have a radio."

"It won't work unless it's up in the air," Rob replied.

"The ranger's tower," Isely countered. "There's a radio up *there*."

Rob looked at Hawks.

"It's seven miles," Hawks said.

"That's half the distance to town," Isely urged.

"And three times the distance to the village," Hawks replied.

"But there's a *radio* there."

"And what's between here and there?"

Isely was stopped.

"Seven miles of open forest," Hawks added, "with trees so thick you can't see three feet on either side. We can't cross seven miles of open forest not knowing where the beast is."

"*I* can," Isely said.

Hawks assessed him with a wary eye.

"I can't carry the pilot," Isely said apologetically. "The only way I can be useful is by going to the tower. You go to the village. If I can make contact, you'll get out within hours."

Rob looked at him carefully, wondering if he realized the danger.

"Let me do this," Isely said. His voice made it plain that it was an act of atonement.

"I'll make a stretcher," Hawks said.

Rob nodded. "Let's move."

While Hawks gathered saplings and torn bits of animal hide to construct a litter, Rob surveyed the bodies that were strewn around, looking for signs of life. There were none, and Rob was relieved; they could not have carried more than one.

In the remains of the car there was a rifle that was undamaged; it had three shells in its chamber. Rob took it, ejecting the shells and putting them in his pocket, then searched through the remains of the tents, looking for his medical kit and anything else, such as a knife or an ax, that could be useful.

He had not stopped to question why he'd emptied the rifle, but now, as he watched Hawks from a distance, he realized he had done so because he feared that the Indian might try to use the gun to put the infant creature to death.

While Rob picked through the remains of the tents, Isely searched the pockets in the clothing of the lumberjack, the sheriff, and the deputy, removing identification and personal belongings to take back to their survivors. On the body of the sheriff he found a revolver and loaded it with bullets from the sheriff's belt. Then he assisted Hawks in the construction of the stretcher, Hawks only grudgingly allowing him to help.

M'rai still sat on the ground chanting, his voice so soft that it was almost inaudible. Maggie and Romona sat near him on the boulders that rimmed the fire pit, their eyes riveted on the shawl-wrapped creature near their feet.

"Is it alive?" Romona asked quietly.

"Yes."

"We must not take it."

Romona reached down and pulled away the cloth wrapping. The small rib cage was still pumping as the creature clung to life.

"We must leave it," she said.

"It will die."

"Mr. Vern?" Romona called. Rob approached and she rose to confront him. "We must not take this."

"We have to take it," Rob answered firmly.

"It's a danger to us."

"I'm not going to lose it."

"Then *bury* it. Come back for it."

"It's *alive*," Maggie responded.

"Then *kill* it," Romona snapped.

Hawks came up and took a stance beside Romona. "Romona is right. It must be destroyed."

"You can't just *kill* it," Maggie pleaded.

"If it makes a noise . . ." Romona argued.

"It can't make a noise," Maggie protested. "Look at it! It can't make a noise!"

Hawks reached for it, and Rob stopped him. Their eyes locked and held.

"You once asked me if I was willing to die for what I believed in," Rob said.

"There are others here."

"I'm aware of that."

"You'd sacrifice them?"

"No." Rob reached down and picked up the infant creature, unbuttoning his parka and placing it inside for safety. "If it makes a noise, I'll kill it. I'll kill it myself. Until then, it stays alive."

Isely approached, sensing the tension in the air.

"You'll agree to that?" Rob asked Hawks.

"If it makes a sound, it dies."

Rob nodded.

"I'm ready to go," Isely said.

"The stretcher's ready," Hawks said coldly.

"Can we see the ranger's tower from your village?" Rob asked Romona.

"Yes."

Rob turned to Isely. "Once you've sent a radio message, I want you to raise a flag. A shirt. Anything you can find. We'll be looking for it."

Isely nodded. "I'll do my best." Then he turned to leave.

"Mr. Isely?" Rob called after him.

"Yes?"

Rob stood for a moment in silence. "Thank you."

Isely headed off into the forest. They watched him until he had disappeared.

Hawks had found the archer's bow standing untouched beside the tree where he left it the night before; he slung it tightly across his shoulders, along with the quiver containing three arrows. Then he and

Rob moved to the pilot and lifted him onto the stretcher. His weight was more than Rob had anticipated.

"I'll lead," Hawks said, turning his back and moving between the carrying poles. Then they lifted, Rob struggling beneath the weight. With the parcel containing the infant creature stuffed in the top of his parka, he couldn't manage.

"Maggie," he called. "Take this."

"I'll take it," Romona called. But there was defiance in her voice.

"You take the rifle," Rob called back to her. "It's by the fire."

Maggie came forward and removed the shawl-wrapped infant from Rob's parka; she shuddered as she caught sight of the face. The mouth was caked with dried saliva and the skin had begun to sag from dehydration.

"I think it's dead," she whispered.

"It's not dead. Let's go."

Hawks started forward and Rob staggered until he established a rhythm; Maggie fell in line just behind him, her face gripped with tension as she tried not to look at the parcel in her arms.

Romona picked up the rifle and helped M'rai to his feet, holding on to his arm as they followed the group into the forest.

The two miles to the village were slow going; uphill almost all the way. The route was cluttered with fallen timber that they had to crawl over, sometimes under; Rob's neck ached and his arms trembled with strain as he struggled with the weight of the stretcher. Hawks moved in silence, his eyes scanning the forest, which seemed deceptively benevolent. Birds sang and fluttered overhead; squirrels chattered at them from the high branches of trees.

In her efforts not to stumble, Maggie had pulled the parcel in her arms close to her, so she could see

over it to the ground. She tried to ignore the stirring
that she had begun to feel in her arms. Warmed by
Maggie's body and stimulated by the jostling movement, the creature was beginning to awaken. Its muscles had begun to contract and tighten. One of the
transparent eyelids had slipped upward; a single eye
stared out from the warm, protected darkness.

"Got to set it down," Rob gasped.

"Keep going," Hawks urged.

"I can't . . ."

"Romona."

Romona hurried to Rob's end of the stretcher and
reached for one of the handles.

"No," Rob said.

"Let her help you."

"I can do it."

"Help him," Hawks commanded.

Romona laid the rifle in the stretcher and hefted
one of the handles; Rob released it.

"How much farther?" Rob panted.

"At the top of the hill, we're halfway," Hawks
answered.

Within forty minutes they had reached the crest
of the hill and stopped, gazing down at the lake and
the village below. The lake was perfectly still, unmoving; so was the Indian village. There was not a
sign of life there.

"They're gone," Romona whispered in amazement.

Hawks, too, was stunned, and there was despair
in his eyes.

"No one's there?" Rob asked weakly.

"No one."

"The forest has turned against them," M'rai said.
"We have angered Katahdin."

Hawks and Rob set down the stretcher. Rob sank
to the ground and rolled onto his back. He was
breathless. His neck muscles were in spasm, rigid and
cramped, and his hands were blistered and bleeding,
deeply imbedded with splinters where the rough-hewn
carrying handles had rubbed.

"There's the tower," Romona said. Rob struggled to lift his head and saw the small ranger's tower rising above the trees on a distant shore of the lake.

"How long have we been walking?" he gasped.

"Two hours. Maybe less," Hawks replied.

"Isely should be there soon."

"Unless he headed for town," Hawks said.

"Why would he do that?" Maggie asked fearfully.

"He knew he could make it by himself," Hawks answered. "Without us, he could run. He could make it before nightfall."

"He'll go to the tower," Rob vowed. "He'll go there."

Hawks's face was grim as his eyes turned to Rob. "If he doesn't, we're here for the night."

Rob struggled to his feet and they lifted the stretcher proceeding downhill toward the empty village.


Isely had begun his journey at a run but was unable to keep up the pace. He had now established a routine of running three hundred steps and walking three hundred steps, counting quietly to himself in an effort to keep his mind off the danger that he feared was lurking in the trees.

In the course of the journey, he had determined that he would assist Robert Vern in every way he could. If necessary, he would confiscate the files of the Pitney Paper Mill and bring them to Washington. If called upon, he would testify and tell everything he knew. It made him feel safer to think that he would absolve himself of sin.

The ranger's tower was in sight now, its thatched roof spiking upward through the trees no more than a mile away. It renewed his energy and he broke into a run. He dodged through the trees like an infantryman crossing a mine field, until his chest began to burn and his legs ached beneath him. Unable to continue, he slowed, his legs wobbling with fatigue.

He paused and leaned against a tree, gasping for oxygen through a raw windpipe and parched lips.

As his breathing quieted, he began to perceive a sound. It was the sound of flies buzzing, as though there were a hornet's nest nearby. He pushed himself away from the tree and staggered on, finding a narrow footpath that seemed to lead in the direction of the tower. The buzzing sound was louder here, and he saw, on the ground in the middle of the footpath ahead of him, a teeming mound of insects with flies hovering over it, ants converging from all directions.

He moved closer and began to detect an odor. It was the smell of rotting flesh. As Isely continued forward he could see, beneath the glistening shroud of crawling maggots and flies, the pinkish-black color of the carcass they were feeding on. He took a step toward it, and his footfall sent a cloud of flies billowing upward, revealing a shape that caused him to stop.

There, at his feet, was the rotting carcass of an infant creature exactly like the one he had seen in M'rai's camp the night before.

Isely had no knowledge that there had been a second infant creature or that the beast had carried this one away. He stood in momentary confusion, then shuddered as the smell of dampness swept over him. His posture stiffened, and he realized he was about to die.

The movement in the brush behind him was swift, followed by an earsplitting squeal of rage.

Isely did not turn around, for he did not want to see. But in the millisecond after his head hit the ground, his eyes registered the sight of his severed torso being ripped and torn to pieces.

By late afternoon, a light cloud cover had begun to move in over the lake, threatening the group assembled in the Indian village with early darkness. As they had suspected, the village was completely deserted when they entered, all the people and their belongings gone.

Rob had faithfully maintained watch; his eyes were blurred from strain as he continued to stare up toward the distant ranger's tower. It was almost four o'clock now, and there was no sign from Isely.

Romona was inside one of the flimsy cabinlike structures, tending the pilot, who was laid out on the earthern floor. He regained consciousness from time to time and wept, then slipped back into oblivion.

There was a small fire burning in the fireplace. Maggie sat before it, gazing into the flames. The infant creature was still wrapped in her shawl; she had tied the shawl tightly around it to make certain it would not move. She had also draped a piece of the cloth over the small opening at the top, for she had seen the eyes staring out at her.

In a far corner of the small cabin M'rai rocked slowly, uttering his soft, mournful chant.

As Romona knelt over the pilot, applying a wet towel to his forehead, she glanced through the open door and saw that the sky had turned gray. She was worried about Hawks, for it had been over an hour since he left the village to scout for help.

The pilot moaned and rolled his head, waving his hand as if to push the towel away. Romona moved to where she could see his eyes. They were open again and seemed clearer than before.

"The plane . . ." he whispered.

She took his hand and gently massaged it.

"I can fly it," he pleaded.

"We'll be safe soon."

"I can fly us . . . out of here . . ."

"They're coming for us."

"She'll think I crashed . . ."

"No . . ."

He whimpered and his face contorted as he tried to keep his tears in. "I'm sorry . . ."

"You're going to be all right."

He wept, then slipped into unconsciousness. Romona rose and moved outside.

Rob was standing in the center of the village, his eyes fixed in an upward stare.

"No sign?" she asked.

He shook his head. "We should have taken the road."

"We couldn't have carried the stretcher fifteen miles."

"We're going to have to spend the night here."

Each saw dread in the other's eyes. Their silence was broken by John Hawks, who came running toward them through the trees.

"Mr. Vern!" he shouted as he raced into the clearing. "Three quarters of a mile . . ." he panted, "where they're surveying trees, they've left a skidder."

"A skidder?"

"They use it for transporting equipment. They're like tanks, they can move through anything."

"Will it run?" Rob asked urgently.

"I can cross the wires."

"How long will it take?"

"It's flat ground, we can get there in thirty minutes."

"To get to *town*."

"Three hours, maybe four."

"It will be night by then," Romona said.

"It will be night *here*, too," Rob responded.

"We have some shelter here," she answered.

"Those cabins are matchsticks. If we've got to face the darkness, let's be close to town."

"I agree," Hawks said.

"All right," Romona answered.

"Let's go!"

They hurried into the cabin and emerged with the stretcher, Romona once again helping M'rai, Maggie following with the bundled-up creature in her arms. Hawks still had the archer's bow and quiver strapped to his back, and the rifle was in the stretcher. Darkness was descending, but they moved with power now. The possibility of escape had renewed their strength.

Maggie struggled to keep up with Rob; she studied his face as she moved alongside him. The veins protruded on his neck as he fought to keep the stretcher aloft; his jaw was clenched with a sense of purpose. Their eyes met and they exchanged a reassuring nod. Rob was barely able to speak as he struggled with the stretcher.

"We're going to get through it, Maggie."

"I know."

The trees ahead of them looked unending, as deep and dark as eternity. It felt as though they were moving on a treadmill, going nowhere, for there was no change in the landscape to mark their progress.

Maggie felt a quick spasm go through the body of the infant creature, and she looked down, opening the cloth around its face. Both eyes were open, and it stared up at her with a kind of blank affection, the kind of mindless trust one sees on the face of an infant watching its mother. Maggie quickly covered the face and focused hard on the forest. She prayed the creature would not cry out. She could not bare to watch it be slaughtered.

"There!" Hawks shouted.

They broke into a run, reaching the crest of a rise, where they gazed out over an area of forest laid waste by men and machines. The trees had been reduced to stumps, the ground pounded to pulp beneath boots and wheels. Disposable drinking cans and paper garbage littered the ground; a giant vehicle stood in the center, looking like a mechanical king of this domain.

"Look at the size of it!" Rob hissed.

It was made of heavy steel, tall as a steamroller, with rubber tires that were five feet in circumference. A narrow glass-enclosed driver's compartment protruded from the top of it, and a half-dozen stick-shift rods could be seen surrounding the driver's wheel.

"Can you drive it?" Rob asked Hawks.

"I'm about to learn. Wait here till I get it running."

They lowered the stretcher and Hawks raced across

the clearing, swinging himself up into the driver's compartment and disappearing from view as he slipped beneath the steering wheel.

As Maggie watched, a small, muffled sound came from the parcel in her arms. She pushed the shawl down hard toward the creature's face, but caused it to struggle and squeal louder. Rob heard it, and Romona heard it too; she quickly approached, glaring into Rob's eyes.

"You said—"

"Please," Maggie interrupted.

"Maggie . . ."

"It'll stop."

*"Kill it!"* Romona demanded.

But their voices were drowned out by the combustion of the skidder's motor. Exhaust fumes poured from a verticle pipe and Hawks jumped down.

"Let's go!" he shouted, running up and grabbing the stretcher.

"John," Romona protested.

"Let's go!" he demanded, cutting her off.

Romona whirled angrily toward Maggie.

"It's quiet!" Maggie insisted. "It stopped!"

"Let's *go*," Rob commanded.

They raced from the trees to the skidder, Rob and Hawks tying the stretcher on with ropes that hung from the running board. Romona climbed onto the open flatbed at the rear that was surrounded with a heavy metal railing. She pulled M'rai up beside her, Rob did the same with Maggie, and Hawks jumped into the driver's compartment, snagged for a moment by the archer's bow strapped to his back.

"I'll hold that for you!" Rob yelled to him.

Hawks shook his head and eased behind the wheel, pulling levers that made the vehicle suddenly lurch forward, then back. M'rai lost his balance, but Rob managed to grab him before he fell.

"Hold tight to the rail!" Rob shouted over the din of the motor. "Everybody get secured!"

Maggie pulled close to the railing, unwittingly pushing the parcel in her arms close to her face, and she could hear a sound coming from within. It was not a squeal, it was a purr. She could feel the gentle rumbling beneath her chin.

"Give me the rifle," Rob called to Romona.

She grabbed it up from the stretcher and handed it across, then braced her body behind M'rai, gripping the railing on either side of him to hold him in place.

"Everybody set?" Hawks called.

"Go!" Rob commanded.

The vehicle lurched and spun aboutface, the passengers clinging tight until it stabilized and started forward. The sound of the motor was louder when the vehicle was in gear, and it vibrated like a jackhammer as it bumped across boulders that were strewn in its way. Rob climbed over the railing and edged his way to the driver's compartment.

"How do we get there?" he asked Hawks.

"There's a riverbed that leads to the lake. We'll follow the shoreline to the road."

"My car's near there."

"I'd rather travel in *this!*" Hawks answered, pounding the heavy metal dashboard with his fist. Rob nodded and edged back to where the others were, crawling over the railing and bracing his body behind Maggie, as Romona had done with M'rai.

Night was coming fast and a sharp wind had risen, blowing the trees. Perched on their metallic stallion, they felt exhilarated, like soldiers returning alive from battle.

In the driver's compartment, Hawks's body vibrated in every fiber as he clung to the shift levers. He glanced at the gas gauge; it was less than half full. There was a roll of heavy tape on the floor near his feet; he grabbed it, and using his teeth, ripped off a piece and plastered it across the gas gauge. He didn't want to know.

As darkness began to take hold, the vehicle emerged from a thinly forested area, and onto an expanse of rolling hills. Hawks knew that the impenetrable tree line to the right stood between them and the lake. There was a dry riverbed somewhere ahead that ran directly through the trees and down to the shore. As a child, Hawks used to race the length of it, from the top of the hills to the shore, and take flight the last few feet, leaping headlong into the water. It was this riverbed that he was looking for, but in the near darkness the landscape looked suddenly unfamiliar.

He glanced behind them, wondering if he had passed it, and saw that the clouds had parted over the distant mountains, revealing a full, glowing moon. Once darkness fell, it would light the landscape almost as clear as day. The difficult time was now, before the shadows came to define the landmarks along the way. Then he saw a streak of yellow through the trees ahead and to the right. It was the reflection of the moon on the lake, calm and peaceful below them. Hawks could even make out the darkened mound in the center of the water, the island where Rob and Maggie's cabin stood. It was all the more frustrating to see the lake, for Hawks could not find the avenue of access to it.

"There's the lake," Rob called. "It's just below us."

"I see it!" Hawks shouted.

"Where's the riverbed?"

"I've lost it."

"Turn on the headlights."

In his desperation to see in the dark, Hawks had forgotten that the vehicle had lights. He found a switch and snapped it on; a spotlight beamed on the terrain that rumbled toward and beneath them. There was a lever above Hawk's head; he grabbed it and swiveled the spotlight, sweeping the beam through the trees. With sudden relief he recognized a landmark, a huge rock sharply configurated like an arrowhead. They used to call it *M'ahay'ah*, the "protector." The riverbed was only a few hundred yards ahead.

"We're going to make it!" Hawks called back. "We're more than halfway!"

The group on the back of the vehicle looked at one

another in triumph; except for M'rai, whose eyes were on the trees. Rob noticed it and edged close to him.

"Do you see something in there?"

"I see everything in there."

"We're going to make it, old man."

"No," M'rai answered. Then he turned and looked at Rob. "Can you stop the car?"

Rob stared at him in amazement.

"I wish to get out here," M'rai said. "You will be saved if I can get out here."

"*Why?*"

"I can speak with Katahdin. He knows my love for him. I will make him understand about taking his child."

The vehicle suddenly lurched to a stop, the spotlight swiveling in all directions.

"Thank you," M'rai said.

Romona grabbed hold of him. "M'rai!"

"He's waiting for me just there," M'rai complained.

Rob grabbed the old man's arms and held firm. "Why did we stop?" he shouted to Hawks.

"The cut to the lake! It's supposed to be here!"

"It's grown over with ferns . . ." Romona shouted.

"Let me please go down before he gets angry," M'rai protested.

"Tie him to the rail," Rob ordered. "Tie him up." Then he edged to the driver's compartment. "Keep moving! Keep it going!"

"There's nowhere to go if we pass the riverbed!"

"To your right," Romona said. "Look for the ferns."

"Where?" called Hawks, swiveling the spotlight.

"It should be over there!"

From beside Romona, a sharp squeal rose from the parcel in Maggie's arms. Maggie desperately pushed the cloth wrapping down upon the creature's face, but the animal began to struggle, its cry of panic rising in intensity.

"Throw it out!" Romona cried. "It will kill us all!"

"Katahdin is here!" M'rai declared.

"Get moving!" Rob ordered. "Get it going!"

"There's nowhere to go!" Hawks shouted.

"Just *move* it!"

Hawks jerked a shift lever and the mighty vehicle lurched backward, all grabbing the railing to keep from being thrown. The creature in Maggie's arms freed one of its paws, the sharp talons waving viciously in front of her eyes, but as she clung to the railing, she was helpless to stop it.

"Rob!" she called.

"Drop it!" he commanded as he edged toward her.

Maggie stepped back to let the parcel drop, but the talons hooked into her blouse, the creature squealing in loud, piercing cries.

"Throw it out!" Romona screamed.

"I can't!"

"There's the cut!" Hawks yelled. "There're the ferns!"

His spotlight swiveled to one side of them, and Romona gasped in fear. Their heads spun around, and they saw it. The reflection of two huge saucerlike eyes staring back at them from the center of the light beam.

"God!" Maggie screamed.

"*Move* it!" Rob shouted. "Fast!"

"Holy Mother . . ." Hawks moaned as he fumbled with the shift levers. The vehicle lurched forward, Romona and M'rai falling to the floor.

"It's coming!" Maggie shrieked.

She fumbled with the surging bundle in her arms, then looked up to see the foliage explode behind them as the huge specter of the beast charged into the clearing. Hawks pushed the accelerator to the floor, speeding blindly into the darkness, the vehicle bumping and lurching as the beast gained steadily from behind. Against the moonlight it could be seen only as a mountainous shadow, growing larger with each second. Then the skidder collided with a tree stump, knocking everyone to the floor. Hawks fumbled with the gears, and the vehicle spun, barreling downward with the speed of a roller coaster toward the trees.

Maggie sobbed as she clung to the floor, the squirm-
ing bundle pinned beneath her. Rob fumbled in his
pocket, pulling out a bullet and throwing it into the
rifle chamber. Grabbing the railing, he aimed at the
mountainous shadow, but the vehicle swerved as he
fired and the shot went wild. The beast was almost
on them now, the vehicle running sideways on a hill,
tilted at a precarious angle.

"Ram it!" Rob shouted. "Turn and ram it!"

Hawks struggled with the wheel, unable to turn
at this speed for fear of tipping.

"She's *on* us!" Rob shouted.

The face of the beast was just feet from the flatbed;
drool could be seen cascading from between its glinting teeth as it ran. But at the last moment it swung
away, running parallel to them on the uphill side.

"She's going to *tip* us!" Rob shouted.

"Throw it *out!*" Romona sobbed as she crawled
toward Maggie. "*Throw* it to her!"

"Throw it, Maggie!" Rob screamed.

But Maggie was unable to move, clinging with both
hands to the floorboards. Rob reached down and
rolled her over, Romona tore away the cloth wrapping
that contained the infant. With a sudden snarl it
leaped upon Maggie's neck, digging its claws and teeth
into her flesh as it wailed with fear. Maggie screamed
and rolled, Rob grappling to pull the infant off. But
he could not disloge it. Its teeth were buried in Maggie's neck.

"Watch *out!*" Hawks cried from the driver's compartment.

The beast lunged down on them, making jolting contact with the vehicle, and the vehicle tipped, poised,
for an awesome moment, on two wheels in the air.

"*Jump!*" Rob screamed.

In a blur of motion, bodies took flight, spilling out
in all directions as the vehicle crashed to its side with
tremendous force, then began rolling and bouncing
toward the trees. As Rob hit the ground, he saw that

Hawks was still trapped within it, and so was the pilot, tied to the running board. The beast had turned its attack on the vehicle itself, assailing it with full fury as it tumbled through the trees.

It crashed to rest at the base of a boulder, and Hawks struggled to get through the broken glass of the driver's compartment. But he was hung up by the archer's bow that was strapped to his back. The lumbering shadow surged down on the pilot, disemboweling him with a single swipe, and Hawks struggled free, the bow ripping off his back as its string was severed by broken glass. He grabbed it up and raced out into the night, trying to get his bearings in the darkness.

Maggie was running toward the lake, screaming in terror as she attempted to dislodge the creature that still clung to her, its snout deeply imbedded in her neck. Rob scrambled across the ground to get the rifle and ran after her, trying to force another bullet into the chamber as he ran. He spotted Romona as she stumbled through the darkness, screaming for M'rai.

"The water!" Hawks shouted. "The water! Swim to the island!"

Rob caught up with Maggie, attempting to grab her as she ran, but she was hysterical, fighting him off and screaming as she stumbled through the trees. Rob attempted to raise the rifle and point it at the creature, but Maggie kept spinning and lurching, her head swinging by the barrel.

"I can't get it off me!" she shrieked. "I can't get it off me!"

"Get to the water!" Rob screamed. "Drown it!"

Behind them, they could hear the sound of metal being ripped as the beast tore into the fallen vehicle. Rob prayed it would stay there long enough to allow them to get into the lake.

Hawks was the first to reach the shore; he paused, gazing back into the darkened trees. "Romona!" he cried.

"M'rai!" her voice called back. "I can't find M'rai!"

Hawks charged back up the hill and found her, pulling her downward, against her will, to the lake, where he threw her into the water.

"Don't leave him!" she screamed.

"Swim to the island!"

Hawks ran back up the hill as Rob and Maggie raced by him, splashing into the water.

"The island!" Rob yelled.

"Get it off me! Get it *off* me!"

*"Swim!"*

"I *can't!"*

Rob came up behind her, swung the rifle across her chest, and, gripping it on either side of her, pulled her backward, propelling them into deeper water.

Scrambling up the hill, Hawks saw the figure of the old man standing in a daze, watching the beast destroy the skidder.

"M'rai!" Hawks shouted as he ran toward him. "Come away!"

"I will speak with Katahdin," the old man answered calmly.

Hawks grabbed him and jerked him backward, dragging him down the hill. The beast spotted them and rose to its hindquarters, its massive head swiveling as it honed in on its quarry.

"Swim!" Hawks gasped as they staggered to the shore.

"I will not swim."

"Do you want to die?" Hawks yelled.

"He will not hurt me. I will call him by name."

Hawks grabbed the old man, but M'rai resisted. The trees were cracking on the hill above them; the beast was coming down.

"He will spare you if I speak to him," M'rai said.

Hawks lifted the old man from his feet and hurled him into the water, then jumped in behind him. M'rai immediately turned and started back for the shore.

"M'rai!" Hawks screamed in frustration.

But M'rai proceeded to the shore, wading up to

the bank, where he awaited the arrival of Katahdin.

"Damn you, M'rai!" Hawks wailed.

"I will not go with you."

In anguish, Hawks forced himself to turn away. With the bow and three arrows clutched in his hand, he began swimming hard toward the island.

Rob and Maggie had made it into deep water, and they were in trouble. With his arms wrapped around her, Rob could not use his hands to dislodge the creature, and his strength was ebbing as Maggie cried out and struggled in his arms.

"God . . . God . . . God!" she screamed.

"Lie *still!*"

"It's *killing* me!"

Rob's eyes were level with the creature's; it stared at him resolutely, its needlelike teeth firmly locked into the flesh of Maggie's neck.

"Help me!" Maggie cried, and she began flailing, trying to wrest herself from Rob's grip.

"Maggie, don't . . ."

But she pulled free, the water erupting in a white spray as Rob attempted to grab her.

"Help us!" Rob shouted. "Hawks!"

John Hawks spotted the flurry of white water and swam hard for them, Romona following close behind.

"She's under!" Rob screamed. "She's gone under!"

Hawks released the bow and arrows, and dove; Romona managed to get to Rob and take the rifle from him; Rob disappeared beneath the water, too. They rose instantly, all three, Maggie choking and sputtering, the creature still clinging to her neck.

"Get its face under!" Rob cried as he grabbed Maggie's hair.

Hawks pushed down hard on the creature's face, until its snout was below the waterline. Maggie's eyes were wide and her mouth was stretched open, her face being pulled from above and below.

"Help . . . me . . ." she gurgled through the water that flooded into her mouth.

Suddenly the creature's jagged teeth snapped upward above the water, and Maggie cried out with relief. Rob grabbed her in a cross-chest carry, pulling her away. The teeth of the creature caught Hawks's hand, and he thrust it below the water, grimacing in pain as he reached down with both hands, fighting to keep it submerged.

"The old man!" Romona cried out as her eyes swung toward the shore. There, in the moonlight, the figure of the old man could be seen standing in a posture of calm dignity as the massive form of the beast crashed through the trees and rose on its hind legs, staring down at him.

As Romona watched, she saw M'rai walk toward the beast, gazing straight up at it as though in conversation. Then the beast raised one of its paws and brought it crashing down, smashing the tiny figure at its feet as though it were a fly. Romona closed her eyes. Without looking again, she turned, the rifle held high over her head, and began swimming toward the island.

The darkened mound that protruded from the center of the lake was no more than a quarter mile from the shore; Romona could discern the outline of the cabin as she silently sidestroked forward. She could see Hawks a distance in front of her, the limp silhouette of the infant creature skewered on one of the arrows that he held, with the bow, above him. She could not see Rob and Maggie, for there was a mist forming on the water. It gathered quickly, obscuring her vision, muting all sounds except her own. Within minutes it had fomented into a graceful carpet of haze that floated on the surface, isolating Romona from everything around her.

As she swam, she sensed how effortless it would be to slip silently under. It felt warm and welcoming and peaceful. The world above felt so harsh and cruel. Her swimming slowed, until she was merely treading water. The mist swirled around her, looking like a layer of clouds in the moonlight, and Romona knew that she did not care if she reached the shore. The

death of the old man had robbed her of the one
human being she completely trusted. There seemed
little left now, just an endless battle for which she
no longer had the strength.

"Romona!" Hawks called out.

She did not answer.

"Vern!" Hawks cried in desperation.

"I'm here!" Rob called back.

"Where's Romona?"

"I don't see her!"

"Romona!" Hawks cried, his voice crackling with
emotion. "Oh, God! Romona!"

"I'm here, John," she responded.

"Romona!" he half sobbed.

"I'm here," she reassured. "I'm all right."

She resumed swimming toward the island.

As Rob and Maggie staggered to the shore and
fell exhausted into the mud, they heard the sound
of the beast bellowing from across the lake. It seemed
to vibrate through the water and penetrate the island;
the ground beneath Rob's face reverberated with it
as he clung to the mud. Maggie was beside him, moan-
ing as she struggled to reach dry ground. Rob crawled
to her and took her in his arms.

Hawks stumbled forward, half carrying Romona,
and fell to his knees, able to go no farther. He laid
her down beside him in the shallows and took the
rifle that she still clung to, tossing it, along with the
bow and arrows and the skewered body of the dead
infant creature, onto the shore. Then he helped
Romona to her feet and they came to Rob and Maggie, collapsing into the mud beside them.

The beast continued to howl from the distant shore,
but they knew they were safe now. They lay back,
grateful for the feel of solid ground beneath them,
none of them moving as the sounds of their heaving
breath gradually faded to silence.

The beast, too, had gone quiet now. Save for the
gentle lap of water against the shore, there was nothing to break the stillness around them.

Then Hawks heard a disturbance in the water, a muted splash, as though something had entered and were swimming toward them. He sat upright and gazed into the mist; it rolled and swirled unendingly, into an infinity of darkness. The sound had disappeared, but Hawks remained stock-still, his ear cocked toward the water.

Alerted to his tense posture, Romona sat up. The sound came again. A light splash. This time, closer.

"What's wrong?" asked Rob.

"Listen," Hawks whispered.

Rob sat up and looked into the mist. He could see nothing. The water that lapped gently at the shore rolled heavier, just slightly, but enough for Hawks to sense the change.

"What is it?" Rob whispered, watching Hawks's expression.

"The waves come heavier."

Rob looked at him in confusion.

"The wind didn't rise."

Maggie struggled to a sitting position, her elbows trembling as she followed their gaze.

"It's swimimng," Romona whispered.

"We'd see it," Rob gasped.

"No."

"It can't swim," Rob moaned. "It can't swim . . ."
It was not a statement. It was a prayer.

But they could hear it plainly now, the sound of its breath grunting with exertion; the light splashing of the water coming louder in their ears.

"No . . ." Maggie whimpered.

"Get to the cabin," Rob ordered.

"I can't," Maggie sobbed.

"The rifle . . ." Rob said.

"Up there."

Rob struggled to his feet.

"No," Maggie wept.

"Get up!" Rob gasped.

"There it is!" Romona shouted.

They all turned and saw, through the veil of mist,

two glowing embers moving inexorably toward them. "God, no!" Maggie moaned.

The beast responded with a gurgling wail, the water around it suddenly splashing violently.

"Shoot it!" Hawks yelled to Rob. But at that moment the glowing eyes disappeared, the mist collecting into a solid wall.

"I can't see it," Rob shouted as he pumped his bullet-shells into the rifle.

"Sssh!"

The sounds were gone. The water was suddenly calm, the small waves lapping against the shore in a gentle, regular rhythm. All held their breath in the silence.

"Where is it?" said Maggie. Hawks held up a hand to silence her. But there was nothing to be heard.

"Did it drown?" Rob asked, not daring to believe it.

Maggie slowly stood, so did Romona, all moving together as they gazed out at the calm, unbroken water.

"It drowned," Rob said. "It drowned." He turned to Maggie, his face filled with wonder. "It—"

A huge air bubble broke the surface directly in front of them. Then, in a cascade of white water, the beast suddenly rose, its arms lashing out as it bellowed in rage. In a blur of confusion, they screamed and raced beneath it, the massive talons slashing into the mud as they slipped and scrambled for safey.

"The cabin!" Rob screamed, dragging Maggie behind him.

Hawks managed to snatch up his weapons, flinging the skewered infant off one of his arrows as he ran. Romona stumbled, rolling toward the shore, but recovered her footing, limping badly as she continued.

Behind them the beast paused, lowering to all fours for a brief moment to sniff the cold carcass of its dead infant. It grabbed up the small body in its mouth and shook it in a ferocious spasm, biting it in half, flinging the pieces into the water. Then it rose on its hind legs, turning its attention to the four small figures staggering toward the cabin along the shore. In a wail of vengeance and an explosion of mud, it burst into motion.

The cabin was a hundred yards ahead, its shape silhouetted in the moonlight as the foursome ran desperately toward it, spurred on by the sound of galloping feet splashing through the water behind them. None dared to look back, for they could hear that the beast was gaining.

Rob glanced at Maggie and saw her terrified eyes, blood glistening on her neck, as she straggled farther and farther behind. The beast was running almost parallel to her, crashing through the shallows of the lake shore in an ungainly gait but outdistancing them with every stride. It was pulling ahead now, as though trying to beat them to the cabin.

"She's going to come *back* on us!" Hawks shouted.

They were almost at the cabin, but the beast was fifty feet beyond them, its head swiveling back as it prepared to turn. In a smash of splintering wood, it collided with the dock, the water erupting around it as it wailed in confusion, and spun.

It gave them the moment they needed to reach the cabin. Hawks hurtled the porch railing and smashed through the door, the others racing in behind him.

"Barricade!" Hawks shouted.

"I can't see!" Romona cried.

Rob dashed to where the table was, fumbling to find the kerosene lantern in the darkness.

"It's coming!" Maggie gasped as she stood at the window.

The beast charged with full fury; the entire cabin shuddered as it made contact.

"Board the window!" Hawks yelled.

Rob managed to light the lantern and run to the cupboards where he'd seen a hammer and nails; Hawks grabbed the kitchen table and furiously assailed it, smashing its legs off and plastering it up against the window. Rob raced toward him, but the cabin was hit again; stones clattered down from the fireplace as a howl of anger resounded from outside.

"Boards!" Hawks shouted.

"The bed!" Rob yelled to Maggie.

"The bed?"

"Bedboards!" Rob shouted; then he whirled toward the window and began pounding nails.

Maggie raced up to the loft, desperately throwing the mattress off the bed, and raked up the bedboards into her arms; but the ceiling just above her head began to groan and bend, bowing inward beneath a sudden weight.

"Rob!" she cried.

Rob ran upward as a huge talon curled in between the rafters, ripping one out, exposing the sky.

"The gun!" Rob shouted.

But it was too late. Another rafter ripped away and the beast's massive paw lunged inward. Maggie shrieked and fell to the floor; Rob grabbed a kerosene lantern and hurled it upward.

"No!" Hawks yelled. "Don't light it!!"

The lantern smashed against the ceiling and Hawks charged up the stairs with an ax in his hand. The beast's paw surged downward and Hawks swung hard, a geyser of blood shooting up from where the ax buried deep into the fur. The paw suddenly withdrew, and the cabin vibrated with a thunderous howl of rage. Then everything went quiet.

Rob grabbed Maggie, half pulling her down the stairs; Hawks remained in the loft, ax poised, waiting for more. But all he could see through the opened rafters was moonlight.

Romona had dismantled a ventilation pipe from the stove and peered out through the small hole where it had been connected to the wall. "I can see it," she said. "It's going away!"

Through the narrow opening she saw the hulking figure of the beast moving slowly, limping as it lumbered toward the tree line. When it reached the trees it turned. Then it coiled back and suddenly charged, speeding forward with full momentum.

"No!" Romona cried.

The cabin was hit with the impact of an earthquake. Romona was knocked clear across the room as dirt spewed from between the logs of the cabin wall, and the entire fireplace collapsed in a clattering cascade of boulders. The foundations beneath the cabin groaned, and they all began to slip.

"We're tipping!" Maggie screamed.

Rafters above their heads bent and snapped beneath the strain; chairs and tables slid across the floor. With a sudden jolt, one end of the cabin hit the ground, the entire structure tilting at a precarious angle.

"It won't hold!" Hawks shouted from the loft. "It's going to get in!"

Rob, Maggie, and Romona stood with their backs against the downhill wall; Hawks leaped from the loft and grabbed his archer's bow from the debris. The broken string trailed behind him as he made his way up the inclined floor to where Maggie's cello lay; when he reached it, he raised it overhead and smashed it to pieces, ripping out the strings.

A roar came from outside, barreling down on them like a freight train; the cabin half spun with the impact, the entire front wall splintering as rafters clattered down around them.

"Your gun!" Hawks shouted. "It's coming in!"

Jolted into action, Rob scrambled for the rifle. Hawks braced the archer's bow between his feet, working with his teeth and hands, fumbling with knots that slipped through his fingers as he desperately attempted to mend its broken string. He groaned with frustration, for it was plain that the beast was within minutes of finishing them. Its massive paw burst through the broken front wall and upward through the roof, slicing a path that revealed its murderous eyes glaring down at them. The air reverberated with its earsplitting cry.

Romona pulled Maggie close to her, and Rob raised his rifle; at that moment Hawks's knot connected, his hands pulling it tight with such force that he fell backward onto the floor.

With a single blow, half the roof gave way, revealinf the full form of the beast towering over them, its teeth dripping saliva as it wailed in triumph, extending its arms to reveal the pink skin folds that stretched beneath.

"Shoot!" Hawks cried. And Rob fired. The beast's jaw became unhinged in an explosion of bloody pulp, and it reeled backwards. Rob quickly cocked the rifle and aimed again. Hawks had regained his footing and drew back an arrow, his arm trembling with strain. The beast lunged forward.

"Again!" Hawks cried. He and Rob fired simultaneously. A hole tore into the beast's chest and an arrow embedded into the side of its neck. It staggered, then rose to its full height, its neck expanding in a sudden swell.

"Again!" Hawks cried as he drew back another arrow.

"It's *empty!*" Rob yelled.

With a gurgle that sounded like an oncoming flood, the beast's broken mouth flew open and its stomach contents sprayed out, hitting all beneath it with the milky debris.

Hawks let his second arrow fly and it streaked into the beast's snout, the huge animal screeching with pain as its arms flailed furiously against the cabin, dislodging heavy timbers that began to crash down around them.

"Run!" Hawks shouted. But there was nowhere to run. The cabin was collapsing, beams raining down with such force that they broke through the floor.

Hawks stood apart from the rest, with his last arrow poised, waiting for the precise moment to let it fly. But before he got the chance, the beast's paw swooped in and caught him, smashing him into a wall.

"No!" Romona screamed.

Rob scrambled toward him, but the sharp talons got there first, impaling Hawks and scooping him up, squashing his body against what was left of the ceiling. It stuck there for a moment, then crashed down beside Rob, the bow and arrow still gripped in Hawks's mangled hand. Rob grabbed for the weapon, dislodging the arrow, but the beast's paw swiped inward again.

"Rob!" Maggie screamed.

He turned and tried to run, but the talons caught him, snatching him into the air.

"No!" Maggie shrieked in a bloodcurdling cry. But she was helpless to do anything but watch. The beast had pulled Rob to its mouth and was attempting to *eat* him.

"God! God! God!" Maggie wailed. Then she saw Rob's arm jerk backward, the arrow still clutched in his hand. With full force he plunged it deep into the beast's eye, jamming it down until it hit something solid.

For a split moment, everything stopped. The beast stood paralyzed, and a fine jet stream of blood shot from its shattered eye. It dropped Rob to the ground and squealed with pain. Then it spun and staggered, clawing at its eye.

Rob lay outside the cabin in shock, the beast whirling and dancing above him, squeaking in agony, stumbling, lurching, trying to maintain its balance. It swayed against the cabin, collapsing the front wall. Rob heard the women cry out. Then their voices fell silent.

The beast's arms lowered and its posture sagged. The one remaining eye turned to Rob. Then it dropped to its knees. Its full, maternal breasts scraped the ground as it crawled toward the lake and collapsed in the water.

Its limp body drifted gently outward until a stream of bubbles broke the surface around its submerged head.

Then it sank, disappearing from view.

The lake returned to calm and the night returned

to quiet. The sky was beginning to faintly lighten; the forest echoed with the call of the loon.

The cabin behind Rob was reduced to rubble; he began to hear the sound of movement within. Summoning all of his strength, he managed to roll over and saw Romona crawling out from beneath the debris. Her face was bloodied and her eyes were empty.

"Your wife is in there," she whispered in a deadened tone. "It fell on her."


With the morning sun, a flight of Canadian geese over Mary's Lake broke formation, frightened by the sound of approaching helicopters. The search that began twenty-four hours before, when the sheriff was reported missing, had been interrupted by darkness when the trail of the survivors ended at the lake.

To the men in the helicopters, the sight of the island did little to explain the mysterious trail of destruction. There was just a pile of timber where a cabin had once stood—and two lone figures standing on the shore.

# 13

---

THE CALL THAT Victor Shussette received from Robert
Vern had filled him with alarm. Little of what Rob
said made sense to him, but it was plain by Rob's tone
of voice that it was all true.

Shussette had immediately left Washington and
flown to Portland, Maine, then hailed a taxi to take
him to the hospital where Rob was waiting for him.
He had not told Rob of the recent developments in
the controversy between lumber companies and the
American Indians; he would withhold the information
until Rob was better able to stomach it. A judgment
had been rendered in the Midwest invalidating the
Indians' claim as rightful heirs to the land they were
born on; it set a legal precedent that would likely be
followed in Maine. Although the Pitney Paper Mill
would be fined and forced to shut down their pulping
operation until they could prove that they could meet
all health and safety standards, they would eventually
reopen, and claim Manatee Forest as their own.

As Shussette sat now in the taxi on his way to the
hospital, he looked somberly out at the rain. He wondered how many people, other than environmentalists,
suspected or cared that these were the same raindrops
that had been falling to the earth since the time of
the planet's creation. They would be absorbed into
the soft ground and eventually vaporized, rising once
again into the sky, where they would ionize with the
atmosphere, form clouds, and descend once again

into the thirsty earth. From the taxi window he watched the rain collecting into pools on the hard pavement and running off into sewers at the gutter.

The sky was beginning to darken. Shussette checked his watch. It was almost eight o'clock. Maggie had been scheduled for surgery at six.

Maggie Vern felt the first stirrings of consciousness well after midnight. As she gradually became aware of who and where she was, her mind grasped at fleeting images that represented the passage of time between the beast's attack and now. They drifted in fragments, blending and repeating, as if they existed only in a dream. She saw the cabin tumbling, then helicopters descending over the lake. She recalled Rob's face bending close to her, shouting at her to stay alive. Then there were other faces, partially masked, a light as bright as the sun shining from behind them.

Without opening her eyes she put her hands on her neck and moved them down the length of her body to make sure it was all there. Her torso was tightly taped and she was unable to move. Struggling to raise her eyelids, she saw tubes snaking down from both sides of the bed; at the foot of the bed there were metal weights suspended on strings. The tape meant that she had been operated on; the weights meant that she was in traction.

As her senses continued to sharpen, she became aware of something else. Not from anything she saw or felt, but from what her intuition told her. Her womb was empty. Her pregnancy was gone.

She closed her eyes and floated in darkness, gradually realizing that there was someone in the room. Footsteps had entered and were slowly approaching the bed. They were light and soft, the footsteps of a woman.

"Will she be all right?" a voice whispered.

"I think so."

Rob sat in a darkened corner of the hospital room.

Romona stood beside the bed. Their voices were weak, numbed with exhaustion.

"How about you?" Rob asked.

"I'm going back now. There's some difficulty there." She hesitated, reluctant to burden him any further. "The police are insisting on examining the body. It's against Indian law. It means we can't bury John in the way he would have wanted." Her voice trembled and she paused, waiting for control. "He couldn't live the way he wanted. He'll have no peace in death either."

"There'll be no autopsy."

Romona nodded, unable to summon any more words. Rob rose and came to her; both knew there was nothing left to say. Rob held out his hand and she took it in both of hers. Then Rob hugged her. Their eyes did not meet again as she turned and quietly left the room.

Rob looked at Maggie and slowly moved to the bed, sitting on the edge of it, gazing down at her slumbering face. It was pale and badly bruised; a well-intentioned nurse had tied a blue ribbon in her hair. Rob reached up and gently removed it, and her hair wafted back against the pillow. Then he bent forward and lowered his head.

He felt the touch of a cold hand against his cheek and looked up to see that her eyes were open. They stared at each other in silence, he taking her hand and pressing it to his lips.

"I'll be all right," she whispered.

"I . . . know."

Their eyes held and they listened to the rain upon the windows.

"I lost it . . . didn't I?" she asked weakly. "The . . . pregnancy."

"Yes."

"It feels so empty."

"It couldn't be helped."

"Was it . . . ?" She didn't finish the question, but he understood.

"I didn't see it."

"Did someone?"

He nodded.

"Was it?"

"It was damaged."

She closed her eyes and moisture squeezed out at the edges. Rob wiped her tears away, feeling a swelling in his throat that made it difficult to speak.

"Maggie?"

"Yes."

"You'll have a baby."

"Yes."

"*We'll* have a baby."

"Yes," she whimpered.

"It's going to be different, Maggie."

"I know."

She clutched his hand and he gripped hers tightly.

"I've missed you, Robert," she whispered.

"I'm back."

Her hand gradually relaxed and she drifted into slumber.

In his lofty perch that towered high above the tree line, the forest ranger sat in a rocking chair, his bloodshot eyes watching dawn break over Manatee Forest. The lake beneath him was calm as glass, reflecting the orange tint of the sun's first rays; everything was still, not a breath of wind blowing.

But somewhere within his blurred field of vision he detected movement, and reached for a pair of binoculars. Surveying the vast panorama of green, he focused in on a gray mound of earth tinged with brownish coloration. It seemed to be rolling, as though awakening from slumber.

As he watched, it slowly took shape, rising on its hind legs and assuming its full stance among the trees. It was a vision like one he had seen before. Only this one was larger. More powerful in every way. And there were smaller ones with it. Five of them. They scampered from beneath it and followed the mighty creature as it lumbered toward the lake.

The forest ranger put down the binoculars and closed his eyes, trying to shake the image away. He knew if he reported it, they would say he was drunk.

And he feared they would be wrong.

# Epilogue

IN RETROSPECT, ALL things seem inevitable. It is a comfortable perspective when things have gone wrong.

One can trace a fatal car collision back to the moment the victim bought the car. Or back further, perhaps, to when he first dreamed of owning a car. In this way, the last-minute details of stop signs ignored, speed limits violated, brake systems unserviced can be passed over as being immaterial to the final outcome.

The history of the earth's environment can be seen in this perspective, too; fatalistically, as a matter of unseen but inevitable obsolescence. Or it can be studied in terms of its detail, taking into account the myriad signals, any one of which could have been heeded to avoid the final failure.

The biological environment within a simple home aquarium will fail in a sequence of increasingly evident steps: a decay of the foliation, a fouling of the water, a browning of the glass, and finally the sight of the entire community of fish gathered at the water's surface, listlessly sucking for oxygen. Even to the untrained eye, the unraveling of the life force becomes plain. If we can singlehandedly reverse it, we usually do. If it requires the co-operation of two or more individuals, it will likely be ignored. In fact, the collapse of an environment requires a conspiracy of negligence.

Anthropologist Richard Leakey, in his probing into the earth around the shores of Lake Rudolf in Kenya, Africa, found evidence of human co-operating dating from a time before man could even be called Man. And we must ask ourselves at what stage of human development "co-operation" became repugnant to the human personality. Mystically and psychologically, man seems to follow the dictate of an inner dynamic which has been labeled the "ego"; a mechanism that makes each within the species feel special, like a species unto himself. It is this mechanism that turned the course of evolution into a drive for "upward mobility," an individual striving for comfort and luxury at the expense of the safety of the community.

Lest one think this is a product of intelligence, it must be pointed out that there is another animal species which, by the yardstick of language, has a measureable intelligence equal to and, some say, beyond our own. Within the community of porpoises, whose communication and problem-solving capabilities have been developed to the highest order, the concept of "me" does not, to any detrimental extent, exist. Even if we discard this example, we must wonder in what perverse equation "intelligence" leads to self-destruction. If we have the intelligence to create warning systems, why, then, do we so blatantly ignore them?

The story you have read is based, in its ecological substance, on actual events. It has been widely reported in journals throughout Canada that lumber mills there, have for several years been using methylmercury—the same substance that caused the disaster in Minamata, Japan—and spilling it into the inland watersheds. The failing health, both mental and physical, of the local Indian populations has been labeled drunkenness. The Indians protest that they do not use alcohol.

In environmental drama the term science fiction will soon be obsolete. Our imaginations have limits. And our realities are catching up with them.

# Acknowledgments

I WOULD LIKE to thank Bob Rosen, John Franken-
heimer, Michael Eisner; Robert Lescher, George
Walsh, Gloria Hammond, Mary Ellen Ernest, Barbara
Jacoby and Sylvia Lundgren for their support.

Also my special thanks to Nguyen Van Trung, Thuy
Thi Phuong, Timothy Ethan and Emily Ann.

# FICTION for all seasons... for people of all ages.